Love's Twisting Trail

Trails of the Heart ♥ Book One

BETTY WOODS

Scrivenings
PRESS
Quench your thirst for story.
www.ScriveningsPress.com

Published by Scrivenings Press LLC
15 Lucky Lane
Morrilton, Arkansas 72110
https://ScriveningsPress.com

Printed in the United States of America

Paperback ISBN 978-1-64917-177-1

eBook ISBN 978-1-64917-178-8

Library of Congress Control Number: 2021951935

Editors: Erin Howard and K. Banks

Cover by Linda Fulkerson, www.bookmarketinggraphics.com.

All scriptures are taken from the KING JAMES VERSION (KJV): KING JAMES VERSION, public domain.

characters are fictional, and any resemblance to real people, either factual or historical, is purely coincidental.

To Jesus, my loving Lord and Savior, who gave me the ability to write and found the perfect home for this book.

To my best-there-is-husband, Craig. He's my number one fan who's been with me through the entire years-long publication journey. This wonderful man is my loving inspiration for becoming a romance author.

Also to my three children, Jason, Cherish and Casey who never stopped believing in me.

ACKNOWLEDGMENTS

Marilyn Eudaly. My fantastic critique partner who has read so many versions of this story that we've both lost count.

· Lena Nelson Dooley and all the wonderful people in her critique group. Lena invited me to her group and suffered through my first manuscript that needed so much work. She and the others in the group helped me learn to write well enough to submit manuscripts to agents or publishers.

Everyone one else in this fantastic group, please know I love you all. This page doesn't have enough room to name all the people who have helped me along the way. Plus, I'm sure I'd leave out someone's name.

Julie Gwinn, of the Seymour Agency. My agent extraordinaire who never gave up on me and kept submitting manuscripts and cheering me on.

1

1869 Outside San Antonio, Texas

C‌harlotte Grimes slid her cleaned revolver into the holster lying on the kitchen table, determined to keep her promise to Pa. She had hoped and prayed four-legged varmints or snakes were the only reasons to need a gun, but from what she'd overheard from others, a body had best be prepared for meeting anything or anyone on a cattle drive. Especially a woman intending to go up the trail disguised as a fourteen-year-old boy.

Slinging her gun belt over her shoulder, she grabbed her tied bedroll off the chair. Toby should be back from town soon, so she needed to sneak her things into the barn before her brother returned. So far, God hadn't given her any idea how to tell Toby she'd be going with him no matter how much he didn't want her along.

A welcome spring breeze brushed her cheeks while a mockingbird sang nearby. How could everything around here be the same when her world had turned so topsy turvy? If only Pa hadn't died. If only she could trust her brother again. If only ...

Fretting over what she couldn't change was a waste of time.

A wagon loaded down with a young couple and their goods kicked up dust not far behind Toby. Must be the people he had found to help her watch the ranch while he was gone. Hopefully, they knew enough about ranching to take care of everything on their own.

"What are you doing?" Her brother growled down at her as he reined in his horse a few feet from the barn. His angry brown eyes took in everything from her bedroll to her holstered revolver.

"Getting ready to leave with you." She met his glare head-on. *Well, Lord, I'd hoped for a better way to tell him.*

"What?" Toby jumped to the ground as the wagon pulled into the yard. "My sister and I need to talk. Y'all can have a look around in the house. We'll unload your things later."

Her brother scowled at her in silence until the man and woman with their young child went inside. She frowned back.

"You're not going." He slapped the reins across his gloved hand.

She flinched. In the few weeks since Pa died, they'd had so many arguments. She leaned her bedroll and gun against the weathered barn then turned back to face her brother. Looking him in the eyes was the best way to deal with him, or he'd think she was fixin' to give in.

"Pa left me half this ranch. I'm going." Even with the afternoon sun in her eyes, she could see him wince.

"No woman has any business on a cattle drive."

"You still need a wrangler to care for the horses. Your kid brother can do that."

His jaw dropped. "We haven't had a kid brother since Pete died while I was gone." His voice cracked. At least something could still touch Toby's hardened heart.

"I'm about the same size as Pete. The new men you hired for the drive have no idea you don't have a younger brother named Charlie."

His jaw clenched so tight she could see the muscles

twitching. Every seasoned hand they'd had refused to work for Toby because of his temper. Except Eduardo. The cook stayed only out of loyalty to Pa's memory and to watch out for her. Something else best not to mention to Toby.

Ignoring her pounding heart, Charlotte drew herself up ramrod straight. She'd stand her ground. Stand up to her brother. Going with him was the only way she knew to keep the vow she'd made to Pa.

"Eduardo promised not to tell anyone the truth about me. He says my idea should work since I ride and rope as good or better than most men he knows."

" 'Cept you're no man, and a cattle drive is no place for a lady."

A brittle-sounding laugh slipped out despite how his words riled her. He'd often taunted her about looking more like a skinny version of Pete than a woman of almost twenty-three.

"Me, a lady? You're the one who started calling me Charlie and making fun of me for working the ranch in men's clothes."

"Just 'cause you can dress like a man don't mean you can work like a man."

She stomped her foot before thinking about it. Acting like a child wouldn't help win this argument. She couldn't let him get the best of her and prove him right. This was his first cattle drive too. He'd even agreed to join with another small herd led by a man who'd gone up the trail last year.

But she wouldn't remind such a prideful man of those things. More important to win the present battle.

"I haven't seen any new hand who looks like a wrangler. I can handle the horses, but you won't admit that or a lot of other things."

His eyes narrowed. "What do you mean?"

"How much did you really sell those mustangs for a while back?"

Instead of answering her, Toby kicked a rock so hard it

bounced off the barn. The sharp sound echoed across the yard like a gunshot.

"That's why I'm going with you." She grabbed her gear. "I don't have to hide these now, so I'll take them back to the house." With both hands full, her dress hem swished in the dust.

"That long braid bouncing down your back won't have any man thinking you're a boy. Your fire-red hair shows up for at least a mile." Toby's taunt chased after her.

"My hair will be secured under my hat." She continued on, not giving him the satisfaction of so much as looking back over her shoulder.

"Unless you decide to flirt with one of the men."

"What?" Whirling to face him, she hissed through gritted teeth. "How dare you say such a thing?"

"The foreman of the other herd's not married. He's a couple of years older than me and turned more than one woman's head while we walked the streets in San Antonio."

Decent men didn't flirt with the kind of woman who dared wear a man's trousers and take on a man's work. He had to know how ridiculous he sounded. She glared back at him. "I have no intentions of throwing myself at any cowboy, and you know it."

He shrugged. "I don't know a lot of things about you anymore."

"Then we're even. You don't trust me. I don't trust you. I'm going on this drive."

Leaving him standing with his mouth open, she turned her back to him again and marched away.

She'd won. For now. If only she were as sure of the next couple of months as she'd sounded.

2

I gnoring the dust created by the bawling cows trailing off to her side, Charlotte reined in her horse and shifted in her saddle for one last look at home. The house was only a speck in the distance, but she could see every inch of it in her mind. Smell the sweet scent of the fresh wildflowers she'd left on her parents' and brother's graves yesterday.

Pa and Ma had given all they had for this place. She'd do the same. But would Toby? Doubting the older brother she'd always looked up to made her insides squirm. Whatever the war had done to him, he kept to himself. Pa had fought with Sam Houston and said a man needed time to get over a war, some men longer than others. But Toby had come home four years ago.

Four very long years.

No matter how much she'd rather stay home, she had to go. Sighing, she returned her attention to the herd of horses. The survival of their ranch lay on her shoulders. Every ounce of that weight pressed down hard. *Lord, I hope I'm doing the right thing.*

Shortly before the sun stood straight overhead, Charlotte halted the mustangs near where Eduardo had stopped the wagon to cook the noon meal. Toby rode in the distance, probably waiting for the other herd they were meeting. Since she'd seen them a ways back, they should catch up soon.

Their trail cook grinned as she dismounted. "You make good wrangler."

"Only if I can convince the big roan over there to stay with the rest of the *remuda*." She grabbed ropes from the wagon to make a corral for the mustangs.

"*Sí*, but if anyone work magic with horse, is you." Eduardo's compliment washed over her like a balm.

"You didn't come to talk, *Charlie*." Toby's sneering emphasis on the nickname he'd intended as an insult couldn't be missed as he rode up to them.

"No, but we'll keep the real reasons I'm here between you and me unless you'd like your too-talkative kid brother to tell everyone things about our business you don't want anyone to know."

She bent to tie a rope to the wagon tongue and jerked the knot tight, glad for one way to keep him quiet. He wouldn't want a single hand to know his so-called brother came along as the wrangler only because Toby had wasted so much money he couldn't afford to hire someone for the job.

He glared at her before riding away. Noon wasn't quite here. Their war of words was getting old already. She had to stand her ground or go home before they got any farther away, and without being able to trust him, the latter wasn't something she could consider.

While she tied the last rope for the makeshift corral, Toby returned with a strange man. Must be the foreman of the other herd. Someone else to be an audience for her brother's taunts. She checked to be sure the ropes were taut while Toby and the other man dismounted.

With his ever-present grin in place, the cook set his Dutch oven on the ground as the men approached him. Charlotte swung into her saddle and started herding the horses into the corral. The hands would need fresh mounts soon.

"Eduardo, this is David Shepherd, my new partner," Toby said.

Mr. Shepherd extended his hand to Eduardo. "My cook broke his arm yesterday. Could I trouble you to fix the meals for my men too?"

Eduardo rubbed his chin. "*Señor* Toby, is all right with you?"

"They brought their own supplies, so it's fine with me."

"Then *sí, señor*."

"Thank you." The man's deep southern drawl made her wonder where he'd once called home.

"How many men you have?"

"Eight. I'm sorry about the extra work."

"Charlie help me. Charlie good help." Eduardo pointed toward Charlotte.

Sucking in air, she halted her horse to turn and take more than a side-long look at David Shepherd. No wonder Toby said this man had turned women's heads in San Antonio. His wide-brimmed brown hat couldn't hide his handsome features. High cheekbones and a perfect almost-upturned nose were accented by his kind-looking, tanned face. A winsome smile revealed a most interesting lone dimple on the right side of his mouth.

If he were half as nice as he looked ... *Oh, my.* More than the spring heat warmed her cheeks. She looked away from his direct gaze, hoping he'd mistake her awkwardness for the youngster she was pretending to be.

When she dismounted, Mr. Shepherd turned his attention to her. Charlotte busied herself ground tethering her horse. Her ridiculous thoughts and emotions needed a corral more than the mustangs did.

"I'd like to ask you a question."

"You would?" Her head jerked up. He sounded sincere, but she couldn't believe he wanted to talk to a kid wrangler about anything.

"David Shepherd." He offered his hand.

Good thing she'd worn gloves. All other thoughts, rational or otherwise, flew away as she shook with him and stared into the deepest sky-blue eyes she'd ever seen. Since he wasn't as tall as Toby, she had a wonderful view of the fascinating man standing only inches away.

"Uh, I'm Charlie Grimes." She finally remembered to release his hand. "Toby's my brother."

As he looked her over, his eyes widened for just a moment. She hoped his momentary look of surprise came from Toby maybe not mentioning he was related to his wrangler and not from him thinking the boy in front of him looked a lot like a girl.

"Which is easier for you, combining our horses or keeping them separate?"

She forced herself not to stare at him more than she already had. Toby scowled at her from behind Mr. Shepherd. If it bothered her brother for someone to say something nice to her or if he was worried the man might discover her true identity, she couldn't tell. Worse, she hoped Toby couldn't see how this man affected her.

"Umm ..." She looked down, lest Mr. Shepherd realize how much she'd like to continue studying everything about him. "Keeping the *remudas* separate would be faster for changing mounts since I know our horses and your man knows yours."

Plus, no one would think it odd if this wrangler didn't sleep anywhere near the other wrangler since she needed as much distance and privacy as possible between her and the men at night.

Mr. Shepherd grinned. "Good idea."

"I'd better go help Eduardo." She turned toward the wagon, glad for an excuse to walk away. If she couldn't control the crazy feelings this considerate man stirred in her heart, she'd need to protect more than her identity. The dignified way he treated what he thought was a lowly kid wrangler drew her to him even more than his swoon-inducing good looks. She stared at his back until he and Toby were quite a ways from the wagon.

"He's good one, *señorita*."

Her attention jerked back to Eduardo. "You can't call me that." She whispered even though no one was close enough to hear her. "We don't know who else might speak Spanish."

The cook ducked his head. "*Sí*, I know."

"We can talk to each other in Spanish the way we've always done. Just don't call me anything that has to do with a female."

The customary smile returned as he grabbed a pot hook from the wagon. "Still, that one is good *hombre* to watch."

"I was wondering about a man with such a strange last name for a rancher, not studying him."

"*Sí*, if you say. But I tell you now he good *hombre*."

Charlotte knelt and busied herself with checking the fire. If she weren't careful, the man would cause her problems she'd never imagined could happen on a cattle drive. And judging from the mischievous sparkle in Eduardo's brown eyes, the cook just might help him if the foreman were so inclined.

DAVID LEFT to tell his wrangler to keep the *remudas* separated, but Grimes came with him. Why, David had no idea. They rode in silence since he couldn't think of anything they should discuss.

Grimes cleared his throat. "Don't take anything Charlie says too seriously."

"Why not?" He wondered why the man hadn't mentioned his brother was the wrangler for his outfit, but it wasn't his business to say anything about who the man picked.

"Mostly 'cause he's ... well he's Charlie. He's only fourteen. And he's—uh—a little different."

The boy had looked and sounded intelligent, but something about the too serious expression on Grimes's face kept him from voicing his thoughts. "I'll remember that."

"I'd appreciate it."

As they rode on, Grimes stared straight ahead. "I'll see to my herd."

The man left David to stare at his retreating back. Something about their strange exchange didn't make sense. Grimes had looked as nervous as a soldier on night watch in a dense fog. If he were so uneasy about his younger brother, he should have found a different wrangler. Hiring help was no problem with so many men around here needing work.

Since he had more important things to concern himself with than possible trouble between brothers, he urged his horse into a canter toward his herd. If this drive turned out as well as the last, he'd be the new owner of the Double B Ranch he'd come to love.

Allowing Mr. Bentley, the elderly owner, to live out his remaining days in peace in San Antonio. The godly partner who'd taken him in and treated him like the son he'd lost in the war deserved no less than David's best efforts to fulfill his wishes.

The welcome smell of beans cooking over the fire greeted David and his men by the time they joined the Grimes outfit.

"You barely got enough wood. You're not camping for fun with Pa, Charlie."

While he and his men dismounted, David couldn't miss the harsh, derisive tone Grimes used with his brother. Even from thirty feet away. Surely the man realized the whole camp could hear him. His stunned men exchanged glances instead of words.

He headed to the back of the wagon where Grimes was still berating the poor kid. The brothers' problems were none of his concern, but his conscience wouldn't allow him to let Grimes keep belittling an innocent helper trying to do his best.

"Head home if you can't pull your load."

"No matter how you treat me, I'm going with you."

Charlie's retort was soft enough David wouldn't have heard him if he hadn't been so close. Hands on his hips like a girl, the boy glared up at his brother before stalking off.

"Told you Charlie's different." Grimes's frown signaled he wasn't pleased to have David for an audience.

"He'd do better if you didn't yell at him all the time."

"The kid's got to learn. Pa spoiled him too much." The man shrugged.

Something else that didn't make sense. Grimes's supposed concerns about straightening out his brother sounded insincere, judging by the way he treated him. But rather than cause unnecessary problems, he let his partner's words go unchallenged.

The noon meal passed without another outburst from Grimes, probably because Charlie sat with the cook to eat. Give the boy credit for doing his best to keep the peace.

Once he left the herd to scout for water, David wished he could shove away thoughts of the two brothers. But his mind wouldn't quit going over what he'd seen and heard. A speckled tan lizard jumped off a rock and ran into the brush as his horse approached. He'd better enjoy this peaceful solitude after the explosion he'd witnessed at noon. Good thing he was the one who knew the trail and could insist his hot-headed partner ride point at the front of the herd instead of scouting.

The sun moved west sooner than David wished. He pulled his watch from his vest pocket. Four o'clock. Time to circle back and let the cook know he'd found a good spot for the night.

While the men settled the cattle, David turned his attention to the wranglers coming in with the horses. Catching the boy's eye, he grinned at him. The kid tried harder than he would have under the same circumstances.

He returned his attention to the hands and spotted Grimes heading his direction, still wearing a frown.

"If you're checking on Charlie, I can do that."

"Doesn't look like your brother needs checking. There's already enough wood stacked for cooking supper and breakfast tomorrow."

"I brought him along. He's my worry." Grimes's scowl didn't soften.

Swallowing his words of contradiction, David settled for shaking his head. He was a coward for not defending Charlie any better than he had. How many Bible verses did he know about protecting the young and weak?

But he hadn't had any idea about the boy coming along when he'd partnered with Grimes. The two of them needed each other. Neither of them had enough men of their own to feel safe crossing through Indian Territory. He had too much at stake to jeopardize this drive.

David sucked in a deep breath. Might as well get another unpleasant chore out of the way. "Now's a good time to assign everyone their watches. I assume you'd like the first one with the man of your choice since you know your hands."

"No one expects the boss to do that." Grimes jerked his gaze from Charlie, glowering at David instead.

"True, but your outfit's shorthanded. So until we get to the next town where you can hire someone, you'll have to take your turn."

When Grimes did nothing but draw his mouth tighter, David headed toward the hands unsaddling their afternoon horses. He'd told his partner how many cowboys he needed when they'd talked in San Antonio. It wasn't his fault the man hadn't listened.

Grimes didn't budge from his spot behind the wagon until Charlie finished tying every knot in every rope of the makeshift corral. Strange how he thought he needed to keep such a close eye on his own brother.

"Before we eat, we'll tell you when you're on watch." David didn't speak until his partner stood at his side. "Mr. Grimes will take the first one with whichever man he chooses."

"Miller, since you rode point all day with me, we should be able to handle a watch together." Grimes's stiff posture didn't match the half-smile on his face.

"Sure, boss."

David grinned only on the inside as they finished assigning the night guards. With Grimes out of the way for a while, Charlie should enjoy a short time of peace. Doing one small thing to help the boy eased his nagging conscience a little bit.

AFTER SETTING the horses to graze for the night, Charlotte sat with the cowboys by the campfire only as long as she could stand it. The men's rough language and crude references to women made her want to cover her ears with her hands. Now she understood why the cowboys often stopped talking when she walked up to them while working the ranch. Too bad she couldn't tell them a lady was present now.

She made a show of yawning before making her way to Eduardo's wagon. Better to let the men think she was tired than have them guess she didn't like their company. A wrangler who acted as if he were better than them might be teased or worse, and she didn't need to do anything to draw unnecessary attention to herself.

The stars sparkled in the black sky like heavy dew on a sunny spring morning. She gazed up and concentrated on the beauty God had created instead of the low voices best ignored. Focusing on God's beauty instead of all the ugliness she'd experienced today might help soothe her tattered spirit. Abilene and mid-June would be a long time coming.

"I've watched the stars since I was a kid."

Charlotte jumped at the sound of David Shepherd's voice beside her. "I'd rather look at the sky and listen to the coyotes than the men." She kept her voice low.

"At least half of what they say isn't true." He chuckled.

She shook her head. "Ma would've washed my mouth out with soap if I talked like that."

"Grandmother would have done the same to me. Using coarse language doesn't make you more of a man, especially in God's eyes. Remember that."

"I will." His warm, soothing voice made her feel as if she were wrapped up in her favorite quilt on a cold day in front of their fire at home.

"I'm guessing this is your first drive. I followed you over here to tell you how well you're doing."

"Thanks, Mr. Shepherd." She used his last name not just to keep up her ruse. Remaining formal and distant with this man was a must. His kind tone and words of praise stirred her heart even more than the sky-blue eyes she couldn't see but well remembered.

"You're welcome. I'll leave you to turn in or just watch the stars."

Charlotte stared at his retreating back, wishing he'd stayed. Except it wouldn't have been much of a conversation only talking about horses and cows while guarding her secret. She sighed.

If only she hadn't met such a wonderful man under such unwonderful conditions. But entertaining ideas about any man— even one as nice as Mr. Shepherd—wasn't her reason for being here. She'd come to keep her promise to Pa. To do whatever she had to do to get the money to save their ranch. Her heart's desires, her personal wishes would have to come after the ranch was taken care. Only God knew how these unforeseen, crazy twists could work for her heart's good and to save the ranch at the same time.

3

Throwing her saddle blanket on her skittish roan, Charlotte squinted toward the early morning sun. He jumped just the way she'd figured. There were some advantages to spending so much time with horses that she smelled like one.

"Whoa, fella." She stroked his neck before saddling him.

"Why you bring that one?" Eduardo looked skeptical as he pitched the last skillet into the wagon.

"The wrangler gets what's left. Despite his orneriness, he's strong and smart. With his spirit, it'll be hard for any cow to get the best of him." Charlotte grinned at the cook as she mounted the mustang. She'd worked with this one enough to anticipate his jumps and hops and kept her seat.

Eduardo shook his head as he climbed onto the wagon seat. "*Vaya con Díos.*"

"*Gracías.*" Charlotte rode off to start another long day. Eduardo's blessing for God to be with her reminded her Who was still in charge. God and the loyal cook wouldn't desert her.

"You got all the warning you'll get about pulling your own load." Toby tossed a frown her way as he rode toward the front of the herd.

His disdainful look and harsh tone shot pain through her.

How she hoped and prayed they could someday be friends the way they had been as kids. That Toby would be at peace again with God. She missed the closeness they'd enjoyed until Toby came home from the war.

But that was in God's hands too. She had no idea what to do to make things right with her brother. Or how to help him return to the good, kind man he'd once been.

The *remuda* gave her fewer problems than the last few days. Riding the troublemaker who wanted to bolt had been a good idea. Jumper might become her regular morning horse.

With the mustangs adjusting to the trail, Charlotte had time to think and pray over her troubles with Toby. She understood him resenting her for coming along to keep an eye on him. And she realized why he didn't want Mr. Shepherd to get too close to her and figure out who she actually was. But her brother had no good reason to keep being so cruel. She wanted to save the ranch the same as he did. He should be working with her instead of against her.

Shortly before noon, Charlotte guided her horse into camp, dragging the large tree branch she'd lassoed. The herd kicked up dust less than a mile behind her. Maybe she'd have another half hour of peace and quiet before Toby showed up to eat.

Thoughts of her problems disappeared quicker than a lightning-fast mustang when Mr. Shepherd rode up next to her with his usual bright smile. She looked away before she got caught up in his sparkling eyes. If only she dared pull her hat a little lower and discreetly study him.

"Judging from the way you rope, your father must be proud to have two good hands on a drive."

Charlotte's grip tightened on the lariat as bittersweet memories ran through her mind. "Yes, sir. Pa was proud of me and Toby."

"Was?"

"Pa died last month." She almost choked on her words.

"I'm sorry."

"Thank you." She blinked away the moisture in her eyes.

The foreman nodded. "I'll tend to the wood so you can get the corral ready."

"No need for that." She glanced over her shoulder toward the approaching cattle.

"Your brother has to pay more attention to the beeves than you, in case you're wondering if he'll see me helping you."

"I guess so." His reassurance didn't help her feel any better about Toby, but telling a man she hardly knew about family troubles wouldn't be right or good.

Mr. Shepherd reached over and took the rope from her. Thank God her gloves kept him from feeling her sweaty palms.

"Uh, I appreciate your help, Mr. Shepherd."

"You're welcome." He turned his horse and dragged the limb toward Eduardo.

As soon as she dismounted, she got the corral ropes from behind the wagon. She couldn't see the cook or the foreman from this spot. Anything to keep from watching the trail boss more than she already had. More than she should.

Eduardo greeted Mr. Shepherd in Spanish.

"Sorry, *señor*, but I just spoke one of the few Spanish words I know."

Charlotte grinned to herself as she tied a knot. What a clever way to find out if Mr. Shepherd spoke Spanish. She wouldn't mind if she were the only one who understood the cook. Except talking with the foreman in a language Toby wouldn't bother to learn would be nice. She shook her head. She didn't dare think such things.

The trail boss felt sorry for a mistreated kid, and she couldn't let him think anything else about her. She waited until the man walked over to watch for the herd coming in before heading toward the fire to help Eduardo.

"*El jefe* es *un hombre muy bueno*." The cook placed his hand on her arm.

While he complimented the trail boss, she couldn't miss

Eduardo's emphasis on the words 'very good.' But admitting how much she agreed would be dangerous in more ways than she cared to think about.

Giving any of the men reasons to think she wasn't actually Charlie wouldn't be good. The other cowboys wouldn't want a woman along any more than Toby did. After listening to their lewd comments around the campfire, she wondered if she'd be safe with some of them.

Toby detested the whole idea of her wearing men's clothes. A gentleman like Mr. Shepherd might loathe her even more.

"I pray for you." Eduardo stooped to check the coals heaped over the Dutch oven.

"I need all the prayers you've got time for and more."

As the cowboys rode in, he whispered in Spanish about promising her father to continue praying for Toby and how hard it got some days to keep his vow. "But since God never give up on him, I won't."

"*Sí*, me too." She grabbed the pot hook to lift the lid and check the salt pork.

"Since I can smell the beans and biscuits, you two must be cooking while you're jabbering."

Charlotte jumped as Toby came up behind her.

"Charlie good company and good help." Eduardo lifted the Dutch oven from the hot coals.

"Good for nothing but trouble." Toby continued muttering to himself as he took his leave.

"Thanks for taking up for me." Charlotte finished stacking tin plates and cups on a log.

"Another promise I make your *padre*."

Not that bucking Toby was easy for Eduardo, but she couldn't help wondering if he'd be able to keep his promises to Pa easier than she could keep hers. Toby couldn't find someone like Eduardo just anywhere. But he didn't want or need a sister who planned to be sure he didn't squander a single dollar they made on this drive.

Once they got to Abilene and sold the cattle, she wouldn't let him out of her sight. And *they* would sell the herd together so she'd know exactly how much money they'd make. Something else that would make him furious.

Such thoughts sent chills through her despite the heat from the cook fire. As much as she hated to think about it, Eduardo's pledge to watch out for her might be more necessary than she wished.

No matter how hard she fought them, her uneasy thoughts plagued her the rest of the afternoon. Eduardo did his best to reassure her while they cooked supper.

"I watch you. God watch you. He want you here."

After supper, Charlotte again picked a spot on the edge of the circle of men gathered around the campfire. Since Toby had started his turn on night watch, this might become her favorite part of the day. Especially if Mr. Shepherd continued his habit of saying something nice to her while her brother wasn't around.

She hoped God didn't think she was awful if she prayed Toby didn't find another hand when they got to the next town. Since the time their sister married a few months ago, her brother had become determined to save every cent he could. Until the day he wouldn't explain why he'd come home with so little money from selling horses.

Whatever the reason, she had no intention of trying to keep him from being thrifty if it meant she could spend even a few uninterrupted minutes with David Shepherd every day.

Except enjoying his company wouldn't do her one bit of good in the long run. He was only being nice to a kid he felt sorry for, and she dared not tell such a gentleman the truth about herself. He'd never accept such an unladylike woman—especially one who intended to keep working her ranch after this drive ended.

Ben Tyler, the man who'd been riding drag for Toby, reached in front of her to pick up a stick, startling her from her thoughts. Pulling his pocket knife from his vest, he started whittling.

"I noticed you Double B men switch places every day." Tyler kept his attention focused on his knife.

"It's only fair to take turns eating all that dust." A man Charlotte knew only as Jessup wiped his grimy face with his bandana.

"You know Mr. Grimes better than us." Tyler looked straight at Charlotte as he tossed wood shavings into the fire. "Would he mind us changing out?"

Staring at the red and yellow sparks created from the wood chips, Charlotte swallowed hard. Tyler might as well have tossed *her* into the flames asking her to speak for her hot-tempered brother.

"Ask me those kinds of questions. I can't see anything wrong if y'all do the same as my hands." Mr. Shepherd kept his eyes on her as he answered.

Such a perceptive man to sense her fear and do his best to help her out. Another thing she shouldn't like about him.

While the hands decided who would ride where the next day, Charlotte slipped off behind the wagon and leaned against the rough boards. After several deep breaths, her heart slowed back to normal.

"Are you all right?"

Mr. Shepherd's low voice sent her pulse racing for a different reason.

"Uh, I'm fine."

Her quick denial had sounded too high-pitched for a boy. How she hoped he hadn't noticed. The almost full moon gave him too good of a view. The longer he stared, the longer she wondered what he looked to be studying or thinking.

"I told the men to let me tell your brother about switching places."

"Thanks, but Toby won't ride drag."

"I'll handle that too." He smiled straight into her eyes.

Keep breathing. She should say something back to him. Look away. But she couldn't do either one.

"I had a sergeant like your brother during the war, so I know how to handle him."

"The war changed Toby. We used to be real close. He wasn't like this before." Despite how he'd treated her, she couldn't help defending him. He was still her brother. And she still loved him and prayed for him.

Mr. Shepherd exhaled slowly. "The war changed us all. You were doing a man's work long before you should have been."

The words meant to comfort and praise her brought back painful memories of heated arguments she'd had with Ma about working the ranch wearing Pete's old clothes. Someone had to take her younger brother's place after he died. With no money to hire a man during the war, even if one had been available, she'd done what needed to be done. Even Pa hadn't been able to get Ma to see that Charlotte couldn't work a ranch wearing a dress.

"Ma never understood about me helping Pa to the day she died."

Oh, she shouldn't have said that, giving him any reason to wonder why Ma didn't want her supposed youngest son helping with the ranch. She had to be more careful.

"So you've lost your mother too?"

She nodded as she let out the breath she'd been holding. "During the war, same as my other brother."

Not that she wanted to talk about Ma or Pete being gone, but at least the man focused on that instead of why she and Ma had disagreed.

"Be glad God gave them to you for as long as He did."

She couldn't mistake his sad tone of voice or the way his whole body stiffened. He quickly turned his head as if afraid of giving away his true feelings.

"Thanks." She focused on lowering her voice, hoping to sound more like a boy. "I'll remember what you said."

"Sure, you do that." His words sounded strained. "Uh... I'll see you in the morning."

Once again, Charlotte stared at his retreating form, wishing he'd stayed while wondering why he'd left so suddenly. No matter the reason, he wouldn't want to be anywhere near her if he knew the boy he felt so sorry for was a lying woman telling him parts of the truth and deliberately misleading him about everything else. She'd been so sure God wanted her to make this drive and keep her promise to Pa.

But she hadn't counted on the complications caused by meeting someone like David Shepherd.

DAVID SUCKED IN A SHAKY BREATH. He'd left as quickly as he could without being rude. Talking with Charlie about losing parents reminded him of things he'd tried not to think about for years. He did thank God for the loving grandparents who had raised him. But after almost twenty-eight years, it still hurt that his father deserted him without ever wanting know him. It wasn't his fault his mother died the day after he was born.

The men's laughter jerked him back to the present. He returned to his spot by the fire in time to catch the end of Jessup's tale about a woman who married someone else before he came back from the war. The men's coarse language bothered him as much as it did Charlie, but he couldn't try to influence his hands for the better if he never had anything to do with them.

Shortly before daylight the next morning, David squatted next to his wrangler and tapped him on the shoulder. "Schmidt, time to start another day."

He ambled toward Grimes while the man woke Charlie and the cook. The gruff words to his younger brother grated on David's ears, especially after hearing the kid last night trying to justify his brother's behavior because of the war.

Grimes wasn't the only one who had lived through the nightmares of battle and death then come home to find loved ones in their graves. He had bawled like a child to see the graves —his young wife and newborn son buried next to his grandparents. The sight still haunted him. Leaving him precious little sympathy for using war memories as an excuse for his partner's hot temper.

"I need a word with you while your brother helps with breakfast."

"Sure." Grimes followed him to the edge of the camp.

"While you were on watch last night, your men and I talked about taking turns where they ride herd. I told them it would be fine."

"Without asking me?" Grimes folded his arms across his chest. "I'm in charge of *my* men."

"I never said you weren't." David took extra effort to keep his voice calm.

"But you spoke for me."

"True, but I assumed a man with your military experience understands about keeping up the men's morale."

Even with the breaking dawn barely lighting Grimes's face, David could see his partner's eyes narrow to slits.

"I don't remember telling you about my war experience."

"While we talked about combining our herds, you mentioned fighting in Tennessee. Since you remind me of my former sergeant, I figured you were a leader in your company."

"Yeah." Grimes dropped his arms to his side.

The man's one-word answer spoke volumes. If he'd had a position of leadership, such a haughty man would have boasted about it. At least he didn't appear to realize he'd just been insulted, since comparing anyone to David's hot-headed old sergeant was no compliment.

"Since you understand how to lead men by example, I assume you'll ride drag today." He might as well take the bull by the horns since Charlie was so sure his brother would never ride in that spot.

"What?"

Several heads turned their direction when Grimes raised his voice.

"You're a good enough businessman to know it doesn't hurt to be on your men's good side, especially if we run into hostile Indians after crossing the Red River."

Grimes looked toward the pink and yellow horizon before slowly turning to glare straight into David's eyes. "I know when a man's trying to butter me up. You have the better hand because you know the trail." He paused as if he wanted his words to sink in.

David stared back at the tight-lipped man. "Then you're smart enough to understand what's best for both of us on this drive."

"I'll ride drag. But I won't forget this." Grimes' right hand rested momentarily on top of his revolver before he turned on his heel and stalked off.

4

David slipped off his bandana and wiped the sweat from his face as Eduardo added wood to the cook fire. He hoped the oppressive humidity and heat weren't warning signs of a thunderstorm coming in. The fluffy white clouds on the northern horizon didn't look threatening. But living four years in Texas had taught him how unpredictable the weather here could be.

Still, his biggest threat was the unpredictable man riding drag at the back of the herd. If Grimes smiled, David might not recognize him. He hoped and prayed the man was as full of bluster and as empty of action as his old sergeant.

Charlie's laughter interrupted his thoughts. He glanced toward the cook and the wrangler, talking in Spanish while working together on the noon meal. When the kid laughed, he sounded so much like a girl that he probably couldn't wait for his voice to change. He turned his attention from the oncoming herd as he approached the wagon.

"Could I trouble one of you to teach me Spanish?"

"*Sí, señor*. Charlie teach you. Charlie speak good English and good Spanish." Eduardo's smile spread ear to ear as he added wood to the fire.

"Me?" Charlie turned redder than David's bandana.

"*Sí,* you have time after we clean up at night." Eduardo's brown eyes sparkled.

The wrangler ducked his head. "Uh—I don't know."

"It'd give me a good excuse not to listen to so many tall tales around the campfire." Strange how the kid was acting so shy when he'd never hesitated to talk to him before.

"Um, well, I ..."

Eduardo looked straight at the boy. "*Señor* Toby can no yell at you if you have good reason to talk to *el jefe.*"

The cook's fatherly tone of voice reminded David of Mr. Bentley and his grandfather. So did his good advice, assuming *el jefe* referred to himself. "What about it, Charlie?"

The boy finally looked up at him. "All right."

"I'll take my first lesson tonight." He grinned down at the wrangler.

"Tonight will be fine, Mr. Shepherd."

The boy ducked his head again, but not in time to keep David from seeing his shining brown eyes. Maybe he'd found a small way to help without meddling in the brothers' problems.

When the point men rode in, David went to ask them their opinions about the weather. He kept an eye out for Grimes as he discussed the heat with the hands.

"I been raised here. You never know for sure about this time of year." Tyler's unmistakable Texas accent attested to his words.

"Those don't look like storm clouds to me." Jessup squinted up at the northern horizon.

"There's the boss. See y'all later." As the drag men rode in, Tyler trotted in Grimes's direction.

Even from where he stood, David could see the hard set of his partner's jaw. Grimes dismounted as Tyler approached him.

"Boss, I appreciate you changing up with me and the other boys, even riding drag. Makes me proud to work for you."

Grimes's customary frown reversed to a huge grin. "Glad to hear you liked our idea."

The chuckle David swallowed almost choked him. Somehow he kept quiet through the entire noon meal as the man basked in his hands' admiration. If Grimes got any more puffed up, the buttons would pop off his shirt, and his hat wouldn't fit on his swollen head.

David was still laughing on the inside while he scouted for a good place to bed the herd down that afternoon. The stifling heat and humidity would probably put a quick end to Grimes's good humor. This had to be the worst kind of day for any man riding drag.

But no matter his partner's mood, he had Spanish lessons to look forward to. The wrangler was growing on him. He'd always wanted a younger brother. Maybe this was God's way of granting him that wish for a little while.

After riding into camp for the evening, Grimes and most of the other men wasted no time heading to the nearby creek. David followed them.

Tyler knelt to wet his bandana in the water then wrung it out over his shirtless shoulders. "Might as well cut this air with my knife."

"Yeah. Feels more like August than late April." Wilson lifted his canteen above his head and drenched himself.

As the men cooled themselves down, Grimes scowled. The dust and heat must have taken care of the jaunty swagger he'd had at noon. But at least he was quiet.

Rather than risk a confrontation with his partner, David left before the others. The wranglers were picketing the night horses as he neared the camp. "Schmidt, you and Charlie have time to go to the creek if you want."

"Sounds good, boss." Schmidt grinned.

"I'll help Eduardo." Charlie beat a path toward the wagon, almost stumbling over the brush in his way.

The boy must be more afraid of his brother than David thought if he wouldn't even go down to the creek with him. Grimes had no cause to treat his only remaining flesh and blood so badly.

By sunset, David had other concerns. The clouds looked to be building and coming their direction. He prayed they wouldn't get a thunderstorm. Lightning and cattle didn't mix well, especially at night.

As soon as Charlie and Eduardo finished cleaning up, the kid staked out a spot on the other side of the wagon. A streak of lightning danced across the horizon as David sat with the men by the fire.

"I'd just as soon that doesn't move this way." Jessup looked to the north.

"It's still several miles out." Tyler tossed wood shavings into the fire.

David rose. "I'll keep an eye on things for a while, boys."

He headed in the direction Charlie had gone, glad he could use the Spanish lessons to explain why he was talking with the youngster. Why Grimes didn't want him speaking to the boy still didn't make sense. But he could puzzle over such a strange man for months and never understand him.

The moonlight gave him a decent view of Charlie's smile as he walked up to the boy. "Ready to help me with Spanish?"

"Eduardo would be better."

David shook his head. "Your English is better, so that should help me learn more quickly."

"Can I ask you a question first?"

"Sure."

"Some of the men who went up the trail last year were talking about stampedes while I helped Eduardo with supper. You think this bunch could stampede?"

David nodded. "Lightning can spook a herd quicker than almost anything else."

"You've seen it?"

"Yes. If it happens, you won't have to wonder. This many cattle running would make the ground rumble."

Charlie shuddered.

While looking down at the boy, he tried to think how to reassure him and still tell him the truth. "This herd seems to be a calm bunch, but if they stampede, I want you in or under the wagon as quickly as you can get there."

"What about the horses?"

"We'll round them up later. You get to the wagon. My orders."

"My brother would be really mad if the horses scatter too far."

"I'll take care of him if necessary. Now teach me some Spanish before we both get too tired."

CHARLOTTE DRIFTED off to sleep with the sounds of Mr. Shepherd's deep-South-drawl trying to master Spanish echoing in her mind. If only she could ask him where home was originally. So many things she'd like to know about such a kind man.

Thunder crashing overhead jolted her awake. As she scrambled to untangle herself from her quilts, a jagged bolt of lightning lit the entire sky. No rain yet, but she smelled it.

She sat up and grabbed her hat lying next to her saddle pillow. Save for the oncoming storm, the camp was quiet. A deep rumbling started gradually and increased until the ground trembled beneath her.

"Stampede! All hands and the cook!" David's shout carried through the camp as men jumped up.

Charlotte shoved her feet into her boots then snatched up her bedding and jacket.

"The wagon!" Eduardo yelled as he grabbed her arm and pulled her with him.

"But the *remuda*. We can't lose our horses."

"*Señor* Shepherd say my first job is keep you safe. Cows and horses *segundo*."

After she climbed into the bed of the wagon, the cook tossed her quilts in after her.

"Please stay, *señorita*."

Charlotte hoped he'd interpret her nod as a *yes* since she didn't want to make a promise she had no intention of keeping. The instant the herd cleared the camp, she'd be out and checking on the horses.

"I borrow your saddle." Eduardo tossed on his jacket as he trotted off.

The fatherly cook knew her too well. While rain pelted the canvas over her head, she pounded her quilts with both fists. A strong gust of wind rattled her prison on wheels. The rolling thunder and crashing lightning bolts couldn't drown out the sounds of gunshots and shouts mingling with pounding hooves. Instead of dwelling on terrifying overheard stories of trampled cowboys, she prayed.

Almost as quickly as it blew in, the storm ended. Charlotte scrambled out of the wagon. Peering through the darkness, she made out the forms of a few horses. Maybe the others hadn't wandered too far.

She surveyed the eerily quiet camp. Drenched quilts lay wherever the cowboys had left them. But she couldn't hang anything to dry on the nearby thorny mesquite trees. The wagon tongue would work to drape Eduardo's bedding over. The other men would have to tend to theirs later.

With clouds still hiding the stars, she had no idea how long she paced and listened for any sound of returning men and cattle. Eduardo calling her nickname as he rode back into camp had to be one of the sweetest sounds she'd ever heard.

"Thank God you're all right."

"*Sí, gracias a Díos*." The cook dismounted. "The herd scatter and *los hombres* hunt them, but *Señor* Shepherd send me back. He say cook should get some rest."

"How are Toby and the others?"

Eduardo shrugged. "I ride with *el jefe* and Jessup. We see about others when daylight come."

Sunup couldn't come soon enough for Charlotte.

Since sleep eluded her the rest of the night, she stood a few feet from the wagon and watched the sun rise while trying to work the kinks out of her stiff neck. Not one sound resembling a human voice or a bawling cow. She wanted to yell at the birds to quit singing so she could listen for the men better. Toby had to be safe. *Please, Lord.*

"We start a fire. *Los hombres* be hungry when come back."

She jumped at the sound of Eduardo's voice.

The cook knelt to take several pieces of wood from the canvas sling under the wagon. "Is good you bring so much yesterday."

"I have to round up the horses. Schmidt just rode off after the Double B herd."

"For you, not until light is better. I promise *el jefe* you be safe. Grind coffee first."

Eduardo's tone of voice told her she'd waste her breath arguing. She stalked toward the wagon to grab the coffee, muttering to herself. "Schmidt will have his *remuda* together before I even start with ours. Mr. Shepherd sounds more like my brother than Toby does."

Her sarcastic words caught in her throat. It had been too many years since her brother had been so concerned about her safety. Surely he was worrying about her now when he didn't know what might or might not have happened to her last night.

Doubts about Toby still gnawed at her when Eduardo let her ride toward the horses they'd spotted earlier. Her brother was angry she'd come with him, but he loved her. Didn't he?

Hoping and praying for any other sign of cattle and men, she rode up onto a rise to get a better look. Cows and riders approached from the south. But only three men with a small part of the herd. One of them looked to be Mr. Shepherd. Neither of the others sat their saddles like Toby.

She spurred her horse. The best thing she could do was round up the rest of the Tumbling G *remuda*. The approaching hands would need fresh horses to find the rest of the missing cattle. To find Toby.

About the same time Charlotte drove in the last horse, Wilson and Jessup rode in. The cantankerous Jumper had run the farthest. She secured him in the rope corral while the men dismounted. Their slow, deliberate pace testified to a long night spent in the saddle.

Jessup's tired-looking eyes lit up as he sniffed the air. "Coffee. Eduardo, you're a good one."

"*Gracias*." The cook lifted the lid on the Dutch oven. "Bacon and biscuits for you."

"Thanks." Jessup blew on his steaming cup.

"Where are the other men?" Charlotte couldn't hold back her question any longer.

Jessup gulped the last of his coffee. "Don't know. Took us most of the night to round up the few hundred we've got."

Charlotte turned away to keep anyone from guessing how scared she was. If only she hadn't overheard the story yesterday of a cowboy thrown from his horse and trampled by stampeding cows.

"You eat." Eduardo shoved a plate and a cup toward her. "*Señor* Toby is safe. I pray."

Sitting on a log while balancing her plate in her lap, she managed a weak nod. She doubted she could taste anything, but she'd be of no help to Toby or anyone else if she didn't keep her strength up.

Mr. Shepherd didn't come to eat until after Jessup and Wilson got fresh horses and returned to watch the beeves. "I'll take some of that coffee and food." He grinned as Eduardo filled a cup and handed it to him. "Schmidt, I need your help looking for the rest of the herd since I want Wilson and Jessup to watch the cattle we found."

"Sure, boss."

"I can help too." Charlotte jumped up from the log so quickly she had to catch her plate before it fell to the ground.

The foreman shook his head. "You'll be good help keeping an eye on the *remudas*."

"But I have to find Toby." The words of desperation tumbled out before she could stop them.

THE INSTANT DAVID looked down into Charlie's pleading brown eyes, he wished he hadn't. Schmidt would be better help than a fourteen year-old boy, but the kid's fear was written all over his face.

"Take Charlie with you. Schmidt not missing his only brother." Eduardo's soft voice sounded firm, almost like an order.

Before he gave in to the young wrangler standing in front of him, David turned to the cook. "We all know Schmidt's a more experienced cowman than Charlie."

The cook looked him in the eyes. "Charlie is better than you know. I help Schmidt with horses."

"Please, Mr. Shepherd." The boy's plaintive voice jerked his attention away from Eduardo.

He shouldn't have stared into those big puppy-dog brown eyes again. "Charlie, I ..." The kid could beg better than any woman he'd ever seen and was just as hard to say no to. He exhaled slowly. "All right."

"Thanks." Charlie trotted off to his horse and swung up into the saddle.

Schmidt caught David's buckskin while Eduardo filled canteens for them both.

"*Vaya con Díos*." The cook waved them out of camp.

David looked over at the almost smiling boy. "What did he say?"

"God be with you."

"I'm sure He is. He's with your brother. Don't forget that."

Charlie nodded but didn't look very reassured. Most likely, the kid had the same doubts he did about Grimes's standing with God.

While David checked for cow signs, they rode in silence. "The herd split in more than one direction. There's a lot of trampled brush heading east, so we'll try that first."

The boy turned his horse toward the morning sun.

David kept an eye on the trail to be sure the cows hadn't changed direction.

"Thanks for letting me come." Charlie scanned the horizon as they rode.

"Your brother's all you have left, isn't he?"

"No, my sister and her husband live in Galveston."

That was good to know in case Grimes had been hurt or worse. "I'm glad you and your brother aren't alone."

Charlie shrugged. "Belinda never loved the ranch like Toby and me."

"Is that why you stayed with your brother no matter how he treats you instead of going to your sister?" He was meddling, but he needed to know what to do with this kid if Grimes couldn't see to him.

"Pa left the ranch to me too, and I—" Gasping like a girl, the wide-eyed boy clamped his hand over his mouth.

The truth slammed into David like a minié ball. War wounds had nothing to do with Grimes's problems. This kid owned half the ranch once he turned legal age, which went a long way toward explaining why the man was so angry with his father and resented his brother.

CHARLOTTE COULDN'T BELIEVE she'd let such information slip. She dared not allow herself to become so comfortable around David Shepherd. He might figure out more than she ever wanted

34

him to know if she weren't more careful. If that happened, his sympathy for a scared boy would turn to scorn for a lying woman.

"Please don't let on to anyone what I told you. Eduardo's the only other person who knows. Toby would be so mad that he'd ... uh ..." She didn't want to think about, much less say out loud, what her brother might do. She wasn't sure herself anymore.

"He'll do nothing to you as long as I'm around, but I won't give him any idea I know. I promise."

She looked over and stared into his solemn blue eyes. His kind words wrapped around her like one of Ma's hugs. If she'd stayed in camp and watched the horses, her heart would have been safer. She forced her gaze back to the east where it should be.

An hour or so later, they topped a rise. Mr. Shepherd continued studying the trampled trail.

"Look!" Charlotte pointed toward the horizon. "A good-sized bunch of cows and three men."

The foreman waved his hat around his head. One of the men circled his hand slowly in the air. "Let's go, Charlie."

Charlotte wished they could gallop instead of cantering toward the welcome sight. As they got closer, she could see five men. None of them looked like Toby.

"We're sure glad to see you, Mr. Shepherd." Tyler grinned at the foreman and Charlotte.

"Same here. Do you have any idea about the rest of the men? This wrangler would like to know about his brother."

Tyler shrugged. "We ain't seen or heard from anybody else."

"Jessup and Wilson are back at camp holding the few hundred head we rounded up. Drive this bunch there, then three of you scout for the rest of the men and beeves. The boy and I'll check to the south."

"Sure, I'll tell the others."

The foreman headed his horse south, and Charlotte followed.

"Looks like we've recovered over half the herd. We should find your brother soon."

"You think so?"

He nodded.

His broad grin revealed his right side, the lone dimple still visible beneath the growing stubble of a beard. Maybe unlike the other men, he'd shave soon. But she'd be better off if he didn't. Charlotte made herself study the hawk soaring above them.

By the time Mr. Shepherd paused at the top of a small hill, the sun was well over their heads. "I'd hoped we'd have found more than just signs of scattered cows by now."

"Me too." Charlotte glanced up at the sun. "Looks like it's not quite noon yet."

David pulled a gold watch from his vest pocket. "Few minutes after eleven. It's not hard to tell you've grown up on the range."

"Toby has Pa's watch, but it's not as nice as yours." She stared at the ornate timepiece in his hand.

"My boss gave it to me."

"He must think a lot of you." Maybe she'd finally found one advantage to her ruse. Mr. Shepherd didn't look surprised to hear an awed boy blurt out such comments.

The foreman slipped the watch back into his pocket. "The man's like the father I never had."

"What about your ma?" Using her disguise to satisfy her curiosity might not be fair or right, but she so longed to know more about him.

"I never knew my mother."

Her heart ached for him. "That's why you told me to thank God for the time I did have with my parents, wasn't it?"

He nodded.

"I'm sorry, Mr. Shepherd." If only she could sympathize with him in a more adult manner. Pretending to be Charlie could be fine one minute and horrible the next.

He shifted as he looked toward the ground. Fearing she'd said too much, she clamped her mouth shut.

When they topped the next hill, a large group of cattle plus several men looked to be not much more than a couple of miles away. "You think they see us?"

"Only one way to find out." Mr. Shepherd removed his hat and waved it in circles over his head.

A man dressed like Toby signaled back with his hand.

"That's my brother!"

"Let's ride, boy."

Charlotte's heart pounded in a gallop as their horses cantered toward the men and cattle. As soon as they got close enough, she wanted to jump to the ground and run to her brother. But such sudden moves might spook the cows again, so she settled for riding up alongside Mr. Shepherd. Which wasn't bad, the more she thought about it.

Toby guided his horse toward them as soon as they reached the herd. No ear-to-ear grin at seeing her. Only a hint of a smile as he looked straight at his partner. "We didn't lose a single beef. What about the rest?"

"We haven't counted them yet." Mr. Shepherd explained the whereabouts of the other groups.

Charlotte handed her canteen to Toby. He took a long swig without a single word of appreciation.

"Thank God, you're all right." She searched his face for any sign of relief that she, too, was safe.

Not one word of gratitude for her wellbeing, just a stony glare when he'd finally turned his attention to her. Being trampled by a cow might hurt less than looking into his cold brown eyes. A stranger like Mr. Shepherd shouldn't care more about her than her own brother.

5

Charlotte yawned as she stacked clean plates and cups into the wagon box. Instead of gathering around the campfire, most of the men were laying out their bedrolls.

"Let's talk before my watch." Toby stepped behind her and gripped her elbow.

She jerked her arm free and turned to face him. "I'm worn out. Whatever you intend to yell at me for can wait."

"No." He snagged her wrist. The shadows of dusk couldn't hide the hard set of his jaw.

Frying pan in hand, Eduardo stared straight at Toby. He said nothing, but kept the cast iron skillet in his grip instead of tossing it into the wagon.

"We need to talk alone." Toby's voice softened, but his glare didn't.

"Only if you're quick. Like I said, I'm tired."

Rather than risk a confrontation between Toby and Eduardo, she followed her brother to the edge of camp, making sure they stayed in the cook's line of sight.

Toby halted then whirled to face her. "What were you thinking, riding off alone with Shepherd this morning?"

"Looking for you the best way I could." Even though he couldn't see her face very well, she narrowed her eyes as she looked up at him anyway.

"What if you'd had trouble finding us and had to make camp somewhere alone with him?"

She hadn't thought of that but couldn't let him guess as much. "The cows hadn't had time to get that far. If all you're going to do is fuss at me, I'll get my bedroll." Spinning on her boot heel, she started to walk away.

Toby grabbed her arm and yanked her around to face him. "I won't have Shepherd finding out who you are. Never go anywhere alone with him again." His hissing words emphasized his threat.

Shivers ran through her as she jerked her wrist from his grasp. "Did you worry one minute about *me* last night?"

He flinched as if she'd struck him. "You sound like a spoiled child."

"And you care more about losing cattle than family." She hurled the words at him.

"That's not true. Never has been. Never will be."

"Sure seems that way to me."

"Things aren't always what they look to be." So unlike his usual self, his voice remained calm despite her angry words.

Such a nonsensical excuse made her laugh. "We both know that for sure."

Head held high and shoulders straight, she turned her back to him and marched away. Her too-quiet brother made no effort to stop her. If only Toby's concerns over her being alone with Mr. Shepherd had come from him wanting to protect her the way any brother should, instead of wanting to excuse his own behavior. How she longed for the old loving Toby she'd known before the war.

DAVID LET out the breath he'd been holding as he watched Charlie head toward him and Eduardo. If not for the cook telling him to stay put, he'd have gone after Grimes the moment the man jerked his brother around by the arm. The cook finally pitched his skillet into the wagon.

"I'm glad you were right about Grimes not hurting Charlie." He whispered to avoid being overheard.

Keeping his eyes on the approaching boy, Eduardo shrugged. "*Sí*, for tonight. But another time? I don't know."

I know. David didn't voice his thoughts. So much for not meddling in the two brothers' troubles. He'd jump in the middle of whatever if Grimes truly threatened Charlie. When he'd prayed about getting the brother he'd never had, this wasn't what he'd intended to happen.

"Evening, Mr. Shepherd." Charlie's voice sounded strained as he neared the back of the wagon. "Looks clear enough to count every star, so the weather shouldn't cause us problems tonight."

He didn't have the heart to tell the kid cattle were more apt to stampede again after doing it once, and it didn't always take a thunderstorm to get them started. "We should do Spanish lessons another night since everyone needs to turn in early."

"I guess you're right." The disappointment in the kid's voice couldn't be missed.

"You can help me tomorrow night."

"Sure." The boy ducked his head.

Before his emotions won out over his bone-tired body, David grabbed his bedroll. He could sleep on the rockiest ground God had to offer after all the hours he'd spent in his saddle. That is, if he could quit thinking about a young wrangler. Disappointing someone had never bothered him so much until this red-headed kid came along.

Time to throw the herd back onto the trail came too soon the next morning, even though he'd slept better than he'd thought he might. He made a special effort to keep an eye on Grimes while saddling his mount. If someone the caliber of

Eduardo no longer trusted the man, David certainly had no faith in him.

So far, he hadn't heard one cross word from his partner, but he'd wait until Grimes got his horse and rode off before he left to scout the trail. Charlie should have a peaceful day with his brother riding swing and staying ahead of the *remuda*.

Swinging up into his saddle, he let his horse wander closer to the Tumbling G mustangs. Miller and Grimes were the only men who didn't have horses yet. Both of them would be in the saddle soon, the way Charlie roped. He caught the boy's eye and grinned at him.

Charlotte felt her cheeks heating up, but her lips turned up in a smile at the handsome foreman any time even if his attention consisted only of a quick grin.

"Do your job, Charlie," Toby growled at her while scowling at Mr. Shepherd.

Her attention jerked back to the coiled rope in her hand. The lasso zinged in the air and landed around the neck of Miller's black horse as he stepped up beside her.

"I never seen a young'un your age rope like that." Miller's awe was written all over his face.

If he knew who she was, she doubted he'd admire her skills. "I've had lots of practice."

Miller nodded to her before leading his horse off.

Toby moved closer. "I'll take that roan you've been riding. My string needs more rest."

Now she knew why he'd waited for everyone else to get their mounts. He didn't want anyone overhearing his ridiculous excuse for using her horse.

"You don't need Jumper. I checked Smokey's leg. Falling in that gopher hole yesterday didn't hurt him."

"Rope the horse, or I will."

Rather than give him the satisfaction, she coiled her lariat. The rope sailed over the heads of the horses and around Jumper's neck. "He's ornery in the morning. Walk him around and talk to him before you ride him."

"Don't tell me how to handle a horse."

"Suit yourself, but I named him Jumper for a reason."

As he led the roan away, she stared straight ahead. He'd chosen her favorite horse to gall her or get back at her for what she'd said to him last night, but she wasn't about to let him see how much he'd aggravated her.

Just as she roped a horse for herself, Jumper bucked Toby off. His coarse words singed her ears. Judging from the crimson color of her brother's face, the cowboys' raucous laughter and teasing remarks burned him. Even Mr. Shepherd chuckled. Toby picked up his hat, dusted it off, and stalked over to the horse. This time he stayed in the saddle.

"You've wasted enough daylight, men." Toby spurred Jumper and rode toward the herd.

Charlotte turned her back and untied the knots to the rope corral. Her brother would probably let his anger stew all morning. She'd stick extra close to the wagon during the noon meal. Since Toby had to stay in good with their only cook, Eduardo could get by with speaking his mind or protecting Charlotte if necessary.

So can David. She grabbed her saddle blanket. No, he shouldn't—couldn't—be David to her. She suspected he'd watched Toby talking to her last night. But he had to remain Mr. Shepherd. Nothing more.

She spent the rest of the morning reminding herself to be cautious about the foreman. But her mind drifted toward Mr. Shepherd more times than it should. Thinking about him was so much more pleasant than worrying over her problems with her brother, but she couldn't afford herself that kind of luxury.

At noon, Charlotte added another piece of wood to the cook

fire while hoping for a glance of the man she shouldn't be thinking of. "Looks like the men are coming in to eat."

Eduardo reassured her in Spanish that he'd stay close by since he, too, wasn't sure how mad Toby might still be after Jumper had bucked him off.

"Think one day I'll be able to understand you two?" Mr. Shepherd grinned as he joined them.

"*Sí, señor.* You have very good teacher." Eduardo's eyes twinkled.

"The best." Mr. Shepherd winked at her.

"Thanks." Charlotte gave him a quick smile before stooping to scrape the coals off the lid of the Dutch oven.

Anything to stop from gazing into the foreman's eyes. If only she didn't have to pretend it was just his compliment that so pleased her. They'd been on the trail almost two weeks, but her masquerade felt years old already. She glanced up from her spot by the fire in time to see Toby and Miller coming in.

"Looks like you showed the roan who's boss." Miller lightly clapped Toby on the back as they neared the fire.

Toby chuckled. "He's got the makings of a good cow pony. I might keep him."

"No!" Charlotte shot to her feet.

Her brother scanned the silent cowboys staring at him and Charlotte before crossing his arms and glaring down at her. "*You* don't tell *me* no." His low voice didn't disguise his menacing tone. "We'll talk later."

"Jumper's mine. I broke him." She copied his stance, folding her arms over her chest.

Plate in hand, Mr. Shepherd stepped between them. "Eduardo, those beans smell delicious. Boys, we got a river to cross this afternoon."

The cook slid behind her to start serving the food. The rest of the men followed the foreman's lead. She took her plate then sat next to Eduardo. Toby looked fit to be tied. She hoped Mr.

Shepherd's well-meaning gesture wouldn't cause her more trouble later.

Talk turned to the Colorado River. Everyone had noticed signs this area had had more rain than they'd seen a few days ago.

"How high you think the water is, boss?" Jessup asked between bites of biscuit.

The foreman shrugged. "Swimming deep about halfway across. We'll make a raft and float the wagon over."

Sometimes Charlotte wished Jessup didn't know what questions to ask. She couldn't swim, and her most trusted horse needed rest after Toby had ridden him all morning.

The men hurried through the meal. She chose her barrel-chested bay, hoping his sturdy build made him a good swimmer. He wasn't as smart and quick as Jumper, but he'd have to do.

Only half an hour or so after they broke camp, Mr. Shepherd halted the herd. She reined in Red and stared at the rugged, rocky shore dotted with mesquites, cedars, and an occasional cottonwood. Unlike the worrisome thoughts muddling her mind, the water ran clear.

The foreman guided his horse next to hers. "Hold here till I tell you. Schmidt was with me last year. Stay close to him when it's time to take the horses across. You'll do fine, Charlie."

Forcing a smile, she nodded. Her fear must be showing all over her face for everyone to see, but as usual, Mr. Shepherd was the only one paying enough attention to her to notice. Or the only one who cared she was upset.

"We'll find out who's handy with an axe. We've got two, so don't be bashful." Mr. Shepherd grinned at the hands as he dismounted.

The men spent most of the afternoon cutting cedars or cottonwoods and dragging logs to the river bank. The higher the sun got, the worse their language became as they sweated and strained at their work.

Mr. Shepherd wiped sweat out of his eyes with his bandana. "Eduardo, drive the wagon into the river. We'll build the raft under the bed. Once it starts floating, I'll need about a half dozen of you to swim your horses out and use your ropes to tow the wagon."

The men removed their boots and tossed them into the back of the wagon before the cook drove into the water. They lashed the first set of logs under the wheels. The wagon started to float before they finished cross-timbering with the other set of logs.

Swallowing a horrified gasp, Charlotte looked away when the swimmers stripped off their shirts. Her whole face and neck must be bright red, as hot as her cheeks felt. Good thing Schmidt had to pay more attention to his *remuda* than her.

As she listened to the men's exultant words, her ears told her when the wagon made it safely to the other side. She'd keep her eyes on nothing but the horses when the time came to swim them across.

Schmidt rode over to her. "Don't look so worried, boy. Once Mr. Shepherd gives the orders, we'll have every cow and horse across in a half hour or so."

Since the man had no idea what so concerned her, his words gave her little comfort.

"You might want to get ready." Schmidt dismounted and grabbed his jacket. "This works good for keeping things dry." He took off his boots.

To Charlotte's dismay, he removed his shirt. *Dear Lord, what do I do?* She slipped from her horse, taking her time untying the jacket rolled up behind her saddle. She tugged off her boots and socks, then wrapped them inside. Fortunately, her trousers were a little too long and hid her bare ankles that looked nothing like a boy's.

She slowly removed her vest and tucked it into the bundle. If it wouldn't make her look even stranger, she'd leave her leather vest on. Her brother, Pete's, old, loose-fitting shirt would have to do to disguise her body. For the first time in her life, she didn't mind not having as many womanly curves as her sister.

She heard the other wrangler swing up into his saddle.

"Better finish getting ready quick."

Gulping hard, she kept her eyes on her horse while she secured her jacket.

"You swimming like that?"

"Easiest way I can think of to wash dirty clothes." She hoped her forced grin looked natural.

"If you say so, kid." Schmidt chuckled.

The foreman yelled to them to drive the horses into the water then removed his shirt. *Oh, my.* Charlotte forced herself to look away from his well-formed, muscular body. She hoped her hat hid her burning cheeks. All thoughts of the men around her fled when Red started swimming. As the cool water swirled up past her thighs, she gripped her saddle horn and prayed.

The *remudas* crossed faster than the herd of cows. As soon as the last horse stepped onto dry ground again, Charlotte dismounted. She buttoned her leather vest over her wet shirt before pulling on her boots.

As soon as the men took their usual spots around the campfire, Charlotte slipped off to change clothes in the wagon. Before she finished buttoning her dry shirt, Schmidt's mention of Charlie caught her attention. Even without hearing every word, she could tell he was having a fine time telling the others how she'd kept her shirt on.

"Don't know how he got his clothes clean with those cows and horses stirring up so much of the muddy river bottom."

The whole camp joined in his laughter.

Mr. Shepherd said something she couldn't make out. She'd learned his gentle drawl well enough to be sure he'd been the one speaking. The men quieted down.

Charlotte stayed in the wagon until she heard the hands making their way to their bedrolls. Even thoughts of Spanish lessons with Mr. Shepherd couldn't force her to leave her hideaway. She wasn't sure she could face the kind foreman who must have taken her side tonight.

How many more rivers were between here and Abilene, Kansas? If only she knew.

6

D avid glanced toward the Tumbling G *remuda* as he cinched his saddle. Just like yesterday morning, Grimes had managed to be the last one to get his horse. The man leaned close to Charlie and spoke too softly for his voice to carry. The kid shook his head.

Against his better judgment, David led his bay and packhorse toward the brothers. He should be on his way to Austin for supplies and mind his own business. Except his conscience wouldn't let him abandon the young wrangler. Again. He hoped the niggling voice in his head didn't cause him other problems later.

Charlie's lasso zinged through the air and landed around the neck of Grimes's regular morning horse as David came up behind the two.

"I said rope the roan." Grimes glared down at the boy.

"I won't give you *my* horse." Charlie spoke softly despite his forceful words.

The kid had more gumption than a lot of grown men. Another thing he liked about him.

"A man doesn't take another man's string." David kept his voice low as he announced his presence. Best not to let everyone else see the bad blood brewing between him and his partner.

Grimes jerked his attention toward David. "Charlie's no man." His whispered words dripped with contempt.

"Not yet, but he's doing a man's work." David struggled to keep his voice calm as he met his partner's glare with one of his own.

Muttering something under his breath, Grimes stomped off to bridle the horse his brother had roped for him.

"I should catch up to y'all by noon." David swung up into his saddle.

Charlie shot him a quick grin before roping his roan.

David guided the packhorse out of camp. He'd offered to let Grimes ride for supplies in case he wanted to hire another hand. But the man had turned him down. The Tumbling G must have serious money problems.

Maybe that accounted for part of Grimes's short temper. But it didn't explain why he couldn't let go of his anger towards this brother. Or didn't want to. Either possibility could cause a lot of trouble. He knew that too well from experience. If Mr. Bentley hadn't rescued David from himself, no telling what kind of man he might be now. Probably not a very good one.

He turned his attention to more pleasant thoughts and the beautiful country around him. The spring air smelled clean and new after the recent rains. Rolling hills decorated with patches of colorful wildflowers made for reminders of pleasant childhood memories back in Georgia. Grandmother had loved each and every handpicked bouquet he'd brought her.

Thinking about his happy childhood brought his mind back to Charlie. Surely the kid had some good memories despite the hardships the war had forced on him. As he'd done since the first day of the drive, he prayed for the boy and about his problems with the wrangler's brother.

He'd been so sure partnering with Tobias Grimes was God's will. Maybe he hadn't been listening to the Lord as well as he'd thought. But he couldn't change any of that now. At least he'd be rid of him once they got to Kansas. But he hated to think what would become of Charlie after that. The kid was in God's hands. He and his conscience would be better off leaving the boy there.

He soon focused his attention on riding through the streets of Austin, busy with wagons, horses, and people. A few minutes later, he tied his horses to the hitching rail in front of the general store. Then walked in and handed his list to the man behind the counter. "I need a few supplies."

"Sure, mister."

The clerk soon laid the flour, cornmeal, and sundries on the counter. "Anything else?"

Before David could reply, the candy jars in front of him grabbed his attention and refused to let go. Every kid he'd ever known liked sweets. "Give me a dime's worth of the horehound and peppermint sticks."

The words slipped out before he could stop them. A dime was a lot of money to spend on candy. Finding a way to keep his heart from overrunning his common sense or his mouth should have been the next thing on his list.

The sun burned straight overhead when he caught up to the wagon. Grimes had found a spot with plenty of grass. As he rode into camp, David waved to Eduardo and the wranglers.

The cook grinned when he looked up from the fire he was starting. "*Buenas dias.*"

"*Buenas dias* to you." David dismounted.

"Didn't know you could jabber with my cook." Grimes wore his usual frown.

Charlie's face paled as he glanced up while tying a knot in the rope corral. He doubted he'd imagined the warning look in the kid's eyes.

"Eduardo's helping me at night." Fibbing wasn't right but telling half or less of the truth was probably safer for Charlie.

David loosened the ropes holding the supplies on the packhorse. "Show us where you want all this, Eduardo." He handed the sack of sugar to Grimes then grabbed the coffee. "I even got us some dried apples."

"I want a word with you." The hard look in Grimes's eyes signaled he wasn't thinking of a friendly chat.

Neither was David these days. Which didn't please God any more than telling a fib. He set the last of the supplies by the wagon.

"Charlie can put these away." As if that settled everything, Grimes led the way to a large thicket of juniper trees a short distance from camp.

David followed.

Once they were well hidden from sight, his partner whirled to face him. "We need to come to an understanding about Charlie."

"What do you mean?" These discussions were getting old. David worked to keep his voice calm.

"What goes on between me and Charlie is none of your affair." Grimes folded his arms across his chest.

David looked straight into the man's eyes. "What could a kid his age do to make you so mad at him?"

Grimes jaw dropped as he stepped back. "None of your business."

"Until I see you treat your brother with the same respect you give the other hands, I'll make it my business."

"Like I keep telling you, he's different. Stay away from Charlie." Grimes fisted both hands.

David kept his arms limp at his sides. If the man wanted a fight, he wouldn't get one today. But he couldn't allow anyone to keep mistreating an innocent kid. "Different how? Because he rides and ropes better than a lot of grown men? Or because he makes you mad standing up to you?"

Grimes's eyes flamed with anger. "Leave him alone."

"Treat him the way you should, and I'll do that." Turning his back, David left the man mumbling something to himself. Best to quit talking before more than words were exchanged. Just what Grimes meant whenever he insisted Charlie was different, he'd leave alone for now.

CHARLOTTE LEANED against the back of the wagon, staring up at the sparkling stars that never failed to remind her of the loving Creator who cared for her no matter what. Coyotes howled not far away. Some things stayed the same even though she was farther from home than she'd been all her life.

Home with no worries about river crossings, crude cowboys, or Toby ordering her to stay away from David Shepherd. Her brother hadn't minced words before starting his watch tonight. If she closed her eyes, maybe she could pretend she was safe in her bed listening to the night sounds from her open window.

" 'Cept I couldn't keep my promise to Pa if I'd stayed home. And I can't ... I won't quit talking to Mr. Shepherd."

Before she could stop them, her whispered words floated out on a sigh. If only she could be truthful with the man she liked more every day.

She'd keep praying about that and forgiveness for all the lies she'd told and had to keep telling. Despite how sure she was God wanted her to keep her promise to Pa, she was testing God's love and mercy in ways she'd never dreamed.

Twigs snapping startled her from her thoughts. Her eyes flew open as Mr. Shepherd stepped beside her. She couldn't stifle her gasp. Had he heard her talking to herself?

"Sorry. Didn't mean to scare you."

"I ... uh ... was wool gathering and didn't hear you coming." She hoped he didn't notice how high-pitched her first words had been.

"We should work on Spanish."

"Sure."

"I can even pay you a little." He reached into his vest pocket.

"No need for that."

"Do you like horehound or peppermint sticks?" He held up a small bag.

"Either one." She licked her lips. She hadn't had candy since before the war.

He lightly pressed a piece of horehound into her palm.

Popping the candy into her mouth, she savored so much more than the sweet treat on her tongue. His quick touch sent happy shivers through her entire body. "Thanks, Mr. Shepherd."

She added his formal name as a reminder to herself about the distance she had to maintain.

"So, what should we work on?"

"Numbers. If somebody's counting to you in Spanish, you should know if they're telling you the right amount."

"Sounds good."

Laughing at his efforts to count to ten made her feel happier than she had in years. "Be sure you pronounce *nueve* right. If you say *nuevo* instead, you're talking about something new instead of the number nine."

"That's good to know."

If she dared ask, she could think of all kinds of things that would be good to know. Where was he from? Somewhere in the deep South. His fancy vocabulary made her wonder about his former life and why he'd come to Texas.

Oh, but she couldn't let herself think about such personal things. Not here. Not now. Not ever, once he learned the truth about her when they got to Abilene.

"We'd better get some sleep." Mr. Shepherd again pulled the small bag from his pocket. "You can keep this."

"I'd better not. If Toby saw me with candy, he'd want to know how I got it."

"And he wouldn't be happy if I gave you anything."

"Toby doesn't want me around you at all."

David nodded. "He told me at noon not to interfere between him and you."

"Thanks for not letting him take Jumper, but don't make

trouble for yourself. My brother has a nasty temper when he's crossed." As much as she wanted to continue their time together, the foreman deserved to be warned.

"I can take care of myself, but I worry about you. Maybe I should have Eduardo teach me Spanish."

"No." She hoped he didn't wonder why she spoke so quickly. "Toby's no king. Not letting him have his way about everything's usually the best way to deal with him."

He studied her as if thinking about her words. While wishing the shadows didn't obscure the deep blue of his eyes, she took the opportunity to enjoy watching him.

"You're very wise for someone your age."

She had to be more careful with her words. "Pa told me how to handle Toby."

"I'll see you in the morning." David turned toward his bedroll.

As had become her habit, she stared at his retreating form until the shadows hid him from view. She closed her eyes and brushed her lips with the hand he'd touched. Maybe she could chase away her nightmares about river crossings with dreams of David Shepherd.

Eduardo's low chuckle interrupted her reverie as he walked over to her. "You have good lesson?"

The smile in her heart meant there was probably one on her face despite her efforts to stop it. Good thing Eduardo couldn't see her well. "Very good."

He pulled his bedroll from the wagon. "He *muy bueno hombre*. Maybe even answer to prayers, *sí*?"

Reality wrapped around her like a thick, smothering fog she couldn't escape. She shuddered. "He thinks he's protecting an orphaned boy from a hot-tempered brother."

"*Sí*, but you tell him truth in Abilene. Will be good there." Eduardo's whispered comments weren't the least bit comforting.

"How?" Frustration surged through her like a raging river overflowing its banks. She fought to keep her tone low. "He's an honest, God-fearing man trying to do right by a kid. I'm a lying woman doing whatever I have to do to hold onto a ranch that's nothing more than dirt, trees, and cows."

"Land is good. God give Promised Land to His people. God say truth set us free." He patted her arm before carrying his bedding closer to the dying embers of the campfire.

She jerked her quilts from the wagon. Telling the truth would be like putting a noose around her neck instead of freeing her. No telling what Toby might do if he knew she intended to stop him from squandering their money again. And David—Mr. Shepherd. If he found out who she was and what she was doing ...

She couldn't imagine such a decent man wanting anything to do with a lying, brazen woman in men's trousers. Thinking about the possibility of his eyes snapping in anger at her made her heart hurt as if someone had stomped all over it with their spurs on.

Truth was her enemy, not her friend.

7

Charlotte covered a yawn before adding more wood to the fire. No better than she'd slept last night, her bedroll might as well have been full of sandburs. She'd always prided herself on telling the truth. Until coming on this drive.

Eduardo stirred the stew as she stared at the yellow and orange embers, trying to ignore the hungry men coming in for supper. *Lord, what do I do?* She'd been so sure it was right to disguise herself to keep her promise to keep an eye on Toby. But everything had turned so topsy turvy that she wasn't sure if God heard her prayers anymore.

"Charlie, why haven't you brought up the night horses yet?"

She jumped as Toby came up behind her.

"I finish this." Eduardo dropped the lid onto the stew pot.

"Schmidt's already picketed their mounts. Do you know where ours are?" Toby didn't bother to keep his voice down.

"They're grazing down by the creek."

His gruff voice told her she didn't need to turn around to see him glaring at her. Never mind supper was running late because they'd had to travel farther for a place to water the herd.

Without a glance in her brother's direction, she headed over to saddle her bay. Jumper was probably the farthest away, but her main concern was the night horses. And Toby and his temper.

The noises of camp faded away as she reached the tranquil, shaded creek. She'd take her time herding the horses back and soak in a little peace and quiet. She dismounted. Filling her empty canteen without rushing wouldn't hurt anything.

As she reached for her canteen, Red snorted and pricked his ears. A blood-curdling scream unlike any she'd ever heard rent the serene silence, causing the hair to stand on her neck. Her horse reared then bolted through the brush. A mountain lion leaped toward her from the ground-level branch only a few feet away.

Her heart thundering in her ears, Charlotte drew her revolver and fired several shots. The cat fell not far from her boots. Shaking from head to toe, she stared at the lifeless body. She couldn't holster her gun if her life depended on it.

When Eduardo galloped up, she still stood, weapon in her trembling hand.

The cook jumped to the ground the instant his bareback mount halted. "*Gracias a Díos.*" He laid a hand on her shoulder as he took in the sight of the fallen animal.

She bit her quivering lip. How she wanted to fall into Eduardo's arms for a fatherly hug and lay her head on his shoulder like a little girl. But Charlie wouldn't do such an unmanly thing.

"Charlie!" David's unsaddled horse thundered up to them. He jumped down beside her. "Thank God, you're all right." As if to reassure himself of his words, he looked her up and down.

"I'm fine, but our horses must be good and scattered." She tried forcing a smile but doubted her efforts looked genuine.

"We'll worry about them later." David's kind words smoothed out some of her tattered nerves.

She nodded, looking down at the gun still in her hand.

"Better reload that first. Let me have it." The foreman reached to take the revolver from her.

"I told you to leave he—him—Charlie alone." Toby rode up as the foreman's fingers brushed hers.

Did Toby realize how close he'd come to saying her instead of him? "Mr. Shepherd's fixin' to reload my gun for me."

"You been loading pistols for years." Toby marched toward them.

"The kid brother you're so worried about is scared but fine." David glared at his partner.

The hard set of Toby's jaw told Charlotte her brother hadn't missed the sarcasm dripping from the foreman's quiet words. "I'm making sure a mountain lion is the only thing trying to bother Charlie."

"Strange how the cook and I were the first ones here to see about *your* brother."

The angry stance of each glaring man reminded Charlotte of two roosters ready to fight to the death.

"I'd better get me another horse before our *remuda's* gone to who knows where." She said the first thing that came to mind to break the tension.

"*Sí.* Ride back with me." Eduardo placed his hands on her shoulders and turned her toward his borrowed bay.

David trotted behind them. "I'll help you round up the herd."

"Me too. I need my night horse." Toby brought up the rear.

They didn't find the last mustang until after dark. With the *remuda* scattered across the countryside, Toby and David couldn't stay together. She hoped and prayed they'd manage to keep a lid on their simmering differences until the end of the trail.

When she brought the last horse into camp, David was picketing the others. "Thanks for the help, Mr. Shepherd."

"I figured you could eat a little sooner this way." He looked toward the men already seated around the campfire.

"I appreciate that." She dismounted.

"You're welcome." He grinned before walking off to get his plate.

David—no, Mr. Shepherd—had delayed his supper to help her while Toby sat shoveling in his food. If only the war hadn't changed her brother into a man she no longer knew, much less understood. Pa often told her some men buried their hurts deep.

But she had to work hard at having sympathy for Toby, especially after a day like this. If he weren't family, she wouldn't be trying to care about him, much less put up with his temper and cruel ways. She'd lost so many loved ones that she hated to lose Toby for good too. Her growling stomach reminded her she'd better think about other things for now instead of worrying and tying her insides in so many knots that she wouldn't taste anything.

Eduardo rose and grabbed the pothook to slip the lid off the stew pot.

"I could have served myself."

"Is no trouble." He smiled as he ladled stew onto her plate.

"*Gracias, amigo.*" She grabbed the last piece of cornbread before sitting next to the cook's spot. If not for Eduardo, she doubted even one piece would be left.

Miller pointed his spoon in her direction. "Eduardo says you shot a mountain lion almost as big as you."

Chewing a bite of cornbread, Charlotte nodded. She didn't want to talk about her terrifying experience, but maybe that was better than thinking about the unsettling worries over her brother.

"Boss, you did a good job picking your wrangler." Tyler took a long swig from his tin cup.

"Don't make Charlie's head swell." Firelight danced across Toby's face making his rare smile look eerie.

Her brother probably intended for his grin and light tone of voice to hide how disgusted he was about her being here. Such a hypocrite. But calling him out would ruin her ruse and her chances of finishing this trip, so she swallowed her anger and pain along with the stew.

"I don't think you have to worry about this kid getting a big head." David's words sounded non-threatening, but she knew better after the looks he and Toby had exchanged earlier.

The hands didn't act as if they realized there was a silent battle going on between the two partners and kept up the conversation about the mountain lion while she tried to eat. Someone besides her had to notice how quiet her brother was. He'd come to see about her, so he must still care. Except he'd been the last man there ...

Her last bite of cornbread almost stuck in her dry throat. Surely Toby wasn't so determined to do what he wanted with the ranch that he'd like her gone for good? She shivered. An accident with a mountain lion would be the perfect way for that to happen. But if Toby had wanted something bad to happen to her, he wouldn't have come to see about her at all.

She'd keep praying for God to soften his hardened heart.

REVULSION ROSE like bile in his throat as David looked across the campfire at the two-faced Grimes pretending to smile while the men complimented Charlie. The same partner who never said anything nice or encouraging to his own flesh and blood. Who acted as if he were eaten up with jealousy over a kid who'd been left half of the family ranch. How convenient for the man if something had happened to his brother.

But not as long as David was around. He'd keep a closer eye on the boy. Only God knew what would happen to the kid once they parted ways in Abilene.

Such thoughts made his blood boil. He choked down the rest of his stew then rose. The men were used to his nightly walks and paid no attention to him taking his leave. If he stayed around the campfire much longer, he'd say or do something he'd regret. He might have made a deal with the devil partnering with Tobias Grimes. But he didn't want to cross Indian Territory with only his small outfit.

David stayed along the edge of camp until he saw Grimes ride off to start his watch, then went to look for Charlie. Between the firelight and lantern, the night shadows couldn't completely hide the boy's broad smile as David walked up. The kid always looked more than happy to see him. He felt the same about the boy.

"We're almost through cleaning up." Charlie loaded the cups into the wagon.

"Do you feel like teaching me Spanish after what happened this evening?"

"Sure."

They walked a short distance from the wagon where they could talk without the men overhearing them. Charlie seated himself on a fallen log. David took the spot next to him.

"I'm glad you shoot as good as you rope."

"Me too."

He couldn't miss the quiver in the kid's voice. "I brought your gun back."

Charlie holstered the revolver.

"Be sure you keep it loaded and with you all the time."

"I always do."

David prayed the youngster wouldn't need the gun for anything other than snakes and varmints. But he trusted Grimes about as much as a silent copperhead hidden in the brush waiting to strike.

"Thanks for all you've done for me, Mr. Shepherd."

"You're welcome." He patted his vest pocket. "I have candy left."

"You didn't have to save any for me."

He retrieved the bag and placed it in the kid's hand. "I bought it for you."

"You did?" Charlie ducked his head as he gripped his treat.

The boy's squeaky words sounded more like a surprised, breathless girl. Embarrassment over the way he sometimes sounded must be why the youngster looked away from him so often.

"I appreciate how nice you treat me."

"If I had a little brother, I'd want him to be a good kid like you."

"You never had a brother?"

David shook his head.

"Don't you have anybody besides your grandparents?" Charlie gasped. His hand flew over his mouth. "I'm sorry. I shouldn't ask such a thing."

Another girlish reaction. But he wouldn't think of saying such a mortifying thing to a young man. He talked with the kid so much to help him feel better, not humiliate him.

"I never had anyone but my grandparents."

"Oh. Guess I'd better help you with more Spanish."

Nice how the boy sensed the need to change subjects. Odd how Charlie often sounded and acted more like a fourteen-year-old going on at least twenty. But no matter how easy it was to talk to the young wrangler, he didn't care to share the bitter details about his family with anyone.

"I heard you practicing counting to ten at noontime, so maybe we can work up to twenty tonight."

"That'd be good."

"*Once* is eleven, *doce* is twelve, *trece* is thirteen."

He struggled to repeat the words. "Your *r*'s sound as good as Eduardo's do. How do you do that?"

"Put your tongue loosely at the top of your mouth when you're saying *r*'s. It kind of vibrates and tickles your tongue once you get it right."

He tried his best to do as Charlie said. The harder he worked at it, the more the kid laughed. David ended up chuckling with him. He hadn't laughed so much in years.

"Maybe the good Lord didn't intend for a man born and raised on a Georgia plantation to speak Spanish as well as you do."

"I've wondered where you're from and what brought you to Texas." Charlie's tone sobered instantly, again sounding more like an adult than a not-quite-grown boy. As if waiting for him to answer, the kid continued looking up at him.

David swallowed hard, glad the shadows hid his face. He couldn't figure out why the youngster was so curious, maybe even concerned, about him. No matter. Georgia held too many bad memories—haunting memories buried in a spot so deep in his heart that he didn't go digging there himself.

"Texas is home now." He glanced up at the stars. "I'd better let you turn in after such a rough day. See you in the morning."

THE MAN ROSE, spun on his boot heel, and marched away as if Charlotte had told him she had the measles. She hadn't even had a chance to give the candy back to him. The night shadows couldn't disguise the way his shoulders slumped. Something terrible must have happened in Georgia. Maybe she could find a way to help him not to hurt as much anymore.

Charlotte Grimes, you can never do such a thing.

Closing her eyes, she didn't try to stifle the groan that welled up from deep inside. She wouldn't think of playing with a scorpion, but her fanciful thoughts would cause her more agony than any scorpion sting if she didn't stop her foolish wishing.

Working the ranch meant enough to her that she intended to continue doing it. Wearing her trousers and boots. A true Georgia gentleman used to delicate southern belles in hoop skirts would never accept so much as friendship with any woman doing a man's work.

What a mess her life was.

She'd shot a mountain lion to save her life. She'd better protect her heart just as diligently. Maybe she should insist Eduardo teach Mr. Shepherd how to speak Spanish.

8

C harlotte glanced away from the biscuits she was putting in the Dutch oven to see Toby watching her again. He'd done the same at breakfast and when they'd stopped at noon. Supper looked as if it would be no different. She deliberately focused her gaze on him. Let him realize she could stare him down as well as he liked to do with her.

He stalked over to her. "We need to talk."

"You want to talk, and I'm supposed to listen while you fuss at me?"

He leaned in close. "I heard you and Shepherd having a grand time while I was on watch last night." His whispered words sounded like a low growl next to her ear.

"What?"

"Finish the biscuits, and let's go for a walk."

With Mr. Shepherd nowhere in sight, Charlotte looked Eduardo's way to be sure he saw them leaving together.

Toby halted behind a mesquite thicket. "What were you doing carrying on with Shepherd last night? I could hear both of you laughing for a mile."

None of your concern. But she knew better than to voice her thoughts, especially when David had led Toby to believe the cook was teaching him Spanish. "Eduardo was tired last night and asked me to help Mr. Shepherd."

"Sounded to me like you were helping him with a lot more than Spanish."

"How dare you say such a thing?" Hands on her hips, she stared up at him with what she hoped looked like a terrible scowl. "We were laughing about how funny he sounds trying to say his r's."

"Yeah, and the South won the war."

Resisting the urge to kick his knee so hard he'd howl loud enough to be heard by everyone, she settled for another glare. "He thinks I'm Charlie just like the other men."

"Until you tell him different, or he figures it out. I've seen the way you look at him."

A brittle laugh escaped before she could stop it. "You hate me dressing like a man. Think what a gentleman like Mr. Shepherd would say if he found out. I have no intentions of letting such a God-fearing man know how many lies I've told him."

"Just so you keep it that way." He turned and left.

She stared at Toby's back. She and Mr. Shepherd had nothing but a friendship based on lies. And that wouldn't ever change. Especially so with a Georgia-raised gentleman who wouldn't truly understand her love for ranching. She'd never have a future with a man who wouldn't accept her as she was.

WHILE HE STILL HAD SOME daylight left, David gripped his Bible as he looked for a solitary place to read. The sounds of the men swapping yarns around the campfire faded. He had to have some time to soak in God's word. Charlie's innocent curiosity about why he'd left Georgia had triggered loneliness and nightmares such as he hadn't been plagued with in a long time.

He kicked at a log, checking for snakes or scorpions before

sitting on it. Taking in the serene rolling landscape spreading all around him eased his mind. He needed peace.

His Bible opened to underlined verses in Job. Not many people understood why this particular book meant so much to him. But David knew too well the agony of losing everything. Like Job, his redeemer lived. God had used Mr. Bentley to slowly restore David's wounded heart. If this drive proved successful, much of his fortune would soon be restored with a ranch of his own.

"I've been looking for you." Grimes's shadow fell over the pages.

David set the precious book beside him. "I'm here in plain sight."

Grimes kicked the Bible off the log. "A man reading the Good Book shouldn't tell lies." The volume of his voice rose with each word.

David shot to his feet. "What are you talking about?"

"Who's really teaching you Spanish while you're lying to me?" Grimes's fist slammed into David's jaw, almost sending him backward over the log. "Stay away from my ... from Charlie. I won't have you ruining him. Turning him into someone like you."

Sidestepping, David dodged a second blow. "I don't want to fight you."

"Every man and coyote around heard you and Charlie last night."

His partner lunged toward him and landed another punch to his jaw, leaving him no choice but to defend himself.

"No!" Charlie reined in his galloping horse. Jumping down, he ran toward his brother. The kid grabbed Grimes's arm in time to prevent a blow near David's eye.

Grimes shoved the youngster to the ground then charged David with full fury. David landed a hard enough punch to cause his adversary to stumble and give the boy enough time to get to his feet.

"Toby, stop it! Now!" With both hands, Charlie snagged his brother's arm and jerked him back.

Gulping in air, Grimes glared at the youngster. "I'm not the only one in this fight."

"You started it. I saw everything while I was rounding up night horses."

"You're taking up for someone you barely know instead of your own family?"

"He acts more like my brother than you do." Charlie hurled his words with a venomous tone.

As he clamped his open mouth shut, Grimes's face paled. The man looked as dumbstruck as if the kid had hit him hard enough to send him reeling.

"I don't care if Shepherd treats you like you were the president. I don't want you anywhere near him. He knows he's supposed to stay away from you."

Charlie straightened his narrow shoulders, drew himself up to his full height, and looked his brother in the eyes. "I will teach Mr. Shepherd Spanish any time I choose."

"We'll be in Waco in about a week. I'll find another wrangler then put you on a stage home."

"No, you won't. I know secrets you'd never want me to mention in front of Mr. Shepherd or anyone else." Charlie's terse, no-nonsense words matched the glare he gave his brother.

Watching the two stare each other down, David had a hard time believing his ears or his eyes. What kind of family secrets were they hiding? If he didn't know better, he'd swear he was listening to two grown men tell each other off.

Without a word, Grimes picked up his hat and dusted it off. He narrowed his eyes as he returned his attention to Charlie. "We'll settle this and more in Abilene."

"You have no idea how happy I'll be to get to Kansas." The boy didn't flinch as he scowled back at his brother.

"Same here." The man looked daggers at David then stalked off.

When David turned his attention to the young wrangler, he noticed a couple of bad scratches on the boy's face. "One more thing, Grimes."

His partner halted and looked his direction.

"Hurt the boy again, and your eyes will be so swollen you won't be able to look up at me from the ground." David fisted both hands.

Grimes shot him a withering look. "If you don't start leaving my ... my brother alone, you might not live to tell about it."

TOO MUCH LIGHT remained when Charlotte brought the night horses into camp. She hoped stopping at the creek to wash her face made whatever damage Toby had caused harder to see.

While she picketed the night mounts, she stole careful glances at her brother and Mr. Shepherd. Neither of them could deny being in a fistfight. Both would have bruises and welts for a few days. But the other men acted as if everything were as normal as could be while sitting around the campfire. Cowboys weren't in the habit of asking questions.

Except for Eduardo. His snapping, dark brown eyes left no doubt the moment he spotted her. The way her face stung, Toby had to have left some marks on her as hard as he'd pushed her down. The quiet man saw so much more than most people realized. The sun had set by the time he cornered her behind the wagon.

He lifted his lantern and studied her. "*¿Que pasó?*"

Giving him the sparsest details she could, she told him in Spanish how she'd broken up the fight between Toby and Mr. Shepherd.

The cook pointed his finger inches from her nose and asked point-blank how she'd gotten the nasty scratches on her left cheek.

Charlotte gingerly touched her tender face. "*No sé.*" An out-

and-out lie. She *did* know. Without a mirror handy, she couldn't tell much about the damage. She wasn't sure if she looked that bad or if Eduardo was just being his usual concerned self.

"*La verdad, señorita. Ahora.*" His stern whispered command left no wiggle room for anything but the truth he demanded right now.

If she didn't comply, he might confront Toby. Eduardo wouldn't stand a chance against her bigger, stronger brother. She kept her voice low as she told him in Spanish how Toby had shoved her, emphasizing he'd done it only once.

Eduardo's brow furrowed.

"I came to talk about Spanish lessons, but if I'm interrupting, it can wait." David stepped out of the shadows.

"*You* never interrupt." The lantern light emphasized the cook's welcoming smile. "You tell me if Charlie says truth."

"About what?"

"About the fight I broke up between you and Toby."

"Oh, that." David rubbed his jaw. "Tobias wasn't happy to figure out Charlie's the one teaching me Spanish."

"*Sí*, but *Señor* Toby push Charlie harder than boy admit. Is right?"

"Most likely." David closely eyed Charlotte as if he were using Eduardo's lantern light to check her scratches too. "But I told him he'd answer to me if he hurt the kid again."

"*Bueno.*" Eduardo nodded. A smug-looking smirk erased his serious expression.

"Maybe you'd better teach me Spanish if I'm causing trouble for Charlie."

"No!" Charlotte blurted out her objection before thinking about her words.

Letting Eduardo take over Mr. Shepherd's lessons was the best way to protect herself from a man who would never accept her the way she was. She should have kept her mouth shut.

"No?" Looking as puzzled as he sounded, the foreman cocked his head as if still studying her.

"I won't cower to my brother like a whipped pup."

"You're sure?"

"I'm sure."

David didn't look convinced.

"Is good. You help each other, no?" The cook's head bobbed up and down as if his enthusiasm could convince Mr. Shepherd to continue learning Spanish with Charlotte.

"*Sí, amigo*, as long as you say it's all right."

"Is right, very right." Eduardo's grin spread from ear to ear.

Charlotte somehow kept from groaning out loud. Mr. Shepherd had no idea what the cook really meant, but she recognized match-making when she saw it. That Eduardo refused to see the truth concerning her and Mr. Shepherd.

The cook set his lantern on the work table at the rear of the wagon. He grabbed his bedroll and walked off, leaving the two of them alone.

"Since Eduardo says it's fine, teach me something more tonight."

As Mr. Shepherd looked down at her, her stubborn heart did a happy somersault. She'd never seen him gaze at her with such intensity, so she took the unexpected opportunity to survey him. The lantern light glinted off his lone dimple. How she'd love to reach up and push his hat back so she could see his eyes more clearly and maybe even touch his wavy, sandy brown hair.

Thinking such things about a man who'd never accept or understand her had to stop. She should turn down the light to keep Toby from seeing them so well, but her heart wouldn't listen to common sense. Especially with the way he kept staring at her tonight.

"Uh, let's see how close we can get to counting to fifty." She forced herself to look away from his penetrating gaze.

CHARLIE LAUGHED at his efforts to make the r's sound right the way he usually did. But tonight, he couldn't laugh with him. Concentrating on Spanish instead of the wrangler talking to him was almost impossible. He thought he'd heard Eduardo call Charlie *señorita* when he came up behind them a while back. One of the first Spanish words he'd learned after coming to Texas.

Señorita? Charlie a lady? Maybe he'd heard wrong. Had to have heard wrong. The skinny kid dressed in trousers and boots looked nothing like a female. Didn't act like a female.

Except ... All the times he'd seen the wrangler with his hands on his hips like a woman. The times he'd stood up to his brother and sounded too much like an adult. The high-pitched laugh that sounded too much like a girl.

But Charlie rode and roped as well as any man. Better than a lot of them. Could gentle a horse better than he could.

After his third attempt to pronounce *cuarenta*, David glanced up at the stars. "I might *be* forty before I get that one right. We'd better get some sleep."

Not really, but he needed time alone to think without letting the wrangler know his true thoughts. Or have him ... her ... guess the questions now whirling through his mind like a fierce storm of doubt.

Charlie glanced up at the sky. "Guess it is time to grab our bedrolls."

Nodding, he turned to leave. If the wrangler wasn't who he said, who was he? She? Preposterous that a woman could fool him and every other man on this drive since April.

"Wait. Your candy." Charlie pulled the bag from his vest pocket. "You'd better keep this."

Yes, he should. If Grimes knew David had given the kid anything, it would cause problems for the boy. The girl?

As he took the sweets, he folded his hand around Charlie's. No matter how work-worn, the fingers he held were too slender, too delicate and feminine to belong to a boy. His heart thudded so hard he could hardly breathe.

He tightened his grip on the wrangler's hand when he or she tried to slip it from his grasp. "Charlie."

"What?" Whoever this person was, swallowed hard while staring up at him.

Glad they hadn't walked away from the lantern Charlie usually turned down, he studied the supposed boy in front of him. The light illuminated delicate cheeks, full feminine lips he'd ignored or missed seeing because of shadows from her hat. He sucked in air, trying to slow down his pulse. Trying to make sense of the strange turn things had taken.

"You aren't really Charlie, are you?" He ran his fingers over hers.

Gasping, she jerked her hand from his. "W—what ... what do you mean?"

"I've figured out what you meant when you threatened to tell secrets Tobias wouldn't want you to mention if he found another wrangler."

She swallowed hard.

"Who are you, really?"

Her mouth dropped open. She clamped it shut.

How he managed to sound so calm, he'd decipher later. He'd never wanted an answer to a question as badly as he did now. What sort of woman would do what this one had? Could deceive him and everyone else so well?

"No, don't tell me your real name. If I know that, I might say it accidentally in front of everyone and cause you all sorts of problems."

"How did you figure me out?" She bit her trembling lip.

"I thought I heard Eduardo call you *señorita* when he asked you about the fight. Holding your hand confirmed I heard him correctly."

She sucked in a deep breath. "So, what will you do?"

He had no idea.

No lady should be on a cattle drive. But a real lady wouldn't think of dressing like a man, much less be able to work like one so well that she could easily pass herself off as a boy. The multitude of questions racing through his mind made it hard to think. Amazing he could carry on any kind of conversation with her, much less sound so calm.

"Nothing right now."

"What about later?"

He shrugged. "I don't know. I'll pray about it and sleep on it a while."

"I *have* to stay on this drive."

"Like I said, Charlie, I don't know." He stopped short of tipping his hat to her before turning to walk away.

Sleep wouldn't come easy tonight, if it came at all.

9

Charlotte spent the next several days doing her best to avoid David. He obliged her by not seeking her out for Spanish lessons or anything else. When Eduardo mentioned David hadn't come around, she let the cook think she and the foreman were staying away from each other a while to appease Toby's temper. Another lie. No wonder David wanted nothing to do with her.

She shouldn't be thinking of him as David. Not at all. But her silly heart wouldn't listen to her mind.

Keeping her promise to Pa had seemed so simple and so right the day they'd started this drive. Now she wondered if saving a piece of land was worth all her lies and trouble.

After making sure Jumper wasn't grazing too far away, she took her time checking on the rest of the *remuda*. Dusk settled in around her as she gazed at the pink and orange sky. She headed toward the campfire rather than risk David finding her alone with only the horses.

"We're making good time. We should cross the Brazos tomorrow." David said.

Words about the Brazos jolted Charlotte from her thoughts as she walked up to the men. Another river. She tossed up a desperate prayer for help, forcing herself to sit next to Eduardo and act calmly while her insides squirmed.

"Since we haven't had rain the last few days, this one shouldn't be running like the Colorado. Right?" Tyler picked up a stick to whittle.

"Probably not. I'll know after I check it tomorrow."

Charlotte hoped no one had had a lot of rain upstream. How she'd like to leave her vest on while crossing horses across a calm, shallow river with no worries about not knowing how to swim. And to be able to concentrate only on the *remuda* instead of diverting her gaze from shirtless men, especially the one man who so intrigued her.

But the fanciful dreams she should have never entertained had been dashed the night he'd figured out her secret.

Except David. No ... Mr. Shepherd was so easy on the eyes with the firelight dancing across his tanned face. She had to get control of her emotions. Regardless of what Eduardo kept saying, she had no possibility of a happy future with a man who must hate her.

He caught her staring at him but didn't grin at her the way he'd done when he'd thought she was a boy. Pretending to flick a wood chip from the leg of her trousers, she ducked her head.

The cowboys soon switched from talking about the Brazos to a woman one of them had known from Waco. Charlotte stretched and went for her usual walk, praying Mr. Shepherd stayed by the fire the way he'd done the last few nights.

DAVID LISTENED to the men a little longer before going in search of Charlie. No matter how much he'd prayed, he still wasn't sure what to do with a female unlike any other he'd ever known. Who had shocked him as no other woman had ever managed to do. But if he kept avoiding her, the men might wonder why. Nobody needed to start wondering anything about the supposed kid wrangler.

The one thing he did know, he'd keep her secret from the others. They wouldn't consider her a lady any more than he did, which meant she might be in danger from a couple of the rougher hands. And no telling what Tobias might say or do if he realized David had figured out the Grimes's secret. He couldn't wish any harm on a woman, no matter what kind of woman she might be.

Plus, he couldn't jeopardize this drive. He needed the money to finish buying out Mr. Bentley. He kicked at a rock in his path. God already knew about the crazy twists this trail would take, but David would have never dreamed of such things.

He spied Charlie about fifty feet from the back of the wagon. "Maybe we should try Spanish lessons tonight." He alerted the wrangler to his presence to keep from startling her. No one needed to hear her cry out like a scared girl.

"What do you mean?"

"Doing what we've been doing looks normal and keeps anyone from wondering if something's going on." He rubbed his hands along the legs of his trousers. Still hard to believe he was staring at a woman instead of a fourteen-year-old boy.

"Why are you so willing to keep my secret?" Her voice was so low he had to strain to hear her.

"I can't think of any other way to handle things for now."

"For now?"

He nodded.

She folded her arms across her chest. "So since I have no idea what you'll say or do when, I have to be as careful of you as my brother now?"

"No. It's not like that." He held out his hands to her, palms up. "I want to do what's best for you, for any woman the way a man should."

"What's best is for me to stay on this drive." Her pleading tone contrasted with her stiff posture.

77

"Why?"

"Why should I share more family secrets with a man I'm not sure I can trust?"

"You can trust me." Frustration surged through him. He fought to keep his voice low. No matter how much he shouldn't, he wanted to retain her trust.

"How do I know for sure?"

"Because I ..." *I care.*

No, he didn't. He couldn't. Thank God he hadn't finished that sentence out loud. He'd come to like the hard-working, spirited kid he'd thought she was. The woman in front of him still maintained those admirable traits. Except he shouldn't continue to admire such an accomplished liar. But he did.

"Because I do want what's best for you."

"We'll see about that." Her sharp tone signaled her doubts.

This conversation was not going the way he'd hoped. He let out a ragged breath. Liking the most unladylike woman he'd ever met confused him as much as he confused Charlie.

"I'll prove myself to you. Then we'll talk. Until then, we need to continue Spanish lessons, so no one thinks there's anything wrong."

Her long sigh floated into the night air while she dropped her arms to her side.

As if everything were as normal as could be between them, he held out the last two pieces of candy. "Might as well enjoy these."

She stepped back. "You paid for them, so they're yours to enjoy. It's Toby's turn to pick up supplies. He won't buy candy."

"I'm going into Waco tomorrow. Tobias said he'd settle up with me at the end of the trail."

"He did?"

He nodded. "So I'll buy more candy to pay my teacher." He shouldn't make such a promise, but until he figured out what to do with the fake cowboy in front of him, he had to help her continue her ruse for her own safety.

"I don't expect pay."

"I know." Out of habit, he placed a piece of peppermint in her palm. He should have thought about it first. Shouldn't be touching her at all, much less enjoying it.

Taking her time sliding her hand away from his, she put the candy into her mouth. He tried to savor the other piece. He should be kicking himself, instead, for thinking about how well her hand fit in his. The shock of finding out the truth about her must have addled his brain. Only God knew what kind of woman stood in front of him.

"Since we have a river to cross tomorrow, we should call it a night." He hoped such a mundane comment would bring things back to normal for a little while.

"Yeah, we should." She reached for her bedroll propped against the wagon wheel.

Hoping his jumbled-up thoughts would let him sleep, he headed off toward his own quilts. The best thing he could do for Charlie was drag her, if necessary, to Waco tomorrow and put her on a stage home. Especially since Eduardo had told him Charlie couldn't swim.

Except the way she kept insisting she had to stay on this drive made him want to know why. Made him want to help her if at all possible. Maybe he should hear her out if he could get her to tell him her reasons honestly.

If she wouldn't, he could put her on a stage in Fort Worth. He didn't like the idea of a lady traveling alone, but staying on this drive had to be more dangerous. Plus, Charlie was no ordinary woman.

CHARLOTTE SQUINTED as she looked toward the late morning sun while helping Schmidt stop the *remudas* at the edge of the Brazos River. The sticky, humid air hinted at rain. So far, only a few innocent-looking, puffy white clouds floated across the blue sky.

After scouting the river earlier, the foreman had promised her an easy crossing. Watching the water running gently past them was an answer to her or Mr. Shepherd's prayers. With all the lies she'd told, she wondered if God heard her words to Him anymore.

"Eduardo, after you cross the wagon, find a good place to stop," David called to the cook as he rode toward the wranglers. "That way, you can start cooking and have dinner ready somewhat close to on time."

"*Sí, señor.*"

"Schmidt, you and Charlie take the horses across now, so Eduardo has the help he needs." He looked straight at Charlotte. "I'll head into Waco after I see you and your mustangs have crossed. I'll be back in time for supper and Spanish lessons."

If only she could ask him why he hadn't left for Waco already. His waiting didn't make sense. Neither did the way he was being so careful to see she got across the river with no problems.

"Charlie, we're supposed to cross *today*." The other wrangler interrupted her thoughts.

"Sorry." She hoped Schmidt didn't notice her voice was higher than it should be. No matter how much she dreaded another river crossing, she had to get hold of herself.

The *remuda* made it to the other side with no trouble. Charlotte turned her back to the cattle in the river and herded the horses. She glanced toward the other bank of the Brazos. True to his word, Mr. Shepherd was heading his horse toward Waco. He'd looked out for her at the other crossing. Maybe he intended to keep doing that. But why?

Dark clouds building on the northwest horizon sent her thoughts in another direction. If it rained, the heat and humidity would make wearing a jacket stifling. Sweat already had her back soaking wet. After experiencing one stampede, she didn't care to see lightning or hear thunder until after they'd sold every last cow in Kansas.

By the time she guided the *remuda* toward the spot Eduardo had stopped to fix supper, roiling clouds blotted out the sun and every inch of what had been a bright blue sky. Thunder rumbled in the distance. Lightning danced across the darkening sky.

"You might need that jacket you been carrying around since noon." Schmidt grinned at her as he dragged a large branch over to the fire.

Charlotte dismounted then trotted behind the wagon. She'd do whatever necessary to keep from having wet clothes clinging to her body. Slipping off a glove, she checked hidden pins beneath her hatband. If the wind got up, she couldn't risk losing her hat. Raindrops so large they felt and sounded more like hail pelted her. She tossed on her jacket.

A crackling bolt of lightning crashed to the ground near the front of the herd. Shouts and gunfire erupted as the ground rumbled beneath the stampeding cattle. She ran toward the horse she hadn't had time to unsaddle. This time the Tumbling G *remuda* wouldn't be scattered across the countryside.

———

DAVID HEARD the commotion before he caught sight of the hands trying to turn the rampaging cattle. He ground-tied his packhorse, praying the animal was far enough away to be safe and would stay put while he did what he could to help control the stampede.

By the time the men managed to get the herd settled, stars twinkled in a clearing night sky. David led his horse toward the wagon. A cook fire had never looked so good. His grumbling stomach reminded him it was long past suppertime.

Eduardo trotted his direction. "You see Charlie?"

"He's not with you?"

"He ride off to take care of *remuda* before I can stop him." The cook's furrowed eyebrows signaled his concern.

"Which way?"

"East. Schmidt just bring in your horses. He not see Charlie after stampede start. *Señor* Toby say not worry, that kid knows way back."

David swallowed hard. "I'll get a fresh mount and head out to find the boy."

How easily such words still slipped off his tongue. He was getting as good at lying as Charlie. But he'd keep his promise not to give away her secret.

"*Gracias, señor.*"

East covered a lot of territory, especially when it was too dark to track someone. David prayed for Charlie's safety. What he wouldn't give for one of Grandfather's hounds right now. The moon escaped from the thinning clouds about the time Eduardo's roaring fire was the only thing he could see of their camp.

An hour or so dragged by as he scanned every bush and gully for signs of a woman and horses, praying he was looking in the right spots. A horse nickered in the distance.

David rode toward the next rise. "Charlie!" He called to the shadowy figure riding less than half a mile away.

The wrangler waved. Too bad it wasn't daytime so he could gallop his horse toward her. He settled for being cautious and meeting her halfway. Being so concerned for a woman who could look him in the eye and lie the way she'd done wasn't smart.

A lying soldier bragging about shooting skills he didn't have had almost cost several lives in his company. That incident left him with no tolerance for people pretending to be what they weren't. But his heart wanted to make an exception for Charlie when his head said he shouldn't.

"Are you all right?" He looked her over as best he could in the moonlight.

"I'm fine."

"How'd you get way out here?"

"Jumper stampeded our horses. Red stepped in a gopher hole not long after I found all of them, so I had to switch mounts and take my time coming back."

"I told you to be in or under the wagon, remember?"

"That's not what I signed on for." Again her words sounded too much like something a man would say. Another reason she'd fooled him as well as she had.

"We'll talk about that later."

"I won't run like a coward." She sat as straight and tall in her saddle as her slight stature allowed.

"Not now, Charlie. We'll talk tomorrow."

"We will?"

He nodded. "Our beeves ran off too many pounds tonight. We'll trail them slower in the morning and rest them in the afternoon."

They rode in silence the rest of the way. David spent the time thinking how to convince Charlie to stay out of the way if the herd stampeded again. Or better yet, how to manage putting her on a stage when they reached Fort Worth. No woman, whatever sort she was, should be in such danger. One of the few things he knew for certain after the way she'd duped him.

At noon the next day, David had Grimes announce they'd rest the herd.

"I'm going down to the creek and get myself so clean I'll smell like a human being instead of a cow." Jessup grinned before popping his last piece of biscuit into his mouth.

"Charlie, you can wash your clothes without wearing 'em today." Schmidt winked at the other wrangler.

Her face reddened. "You fellas go ahead. I'll help Eduardo first."

The creek was such a busy place that David walked upstream to look for a more solitary spot. After washing himself and his dirty clothes, he donned clean ones, then found an inviting-looking oak to lean against and pulled out his Bible. Maybe he'd enjoy a short rest too.

Nearby laughing voices speaking in Spanish jolted David from his nap. Charlie and Eduardo must have come down to the creek to clean up. He pulled out his watch. Four o'clock. He'd slept much longer than he'd planned.

Now should be a good time to speak to Charlie about staying in the wagon during stampedes. Best to keep his thoughts about sending her home to himself.

He followed the sounds of Spanish a little farther upstream to a spot even more secluded than the one he'd found. So many trees, bushes, and boulders blocked this bend in the creek from view that he wouldn't know anyone was here if he couldn't hear the two friends talking.

The voices sounded closer. He stepped to the side of a large cottonwood tree and froze.

In her man's shirt and trousers, Charlie sat with her back to him brushing beautiful, flame-red hair that hung halfway down her back. Eduardo said something else in Spanish. The woman laughed. His heart sped up the way it had the night he'd discovered the truth about her.

David jumped behind the tree. He dropped to his knees, careful to peek through the brush to keep anyone from seeing him soaking in the stunning sight in front of him.

The lady shifted, giving him a good view of her face. He sucked in a breath. Without her usual hat pulled down low and no leather vest to hide her womanly figure, he couldn't help staring at the pretty little secret he was protecting.

Except that pretty little secret could lie like no one he'd ever met, other than the one bragging soldier. He swallowed a groan. So much for talking to her now. He'd never be able to take his eyes off her face or the flowing hair he itched to wrap around his fingers.

So he slipped away before she or Eduardo could catch him staring and marched himself off to pray and think. He had to get hold of himself. Just being friends with Charlie was risky. Anything more was out of the question.

By the time David returned to camp, the men had lined up for Eduardo to fill their supper plates. Dozens of questions about Charlie kept running through his mind, but not one answer chased after his questions.

If only God would open the sky and explain everything to him. He'd especially like to know what to do with, what to say, to the imposter now handing him a biscuit to go with the stew on his plate.

Charlie grinned at him. "I hope you got some rest."

"Uh, yeah."

He looked down into her big, expressive eyes. How a woman deliberately living a lie could look so pure puzzled him worse than the changing Texas weather. Maybe she was so used to misleading people that she had no conscience left. Or maybe she had a very good reason for doing what she was doing. Much more than he should, he'd like to believe the latter.

He forced himself to walk away. Staring at her too long might be more dangerous for him than another stampede. Caring for people was too risky. Too painful. Losing every family member he'd loved was more than he'd ever endure again.

Sitting cross-legged on the ground, he chose a spot where he could keep an eye on Charlie as she ate. Maybe watching her would give him some answers to the questions that pestered him worse than a persistent horsefly.

The rested cowboys were more talkative than usual. David barely heard a word anyone said. Darkness settled around them. With such a bright moon, he didn't need a lantern to see his watch. Charlie had long since walked away from the salty language. Soon the men would be shaking out their bedrolls

Doubts and questions pinned David to the ground as if he were staked there, ruining his desire to learn Spanish tonight. The new sack of candy in his vest pocket felt as heavy as a bag full of lead bullets.

"I like the looks of the Big Dipper without a cloud in sight." Jessup propped himself up on one elbow.

Tyler stretched out his long legs. "Me too. I'd just as soon not have any more stampedes."

David suppressed a groan. If the herd stampeded again, he absolutely had to find a way to convince Charlie to stay in the wagon. No man worth his salt would ever allow a woman to be in that kind of danger.

His feet took several minutes to obey his conscience and move in the direction Charlie had gone. He spotted her a short distance from the wagon.

"I need to talk to you." He kept his voice soft as he approached her.

Charlie turned toward him. Despite the hat shadowing the remainder of her face, the moon lit up her lips. "About what?"

"About where you're supposed to be during a stampede."

Squaring her narrow shoulders, she stared straight up at him. "I'm supposed to be with the *remuda*."

"Not according to my orders."

"We can't drive cattle without horses."

Since she wasn't a foolhardy kid, he couldn't understand why she would put herself in such danger. "You found them all after the first stampede. You can do it again."

"Maybe. Maybe not. I might not be so lucky next time."

"Luck had nothing to do with it. The Lord helped you."

Stubborn woman. She knew what he said was true, but she was bound and determined to risk her life to see to a bunch of mustangs. How he wished he knew why.

"The Lord kept me safe from a cougar. He'll watch out for me during a stampede, won't He?"

Resisting the urge to shake her took every bit of willpower he could muster. He had to convince her to do what he'd told her to do. Living with himself would be impossible if she were injured or worse. "A young kid in our company got shot through the heart when he didn't follow my orders. I never want to see anyone so innocent die like that again. Understand?"

Dredging up that horrible memory wouldn't help him sleep tonight, but keeping Charlie safe would be worth it. *She* might not have a conscience, but he did. Especially when it came to taking care of a woman.

"I understand you. You need to understand me." Her lowered voice couldn't disguise the pleading tone of her words.

"What do you mean?" He braced himself for her answer. No matter her explanation, he'd win this battle with her. He had to, for her. Maybe for his own good, as much as she affected him lately.

"If Toby doesn't have the money to buy supplies, then we can't afford to replace even one horse. If we can't finish this drive and sell our cows ..." Her voice cracked. She ducked her head.

His heart tightened in his chest. This open, honest side of her confused him more. For reasons he couldn't fathom, she was willing to risk her life to get to Abilene.

"Let me or your brother take care of all that."

Her bitter laugh sounded more like a cackle. "Trust my brother? The man who doesn't care if a bad accident helps him get rid of me?"

"Then trust *me* and listen to what *I* say."

An owl hooted nearby. The woman in front of him didn't say a word as she continued to stare up at him.

"I'd like to, but ..."

"Believe me when I say I'm dead serious about you hopping in that wagon."

"And I'm just as serious about why I can't." Her defiant tone left no doubt she'd risk whatever was necessary to get the money she needed.

Looking into the brown eyes he couldn't see, he took a deep breath. "Disobey my orders again, and I'll put you on the next stage to San Antonio the minute we get to Fort Worth."

She gasped. "What? You can't do that."

"I can, and I will. Even if I have to drag you. That's one thing Tobias might help me do."

He spun. He'd said more than enough. So much for their friendship. Except there never had been a true friendship when everything about Charlie was a lie. The pretty redhead would be doing herself a favor if she gave him the needed excuse to put her on a stage toward home.

Except he'd miss her.

He had to send her home for his sake as much as hers. Entertaining thoughts about liking such a deceptive woman was dangerous. He'd promised himself he'd never again risk the pain of losing someone he cared about. Keeping that promise was the only way he knew to keep his heart safe. Which was in more danger every day since his heart too often didn't want to cooperate with his mind and be sensible about a certain wrangler.

10

Charlotte pressed her trembling fist against her mouth to keep from screaming out loud at David's retreating form. Whether in frustration or pain, she was too confused to tell at the moment.

Threatening to send her home on a stage meant he didn't want her around any more than Toby did. Might even betray her at any time like her brother. So much for his empty words about trusting him. Charlotte marched toward the wagon, out of sight from the others where she could be alone with her maddening thoughts.

How foolish she'd been to enjoy his company, to allow herself to wish Eduardo's fanciful ideas about love might somehow come true. David wanted to be rid of her, which meant he loathed her as much as she'd feared he would when he learned the truth about her.

Squeezing her burning eyes shut, she hugged her quilts close to her aching heart. She wouldn't cry. A man who could turn against her so quickly wasn't worth one tear. Her pain was her own fault. The sooner she got over it, the better.

A hand lightly tapped her shoulder. She jumped.

"*¿Que pasó, señorita?*" Eduardo whispered in her ear.

What happened? She had no idea, except she'd be hurting less if a horse had kicked her in the chest.

The cook placed his hand on her arm. "We walk."

He led her away from the camp, toward the creek. When he halted, the fire flickered like a distant beacon. "*Digamé ahora.*"

Tell him now? Maybe she should. "David, Mr. Shepherd, he ..." She repeated her conversation with the foreman, finally telling Eduardo how David had discovered her secret. "I can't figure out why he bullied me like that. He's no different than Toby."

Eduardo shook his head. "*Señor* Shepherd honest *hombre*. He need to know the truth from you. Whole truth why you here."

"Why? After all the lies I've told him, he wouldn't believe me if I told him."

"He care about you."

"He cared about a pretend boy he felt sorry for, not a woman who deliberately deceived him."

"He care for person behind pretend boy's face. Your hat hide face, not true heart." Eduardo pointed to the sky. "I pray. For you. For him."

"I don't know about God or anything else anymore. Maybe God's mad at me for pretending to be a boy. Maybe I was wrong coming on this drive—"

"*No, chiquita mía.*" Placing his hands on her shoulders, he looked into her eyes while quoting in Spanish the verse about God working in mysterious ways.

He hadn't called her his little girl in years. Wishing his comforting words could soothe her agitation the way they had when she was small, she closed her eyes. Eduardo's faith had never wavered, even after losing his wife and young daughter so long ago. If only she could be as sure of God as he was.

"But David's still mad at me."

"He want best for you. I want best for you. Do what he say if cows stampede." He dropped his hands to his sides.

Except Toby would be so angry with her she feared what he might say or do, and she wouldn't dare tell him she'd followed his partner's orders. The other men wouldn't think much of her if she ran into the wagon like a coward. She sighed. No use arguing with Eduardo or David. She'd have to figure things out on her own if the herd stampeded again.

"Think and pray. God show you."

She nodded. She'd pray for no more stampedes. If God answered that request, then maybe He wasn't as upset with her as she feared, and He still cared.

Two days farther up the trail with no problems from the herd should have brightened Charlotte's dark mood. The men's voices from around the nearby campfire drifted her way. A hundred feet or so to the north, her ears caught Toby's and Miller's lullabies to the cows. Leaning against the wagon, she stared up at the countless sparkling stars in the endless black sky. So many stars that one falling wouldn't be missed when it fell. Just as no one would miss her if she left, or worse. She was alone.

Alone and unwanted.

Toby continued saying and doing whatever he could to remind her he didn't want her along. If David ... Mr. Shepherd ... looked her way, he had no smile or wink for her. He hadn't said a dozen words to her since he'd threatened to put her on a stage to get rid of her.

If she hadn't been so foolish over Mr. Shepherd, she wouldn't be hurting like this. She had only herself to blame for her troubles.

"No company or Spanish lessons again tonight?" Toby's whispered sneer made her jump as he rode up behind her.

"Mr. Shepherd and I are only friends." She fought to keep her voice from betraying her emotional turmoil.

"Not from the way he's been eyeing you lately when he thinks no one sees him."

"And you think *I'm* crazy." She hurled her sarcastic words at him.

"I'm not blind. Neither is he."

"What?" Now she truly wondered if her brother was in his right mind.

"You be careful around Shepherd. He's up to no good, especially concerning you and our ranch we're fighting to keep. That's why I'm watching him watching you." He clucked to his horse then rode back to his watch.

Charlotte stared after Toby even though night shadows soon obscured him from view. The more she thought about his words, the less sense they made. Lately, David had paid more attention to the monotonous beans and biscuits they ate every day than he had to her. The foreman was watching her only in Toby's imagination. The only bad thing David was thinking about doing to her was sending her home.

Gritting her teeth, she balled her hands into fists. She had to quit thinking of that man as David.

DAVID LOOKED toward the dust kicked up by the herd a mile or so out from the campsite he'd picked for the night. They'd made good progress the last couple of days. If only he could say the same about his broken friendship with a certain lady wrangler.

Just on the other side of the wagon, Charlie and Eduardo talked in Spanish while getting the fire going. Or rather, Eduardo talked. The pretty woman with the flame-red hair spoke in one-word sentences if she answered at all. He couldn't miss the listless tone of her voice. The wagon blocked his view of her drooping shoulders and sad eyes, but that didn't stop his mind from picturing them.

He huffed out his breath. Maybe he should try to talk to her. He had time before Grimes brought in the herd.

Not a good idea. No need doing anything that might cause her to think he'd changed his mind about the stage. A real man kept a woman safe, whether she appreciated it or not. Even one who couldn't be less thankful for his efforts.

The misery in those beautiful eyes had cost him a lot of sleep lately. She had enough problems dealing with her hateful brother without David causing her more. Except she'd brought on her own troubles disguising herself as a boy and coming on this drive.

If her brother would leave her alone, he wouldn't have to worry about her unless the beeves stampeded or they had to swim another river. He'd seen Grimes leave the herd to talk to her again last night. If that sorry-excuse-for-a-man hurt Charlie ... He fisted his hands.

What happened to her shouldn't matter to him, but it did. Too much. He had no intention of ever standing over another loved one's grave, of barely living through so much pain. He might as well have stepped into a rattler's den. And only God knew how he'd keep from getting snake-bit.

He wiped the sweat from his face and neck with his bandana. Shade was getting harder to find the closer they got to the prairie, but the late afternoon sun had little to do with his discomfort. If he didn't watch over a lady, he couldn't live with himself.

Lady? He didn't dare think of Charlie like that ... unless she really was a lady, with good reasons for what she was doing.

Maybe he'd better find a quiet spot and pray some more before trying to talk to the wrangler he couldn't figure out. He jumped to keep from stepping on a horned toad in his hurry to be anywhere other than the place he stood.

The answers he craved might as well be hiding on the moon. As soon as he found a rock to sit on, his Bible fell open to the verses about going to a wronged brother. *Charlie's the one telling lies.* He had plenty of good reasons not to say one word to someone who lied as easily as she could. But God didn't seem to want to hear any of them. All the way back to camp, he itched to kick at every rock in his path.

Supper tasted as if someone had sprinkled dirt on it. Charlie stayed as far away from him as she could manage. How was he supposed to talk to someone who didn't want anything to do with him? The woman walked away from everyone as soon as she and Eduardo finished cleaning up.

"Looks like my Spanish teacher is ready to help me make a fool of myself again."

David forced himself to stand and put one boot in front of the other. He hoped his light-hearted words weren't about to come true. Maybe he could sleep tonight if he followed God's leading to be nice to the pretend cowboy. He hoped that was God's idea and not his.

No matter how much danger she'd put herself in, he had too much at stake on this drive to be taken in by a scheming woman. He had to figure a way out of this predicament. But he was running out of time to solve his problems with her. Fort Worth was the last town between here and Kansas. He had to come up with something. Soon.

He traipsed to the other side of the wagon. No Charlie.

"Charlie go north." Eduardo pointed past the wagon tongue.

"Thanks."

He heard her praying before spotting her at the edge of camp behind a clump of bushes.

She had her back to him. He shouldn't be here, but his stubborn feet refused to move. It was one thing to let an unfortunate kid get under his skin, but quite another to let a lying redhead turn him into a soft-hearted fool. No more than she'd said to him the last day or so, she probably didn't want to talk to him. But his boots stayed put as if weighted to the ground.

"You sure it's a good idea to be this far from camp?" He should have kept quiet and slipped away before she saw him.

She jumped and clamped both hands over her mouth as if stifling a scream. That wouldn't have been good for either one of them. He had to be more careful.

"Sorry. I didn't mean to scare you."

"I can still hear the men around the fire. Someone would hear me if I yelled." Her defiant tone grated on him.

"Don't go any farther off. Last night's not the only time your brother's left the herd to talk to you, is it?"

"No."

"Has he threatened you?"

Kicking away a rock, she ducked her head.

If Tobias meant her harm, he certainly needed to put her on a stage. He feared what might happen to her once her brother returned home, but a woman as determined as Charlie should be able to take care of herself. Good thing no one could hear the crazy, contradictory thoughts running through his mind. He wasn't making sense even to himself.

Getting his and her mind on something else would be a good idea. He yanked the sack of candy from his vest pocket. "I have a little bit left."

Pressing a piece of horehound in her palm, his fingers lingered over hers much longer than his mind told them to. He *really* shouldn't be here.

"Thank you." The shadows from her hat hid her face, but her lilting tone indicated an ear-to-ear grin he wouldn't be able to miss in better light. "We're still friends?"

The happier she sounded, the faster his heart beat. *Think, man. Look away from her. Think.* He had no idea what kind of woman stood in front of him, and he'd best remember that no matter how beguiling she was.

"Yeah, but I still expect you to follow my orders."

She stiffened. "I can't promise you that."

"Then I promise I'll put you on a stage if the herd stampedes again." And for any other reason he could find to get her off this trail.

His feet finally listened to his brain and marched away from her. If he couldn't find a way to send her home, he might be in more danger than Charlie. Talking with her more or understanding her better might give his wayward heart reasons to go against the promise he'd made to never care for someone again.

The sooner the herd got to Fort Worth, the better.

"WHICH HORSE DO you want to ride to Fort Worth this morning, boss?" Schmidt's words caused Charlotte's heart to pound.

The other wrangler set his empty plate down before heading toward the Double B *remuda*.

"Rope my bay." The foreman followed him.

She scurried to pick up the dirty dishes. Just because David had again ignored her at breakfast didn't mean he wasn't scheming to drag her to Fort Worth and put her on a stage. She dumped the plates next to the dishpan Eduardo was filling with water.

She held her hands to her stomach. "I'm not feeling so good. I'll be back in a little while." She spun on her heel, hoping to get away from camp as soon as possible, before David noticed she'd left.

Eduardo called after her in Spanish, asking where she was going and what she was doing.

Instead of answering, she prayed the cook didn't come after her. If Eduardo didn't know where she was, he couldn't tell David anything when he came looking for her. She made sure the wagon blocked her from view as long as possible then took off in a run.

Sucking in air as she reached the creek, she stopped to scout the trees along the bank. One cottonwood had a low-hanging limb in reach. She used it to scramble up into a leafy hideaway.

Climbing a tree was childish, but avoiding David and staying on this drive made such a desperate move necessary. Jessup had unknowingly given her good news when he'd mentioned Fort Worth was the last town for buying supplies until they got into Kansas. If this little scheme worked, she'd be able to stay and be sure Toby didn't do something foolish in Abilene.

David—no, Mr. Shepherd—would be furious if she succeeded in eluding him, but she'd managed so far dealing with her angry brother. Another man upset with her shouldn't be too much more trouble. Keeping her promise to Pa would be worth whatever problems either man might cause her.

She hoped. Repeating those words to herself over and over the last several days still didn't make her feel as sure as she wished.

She stayed put until she was certain Mr. Shepherd was well on his way to town. A little ways from the wagon, the men who weren't needed to hold the herd were playing cards, enjoying their rare morning of rest the foreman and her brother had decided they needed. Toby wasn't with them. Good. He must be watching the cattle.

She quietly took the long way around them to the wagon. Eduardo sat propped against the wheel, eyes closed as if taking a well-deserved nap.

"*¿Como estas?*" His eyes fluttered open when she got within a couple of feet of him.

"I feel better now." She answered his question about how she was doing in English in case any of the card players overheard her. Best to let everyone think she'd had stomach problems this morning.

Eduardo nodded, sitting up straight. She took a spot on the ground beside him. He told her in Spanish that David hadn't come looking for her.

"*¿De veras?*" She shook her head in disbelief. "Really? Why not?"

He grinned before telling her David cared about her and God was working everything for good.

"*No, amigo.*"

"*Sí, hija mía.*" He nodded vigorously.

Any other time, she'd feel good to hear Eduardo call her his daughter. Not now. "You're impossible."

"Nothing impossible with God. Now we rest. Will be time to start noon meal soon." Looking as if he didn't have a care in the world, Eduardo pulled his hat over his eyes and leaned back against the wheel.

Charlotte tried to take Eduardo's advice but couldn't sit still long enough to relax, much less take a nap. She checked on the horses, gathered kindling, and walked around until Eduardo decided to start cooking.

About the time the fire was going, Mr. Shepherd rode into camp, leading his loaded-down packhorse on his return from Fort Worth. She pretended not to notice as she cut biscuit dough. He'd hardly said two words to her the last week.

Which was fine, since all he'd done lately was try to bribe her with candy and then hunt for an excuse to be rid of her. She'd had no idea he was so much like Toby. *Men!*

Even though Mr. Shepherd had gone alone, they were still too close to town for her to be safe from his threats to send her home. Maybe after they crossed the Trinity River this afternoon, she could relax a little. She lugged the heavy Dutch oven full of biscuits over to the fire, careful to keep her back to the trail boss as he rode up to the wagon.

"I go unload supplies." Eduardo set the lid on the beans he was stirring.

"Do you need help?" Hopefully not. She didn't want to go anywhere near the foreman.

The cook shook his head.

Glad for a good excuse, Charlotte busied herself getting the meal ready. The fire burned down faster than it should. Mr. Shepherd was still helping Eduardo stow things in the wagon, but she had to get more wood from the sling underneath. She stooped to grab whatever she could from the front as quickly as possible. Careful to keep her back to a certain blue-eyed someone, she rose. The heavy load strained every muscle in her arms and back, but one trip this close to the foreman had to do.

Before she managed two or three steps, the man she had hoped to dodge trotted around her and right into her path. "Let me help."

His strong hands slid under the wood and over her arms as he took the logs from her. She almost dropped the whole load. As her crazy heart reveled at his short-lived touch, her feet refused to move.

"Uh ... nothing wrong with making more than one trip to stoke a fire." David stared into her eyes for a brief moment before stepping back.

He dumped the wood by the campfire. Trying to ignore him, Charlotte bent to add kindling. She needed for him to go away and finish helping Eduardo.

"I scouted the Trinity on the way back. It's swimming deep in the middle, but the water's not running fast enough to cause any problems crossing."

"That's good." She focused on the fire as she heaped more coals on top of the Dutch oven.

He leaned in close, too close. "We need to talk after your brother's on watch tonight."

Chills skittered up and down her back as he spoke almost in her ear. "Sure." Not really, as unsure as she was about him and his motives. But at least her voice cooperated with her and sounded as nonchalant about talking with him as she pretended to be.

Her heart thudded in her chest as she watched him saunter toward Eduardo. What a strange man. Threatening to force her onto a stage one day, helping her carry wood the next. He'd even made a special effort to assure her she'd be all right crossing the river this afternoon. As if he intended to let her stay on the trail? But no more than she trusted him now, she couldn't let her guard down. Fort Worth still wasn't that far away.

That night she sat near the campfire, her puzzling thoughts about David Shepherd blocking out the cowboys' coarse language. She stretched and got to her feet. Might as well get her conversation with the trail boss over.

Coyotes howled nearby. Like Mr. Shepherd, they sounded more threatening than they were. Whatever his reasons, she was thankful he'd let her stay.

So far. Unless he was deliberately misleading her, so she'd let her guard down to be hauled back to Fort Worth in the dead of night after everyone else had gone to sleep.

She turned her back to camp and stared up at the stars. Almost two weeks without a stampede, plus she might have managed to remain on the trail. Maybe God still cared about her despite all the lies she had to live to survive this trip and keep her promise to Pa.

"Charlie."

Even knowing he'd follow her, she still jumped at the sound of Mr. Shepherd's voice behind her and whirled to face him.

"Can we talk?"

"About what?" She couldn't imagine what was so important or why he was being so attentive to a woman he had to hate, unless he was still trying to trick her.

He stared straight into her eyes as if he could see them clearly in the dark. Her heart raced like a runaway horse, refusing to listen to her head about the danger of letting this man have such an effect on her. Doing her best to focus on a nearby clump of brush, she looked away.

"We're heading onto the most dangerous part of the trail."

"*We* are?"

"Yes, *we* are."

If only she dared satisfy her burning curiosity and ask why. But leaving all that unsaid and not pressing him might be best.

Pulling a piece of candy from his pocket, he pressed it into her palm. His hands enfolded hers longer than they should. Her imagination had to be playing wishful tricks on her.

"Can we call a truce and be friends again? Let you teach me Spanish?"

"I don't know."

She should quit staring up at him, but her heart refused to be sensible. According to Eduardo, Mr. Shepherd had bought enough candy to last until Kansas. Why? Nothing this man had done today made sense.

"All I want is to keep you safe. Understand?"

"No. I don't understand a lot about you the last couple of weeks."

Without taking his eyes off her, he blew out his breath. "If the Red River is running bank full like it was last year, it could be the most dangerous crossing we'll make."

She swallowed hard, still unable to quit looking at him. Night shadows or not, she'd memorized his face.

"Once we get to the other side of the river, we'll have to watch out for Indians."

"I knew that before we left. Are you trying to scare me into quitting before we get any farther from Fort Worth so you have a better excuse to get rid of me?"

"It's too late for that."

"Why?"

"Did anybody tell you the Indians sometimes stampede the herd so they can steal horses?" He kept staring down at her.

"No." He *was* trying to scare her into leaving, especially since he couldn't or wouldn't give her a reason why he was letting her stay.

"I don't imagine you've heard how fascinated Indians are by bright red hair like yours, even the little bit that shows under your hat?"

She shook her head.

"Please, Charlie. If we run into any kind of trouble, do what I say so you'll make it to Abilene safely."

"Wh—what do you mean?"

"If the Indians stampede the herd, get in the wagon and stay out of sight. I don't want some savage carrying you off for that red hair or, even worse, finding out you're a female."

Even if she couldn't see his eyes, the kind tone of his voice told her he was dead serious She shoved her trembling hands into her pockets. "You really think I should hide?"

"Absolutely. And don't worry about Tobias. I'll take care of him."

Indians weren't the reason her heart pounded in her chest. She had to look away from him, quit listening to his gentle words that soothed her like a verbal hug. But her eyes wouldn't do what her mind screamed she should.

"Please, Charlie." If it had been light enough to see clearly, he was probably staring a hole in her right now.

"All right."

"Thanks." He slowly exhaled.

Imagining the fascinating single dimple she couldn't see was no problem as he stared down at her a moment or two longer. Then headed back to camp.

Charlotte stared so intently at his back that she wondered if he could tell her eyes were on him. Or realize how fast her head was spinning trying to figure him out. Instead of dragging her onto a stage bound for home, he was preparing her for going through Indian Territory.

After Eduardo learned David was letting her stay on the drive, her friend would be more certain the foreman cared for her. Especially if he'd heard the man's gentlemanly concern for her safety.

Except any Georgia gentleman raised on a plantation would never think romantic thoughts about a woman wearing trousers and working like any other cowboy. Most certainly not a woman who intended to continue working a ranch that was half hers. So entertaining any kind of dreamy notions about someone who wouldn't accept her for herself was out of the question.

She sighed. If God still cared about her, she wished He'd quit dangling a man in front of her who would never belong to her.

11

D avid gripped his saddle horn. The afternoon sun glinted off the red, bluff banks of the Red River. Swirling, angry, rust-colored water mocked him about a pretty wrangler who couldn't swim. He should have kidnapped her, hog-tied her, and thrown her onto a freight wagon or any other conveyance leaving for San Antonio.

But growing wings and flying to the moon would have been easier than going against her. He had to be the biggest, most soft-hearted fool ever born for letting a woman get under his skin the way this one had.

For nearly two weeks, he'd prayed for a way to send Charlie home. The Lord might as well have gone deaf. He'd seen her scampering off from camp as he swung into his saddle to head to Fort Worth a few days ago. Instead of going after her, he'd ridden the other direction.

Like him, she had to have good reasons for coming on this drive and risking so much. He wouldn't want someone yanking his dreams out from under him. So he didn't have the heart to do such a thing to her.

At least that's what he'd told himself. What had really spooked him was seeing the fear in her big eyes whenever anyone mentioned Fort Worth. Imagining those eyes filled with pain and agony caused by him if he sent her away, undid him. He had to be the biggest coward in the world to not stand up to her.

Grimes rode up beside him. "This the best spot you could find to cross?"

"Yeah." The better place had been too close to a freshly dug grave. He wasn't about to let Charlie see such a thing. He'd scared her enough the other night and didn't want the woman who couldn't swim to panic and put herself in more danger.

"Looks like it could be worse." Grimes glanced toward pieces of driftwood lodged overhead in a nearby tree.

David nodded. "This river's earned its bad reputation. Let's get the wagon ready to float."

How he wished it wouldn't look strange for Charlie to ride with Eduardo. But insisting on that kind of special treatment would cause her a different set of problems. She didn't want or need the extra attention. And he had to be careful not to let his partner figure out he'd discovered Charlie's secret.

As soon as the men got the first beeves into the water, David rode over to the wranglers. "I expect you two wouldn't mind an extra hand."

"We sure won't, boss." Schmidt's usual grin was nowhere to be seen as he finished securing his shirt and boots in his rolled-up jacket.

When she fixed her gaze on him, Charlie's pale face made her huge brown eyes look almost black. He reminded himself to focus on her face instead of her oversized loose shirt hanging off her narrow shoulders.

He rode up next to her. "I won't leave you."

"Thank you."

Her weak smile made him want to swim the river with her sitting in his saddle in front of him, but he had no business thinking such things about a woman he still needed so many answers from. Answers to questions he hadn't found the courage to ask.

He dismounted then pulled off his boots. When he unbuttoned his shirt, Charlie looked away. He hated to subject her to such things, but keeping her safe was more important than protecting her female sensibilities.

The horses soon plunged into the rushing river. He hadn't prayed with such intensity since going into battle during the war. While the wranglers concentrated on the *remuda*, he did his best to stay within a few feet of Charlie.

Before they reached the middle, every animal was swimming. Water swirled around his legs. The strong current pushed him and his bay downstream, farther from Charlie than he wanted to be. The look of sheer terror on her face robbed him of his breath, but he couldn't swim his horse upstream toward her.

A thick branch slammed into her and knocked her out of her saddle. She screamed.

"Charlie!" David's pulse roared in his ears. An eternity later, he saw her head pop to the surface. "Kick your feet! Grab onto a horse or that branch!"

He plunged into the river as she floated toward him, her arms flailing while she fought to keep her head above water. He managed to snag the back of her shirt in one hand and jerk her close enough to him to keep her from going under again. Praying for strength, he struggled to paddle with the other hand and kick hard enough to keep them both afloat.

The current shoved his horse toward them. He grabbed the tail and hung on. "Keep kicking, Charlie." He tightened his grip on her.

A mile or so downstream, with an exhausted Charlie in his arms, David stumbled onto the riverbank. Together, they collapsed to the ground, her limp body pressed against him. Cradling her head in the crook of his arm, his fingers itched to touch the loose strands of red hair brushing her pale cheeks.

He tried to push her crumpled hat back to get a good look at her face. His hand brushed against a pin hidden beneath the band. So that's how she managed not to lose her hat when she went underwater.

Her eyes fluttered open, but she didn't pull away from him. "Th—thank you."

The sound of her quivering voice made his heart soar higher than the wisps of clouds floating over their heads. "You're welcome."

One look into her luminous eyes drove away every question he'd intended to demand answers for. He'd risked his life for this woman, and he'd do it again. He was either crazy in love or just plain crazy.

The latter made more sense, especially after the promise he'd made himself to never risk the pain of loving anyone again. He'd burned the letter telling him his wife had died during childbirth, that his infant son was gone two days later. The pain still seared his heart. He couldn't risk losing another woman. Yet no matter how much he shouldn't, he wanted Charlie.

"The last time I held a woman this close, I kissed her." The exact moment he'd said such words, he wished he could take them back.

"You what?" She jumped up so fast he almost fell back into the water.

He scrambled to his feet. If only he'd kept his mouth shut.

Barefoot, she scampered off along the riverbank like a scared rabbit.

David stared at her back. If he had any sense, he'd let her go. But being sensible hadn't been his strong suit lately.

He ran after her.

"CHARLIE, STOP!" David yelled from not far behind her.

Trying to ignore her sore ribs and protesting bare feet, Charlotte did her best to run faster. She couldn't stop. His words about kissing her, a woman he barely knew, proved he didn't consider her to be any kind of lady. No gentleman ever said such things to a woman he respected. Her worst fears had been realized long before Abilene.

"I'll bring you down like a runaway calf if you don't stop."

A comment like that left no doubt how he truly felt about her. She tripped on a tree root and landed face down in the red dirt. Before she could completely sit up, he stood over her.

"Are you all right?" He gasped for breath as he looked her over.

"Of course not! I'm all wrong. Everything's all wrong." She covered her face with her hands, wishing she had the strength to run again. Praying for the strength not to cry.

He knelt beside her. "We have to keep anyone else from finding out who you are."

"I don't understand you at all."

"We'll talk later. Right now, stay here where the trees hide you." He sucked in another breath. "I'll see if my bay is where we left him. Then we'll ride to the wagon where you can change clothes before the others get into camp."

Heat rushed up her neck to her face as she looked down at the soaking wet clothes clinging to every curve of her body.

"I don't have any other choice, do I?"

He shook his head as he rose. "You might want to get some of that red dirt off your face. You look like you're wearing war paint."

She used her time alone to tuck her hair under her hat and wash her face. David ... She groaned. Mr. Shepherd had saved her life. But he was the kind of man who would do that for anyone, good or bad. And he must think of her as bad, or else he wouldn't have made such a forward suggestion about kissing her. No cowboy she knew talked like that to any woman he considered a lady.

Too soon, Mr. Shepherd rode up. "Riding double is better than walking any day."

He reached down and tugged her up in front of him.

She winced. Maybe he wouldn't notice since he couldn't see her face. She'd have a nasty bruise where the tree branch hit her. "I can ride behind you."

"True, but this way I can hide you from view in case we come across any of the men."

"Thank you." She hated not being able to control the quiver in her voice. Watching over someone he had to despise made less sense than all the other crazy things he'd said or threatened lately.

His fingers brushed her neck as he reached around her to take the reins in his hand. "I can see where we're going better if you lean back against me."

Every inch of her body stiffened. She'd never do such a thing with him or any other man she barely knew. Despite what he thought about her, she was still a lady.

"I'm sorry. Bad idea." He urged his horse forward.

They rode in silence until they spotted Schmidt a few hundred feet away, heading both *remudas* toward the wagon.

The other wrangler whistled and waved his hands in the air. "You got the boy?" His shout carried over to them.

"Sure do. He's all right." David leaned toward Charlotte's ear. "Lie back against me in case he rides this way so I can shield you with my arms."

If only she could shield her heart. His muscular arms went around her as she pressed her cheek against his broad, shirtless shoulder. The half-mile ride to catch up to the wagon felt like half a day. Her heart relished David's nearness, his gentle touch while her mind chided her for being such a foolish daydreamer.

Eduardo halted the mules pulling the wagon as soon as he saw David and Charlotte riding toward him. By the time they reached him, he'd jumped to the ground and was trotting their direction.

"*¿Que pasó?*"

"She got knocked off her horse and nearly drowned."

Eduardo's dark eyes widened. "*Gracias a Díos* you save her."

"Yeah, thank God. I couldn't have done it without Him."

Charlotte slipped off the horse. "I need to change clothes." She scampered to the wagon and scrambled into the back. The quicker she could hide from view, the better.

"I'll find your horse so I can get your jacket with your boots and vest. Then Eduardo can toss them in to you," David called to her.

Her whole body shuddered as she slumped down and leaned her head against the side of the wagon. She closed her eyes and groaned. If only she could stay here away from everyone else or throw herself into Eduardo's arms for a fatherly hug. She wasn't sure which ached more, her heart or her sore body.

She took as long as she dared to leave her sanctuary. Eduardo needed her help, and she couldn't act manly and pretend she was fine if she didn't do her share of the chores. Even at fourteen, Pete had done his best to behave like a man instead of showing pain, so Charlie had to do the same.

The cook looked her over as she walked toward him. "*Gracias a Díos* for saving you."

Charlotte nodded before stooping to get logs from the sling under the wagon.

By the time she finished helping Eduardo clean up the supper dishes, her entire body protested. Her feet were sore from running without her boots. The scratches on her face stung. Her bruised ribs made it hard for her to use her left arm.

At least she had good reason not to stay by the campfire very long tonight. She yawned as she took her usual spot next to Eduardo.

"I'm mighty glad to see you here, young fella." Tyler grinned at her before picking up a stick to whittle.

"Yeah, I'm glad to be here."

Charlotte hoped her brief response didn't sound ungrateful, but she didn't want to discuss her near tragedy or the man who had saved her. Thank God David hadn't kissed her. She didn't need more painful memories to try to forget.

"Guess it's a good thing you like to wash your clothes while crossing a river since the boss said he pulled you up by the back of your shirt." Schmidt chuckled. "I might leave my shirt on next time."

The other men laughed with him.

"It's only by the grace of God I managed to grab the boy like I did." David looked straight at her.

She looked away. Her brother scowled her direction. Why he got so angry whenever Mr. Shepherd paid special attention to her, she still didn't know. Surely he wasn't upset that his partner had saved her life. She shivered in spite of the warmth from the campfire.

Talk about the crossing and her almost disaster continued. Charlotte yawned again. She stretched before getting to her feet. "I'll see y'all in the morning. I could use some extra sleep."

Heeding Mr. Shepherd's warning about Indians stampeding the herd, she shook her bedroll out not too far from the wagon. She needed time alone to think. And to keep her distance from the foreman who had said they'd talk later. The man cared enough to risk his life to save her, yet he'd talked about kissing her as if she were no lady at all.

Laying her head on her saddle, she looked up into the night sky. Her rescue had been a miracle from God regardless of who He'd used to do it. Her heavenly Father still loved her. That mattered more than what any man, even David Shepherd, thought of her. A calming peace enveloped her like a warm blanket.

The Lord wanted her on this drive, and He wanted her to keep her promise to Pa.

12

Not long after Charlie walked away, David picked up his own bedroll. He was exhausted too. He glanced toward the wagon, glad to see her stretched out so near the back. The stubborn woman had listened to him about something. It was past time she gave him the answers he needed about why she was on this drive, but he'd let her rest tonight.

As he shook out his quilt, a twig snapped behind him. David whirled to see his partner approaching.

"I want to say a proper thank you for saving Charlie."

"You're welcome."

Grimes shifted from one foot to the other as he looked toward his sleeping sister. "Don't get too attached to someone you won't see again after Kansas. Charlie's my responsibility and stays with me no matter what."

Where else did he think Charlie might go? Not with David. Lately she'd worked harder at avoiding him than she did at anything else. But if he could find out her real reasons for being on the trail ...

No. He shouldn't be thinking about other possibilities for her.

"Uh, yeah. I assumed your kid brother stays with you."

The word brother slipped from his mouth too easily. He'd become as good at lying as Charlie. Like Charlie, he had good reason to shade the truth, as little as he trusted her brother. But only a soft-hearted, soft-headed fool sympathized with someone who lied as easily as Charlie did. He had no business risking his heart for that kind of woman.

"Like I said, thanks. I appreciate it." Grimes walked off toward his night horse.

David laid his head on his saddle and closed his eyes, desperate for one good night's sleep. But his partner's words kept running through his mind. Grimes had the strangest way of saying thanks.

The more he thought about the odd conversation, the more threatening his partner's words sounded for Charlie. And maybe for David, if Grimes thought he was interfering between him and his sister. He had no idea what the man meant, saying she stayed with him no matter what. She was a grown woman and could do as she pleased. He couldn't imagine forcing Charlie to do anything she didn't want to do.

Grimes had no reason to think David might lure Charlie away. He and Charlie were only friends. Every man in camp knew that.

Greater love hath no man than this, that a man lay down his life for his friends.

Jesus's words slammed into him as if he'd been hit with a closed fist. Love? For Charlie? No. He couldn't. Never again. Loving people hurt too much.

Meeting Indians on the warpath would be less dangerous than loving Charlie, or whatever her name really was. She had to remain no more than a friend, which meant he had to be more careful than he'd been lately.

Depending on how she explained herself to him, they might be anything but friends if he could corner her long enough to get answers. Tobias couldn't afford to buy supplies. But needing money couldn't be the only reason she endured all the hardships on a cattle drive. Was she not telling the truth about something else? Discovering she'd lied again would be the simplest way to convince his heart to keep his promise to himself.

Except nothing had been simple with Charlie so far.

CHARLOTTE TOOK her time putting the clean cups and plates in the wagon box. So much time that she was still behind the wagon while the men sat talking by the fire. She'd heard more than enough about Indians from the men the last few days and didn't care to listen to more tonight.

But she wanted even less to hear what Mr. Shepherd intended to say to her. He probably wouldn't wait too much longer to waylay her. Being burned by sparks from the fire might be less painful than enduring the words of condemnation he'd most likely saved up for her.

Walking off too far alone wasn't safe. Too bad she couldn't think of a good excuse for crawling into her bedroll early again.

"Got time for a Spanish lesson?"

She jumped at the sound of Mr. Shepherd's voice behind her. This man was too good at sneaking up on her and her heart, no matter how hard she worked to keep him at a distance.

"The stars aren't even out good. Toby will see us." She kept her back to him.

As he reached over her shoulder and shut the full dish drawer just above her head, his fingers brushed her neck. "I don't have anything to hide. Do you?"

She whirled to face him and wished she hadn't as she looked up into eyes focused only on her. She needed to douse the lantern. Now. He dropped his arm to his side. Oh, he was close. Much too close. "Um ... you want to learn more Spanish?"

"Maybe another night. Let's get a little farther away from the hands."

Wishing she could run the other direction instead, she

followed him to not far from where the night horses were picketed. He wasn't the kind of man to yell or curse, but she doubted his words would be kind despite the way he'd looked at her a moment ago.

He halted and turned toward her. She swallowed hard as he stared straight at her.

"Why are you on this drive?"

"Money." She held his gaze instead of looking away. None of this was his business, yet he kept pressing for her reasons to be here. He was much too curious for a man who didn't care about her.

"What else? I want the truth."

His quiet but firm tone told her he'd accept nothing less. A man who had risked his life for her deserved to know the truth. But telling him everything wouldn't set her free as Eduardo kept insisting. If he were as angry with her as she feared, his condemnation would imprison her instead.

"Before he died, Pa asked me to promise I'd do my best to keep the ranch."

"Why you instead of Tobias?"

She focused on the dark western horizon. Confiding in Eduardo was one thing, but baring her soul to someone who most likely wouldn't accept her or what she'd done was completely different.

Especially when she so longed for him not just to think well of her but to like her. Maybe love her if ... She had to quit letting Eduardo's fanciful ideas stir her crazy heart. David still talked like a plantation-raised gentleman, which meant he might still think like one sometimes and would never accept a woman who wanted to keep working a ranch. They were too different to ever be more than friends, if they could even manage that.

"Please, Charlie. You have to trust me. Keeping secrets while going through Indian Territory could be dangerous."

Dangerous? He had no idea how much danger her stubborn

heart was in already. She sucked in a shaky breath. "Toby sold horses to get money for this drive, but Pa and I knew those mustangs were worth more than he claimed he got. We have no idea what he did with the rest of the money. Pa was afraid to trust him after that."

She ducked her head, waiting for the words of condemnation he had to have been saving up for the untrustworthy woman who had told him so many lies. Words her heart still didn't want to hear.

"Why won't you look at me?"

The men's raucous laughter drifted their way. Coyotes howled to the north. As she struggled to answer his question, every night sound emphasized the uncomfortable silence between them.

"Because I don't want you to distrust or dislike *me*. I've lied just like Toby lied to Pa and me." Before she could stop them, her words tumbled out. She shouldn't risk such honesty with a man she was so unsure about.

"Charlie, I ..."

Waiting for him to finish whatever he was struggling to say, she couldn't help looking up at him. They should have had this conversation in the daylight so she could see his eyes and maybe guess his thoughts or feelings.

"What?" She swallowed hard. "I deserve the truth from you too. What do you really think of me?"

He shoved his hands into his pockets as he looked away from her. "I don't know. I need time to think and pray."

Telling her the truth was that hard? The intense pain squeezing her chest choked back the groan welling up inside. She'd bared her soul to a man who couldn't bring himself to honestly answer her questions. Instead of running toward the quilts she wished she could disappear beneath forever, she turned and forced herself to slowly put one boot in front of the other.

"Charlie, I don't dislike you."

His gentle voice calling from behind her gave her no comfort. She'd told him too much. He'd said much too little.

RATHER THAN SOAKING in the rugged beauty around him, a pair of gorgeous brown eyes with no trace of a sparkle haunted David. He doubted the unspoiled land he rode through had changed much since God created it. He'd spied several deer at dawn and a few buffalo this morning.

The last few days, every time he'd glanced at Charlie she'd looked as if she'd just left a funeral. He hadn't intended to hurt her the other night, but she'd surprised him by asking what he thought about her.

No matter how much he'd prayed, he still couldn't give her an answer. Her good reasons for being on the trail made him feel better about letting her stay. He admired her loyalty to her father. Not many men took making a promise as seriously as she did. A lot of people would have given up rather than endure the risks and hardships Charlie had and would face.

Yet he'd never met a woman who could lie as well as she could. A real lady would never dress and act like a boy, much less pull it off so well. His grandparents would have been appalled that their gentleman grandson would befriend such a woman.

Except she'd been the only help her father had after Tobias left for the war, so she'd had no choice but to do a man's work and had to continue that since her scoundrel of a brother was so unreliable.

Lord, what do I do with Charlie?

He pulled his watch from his vest pocket. Almost eleven. Time to ride back and signal Eduardo he'd found a good place to stop for the noon meal. Maybe he should try again to talk to Charlie sometime tonight. Maybe he'd rope a cloud if he could find one in the clear blue sky. One was just about as hard as the other.

A short time later, Eduardo halted the wagon. The cook jumped to the ground then came straight for David. Charlie must have told him about their last talk. He didn't look mad, but the determined set of the man's jaw told David he'd better brace himself just in case.

"I pray for you."

"I appreciate it." David let his shoulders relax but kept his eyes on the *remudas* heading their direction. Especially on a certain wrangler who wasn't riding tall in her saddle.

Eduardo looked the same direction. "Charlie is good woman, very best kind."

He wasn't so sure, but knew better than to argue with the cook who thought so much of her.

"I'm still praying about everything she asked me. Will you tell her that?"

Maybe he shouldn't have been that honest. He didn't want to give her any kind of false hope and hurt her more.

"I tell her, *señor*."

"*Gracias, amigo.*"

Eduardo's grin lit up his entire face as he headed back to the wagon. After watching his grandmother in action, David knew a matchmaker when he saw one. He suppressed a groan. Giving the cook any kind of message for Charlie was a huge mistake. The cook was definitely praying for different things than David.

***

WHILE SHE HELPED Eduardo finish cooking the noon meal, Charlotte did her best not to look Mr. Shepherd's direction. The foreman made quite a show of ignoring her and the cook by constantly checking the horizon, supposedly to keep an eye out for Indians.

Except she'd caught him watching her every time he thought she wasn't paying attention to him. If someone's eyes could burn holes in a person, her back would be flaming higher than any bonfire by now. Toby would be fussing at her again if Mr. Shepherd kept this up. The foreman knew that, but he persisted anyway. What a confusing man.

The cook chuckled as she again turned her back to the trail boss. "You see I tell you truth what his words to me mean."

She shook her head. David—Mr. Shepherd wouldn't tell her the truth about what he really thought of her. No amount of Eduardo's fanciful thinking could change that. She squared her shoulders. God would help her save the ranch. And He'd give her the strength to survive the trouble she'd brought on herself by wishing Eduardo might be right about Mr. Shepherd's intentions.

The men soon lined up for Eduardo to fill their plates. She reminded herself not to look up at the foreman as she put a biscuit next to his beans, but her heart betrayed her. Sky-blue eyes stared into hers longer than they should with so many people around them. He ducked his head and strode toward the men already seated around the fire. She took her usual spot near Eduardo.

"Seen any signs of Indians, boss?" Wilson took a bite of a biscuit while waiting for David's answer.

"Not yet. But Chickasaws are peaceful. Last year we had no problem convincing them to take only three cows as a toll." As if that settled everything, Mr. Shepherd put a fork full of beans in his mouth.

Charlotte hoped his comments *would* settle things. She didn't like to be constantly reminded of the dangerous territory they now traveled.

"Running across a couple of shaved-head Chickasaws begging for beeves don't bother me. Long-haired Comanches is another story." Jessup stabbed his salt pork with a vengeance.

"So you know 'em when you see one?" Tyler asked.

Jessup nodded. "Anybody who's fought with Comanches does. The men have long braids, and some of 'em paint the parts of their hair yellow or red."

"Jessup knows one tribe from another, but we're in Chickasaw territory." David looked around the circle of men as if to emphasize his words.

"Boss, Comanches been known to war with other tribes, so we'd best stay on the lookout." Jessup pointed his fork toward Mr. Shepherd.

"I have been. As long as we're out in open country like this, we're a little hard to sneak up on."

Several of the hands nodded. Everyone but Jessup looked reassured. They finished the meal without any further mention of Indians. Maybe the men felt better after the foreman's calm statements, but Charlotte didn't. She dreaded seeing any Indian, peaceful or otherwise, since she couldn't forget David's words about how fascinated they could be with red hair.

She prayed for everyone's continued safety while she corralled the afternoon horses. Nothing in sight but a stand of trees over on the next rise. By the time she'd roped the last horse, most of the knots in her shoulders had disappeared. The men prepared to throw the herd back on the trail. She swung up into her saddle, reminding herself Chickasaws were peaceful.

Jessup paused before riding to his spot at flank. He pointed north. "Boss, that ridge of trees just started moving toward us. And they're ridin' like Comanches."

13

"Stand down with your weapons. We can't fire on over a hundred Comanches." Mr. Shepherd barked orders to the men already reaching for their revolvers. "Mr. Grimes and I will deal with them. Y'all stay together. Charlie, stick close to Eduardo."

Hoping none of the Indians paid attention to her movements, Charlotte guided her horse next to the cook, sitting on the wagon seat. David's estimated one hundred Indians looked to be at least two hundred as they charged toward the camp.

"We pray." Eduardo gripped the mules' reins as he looked over at her. He whispered in Spanish for her to pull her hat lower. No need for any Comanche to get a good look at her face or hair.

She nodded as they watched the horde of braves, armed with bows and arrows, surging their direction. Her racing pulse pounded in her gloved fingers.

David and Toby rode in front of the herd then halted to wait for the approaching Indians. Two men with fierce-looking painted faces left the band of warriors and headed their horses toward the cowboy partners. The other braves reined in their ponies to watch the exchange between their leaders and the white men.

Praying for David and Toby's safety, Charlotte held her breath. Every Comanche in sight looked to be armed as they halted not far behind the men she supposed to be the chiefs.

"War paint. They're wearing war paint." Jessup's quiet words sent prickly chills skittering up and down her spine.

Silent, grim nods from the other hands were the only response. They kept their attention focused on the goings-on between their men and the Indian chiefs.

She should keep her head down, but couldn't quit staring at David and Toby. The scowls on the Comanches' faces signaled they didn't like whatever the foreman said.

"Eduardo!" David motioned toward him. "We need your help. Sounds like one of these men speaks Spanish."

The cook looped the reins around the wagon brake. "Charlie, I borrow your horse. You watch wagon."

"All right." Charlotte dismounted then hopped up on the seat.

After swinging into the saddle, Eduardo looked Jessup in the eyes. "Tell others I only one who know *Español.*" The cook's low voice sounded more like a growl. "Any *hombre* give Indians idea Charlie knows *Español,* he meet my knife and God *pronto* if he put Charlie in danger." He reached down enough to pat the top of his boot.

"Whatever you say." As the cook rode toward David and Toby, Jessup shot Charlotte a questioning look.

She shrugged, hoping Jessup would think she was just as confused as he was. "Guess Eduardo's worried about the Indians taking a shine to my red hair."

He nodded. "He ain't the only one. I'll give the others his message."

"Thanks." Her hands shook as she gripped the reins.

Jessup rode closer to the rest of the men. Having an experienced Indian fighter agree with David and Eduardo made her heart race even faster. If only she could disappear inside the wagon. But doing anything to draw extra attention to herself couldn't be a good idea.

A long few minutes later, the trio of cowboys turned their mounts toward the wagon. Charlotte swallowed hard when they got close enough for her to see the somber look on each man's face.

Blood-curdling yells the likes of what she'd never heard raised the hairs on the back of her neck. Like a horde of grasshoppers, the Comanches swarmed around the hands and the herd.

"What do we do, boss?" Wilson spoke above the chaos erupting around them.

David looked over them all. "Keep your hands away from your guns."

Wilson shook his head. "That's all?" Arrows zinged through the air as he spoke. A cow fell less than fifty feet away.

"Yep. Unless you'd like an arrow in your back." Toby looked Wilson in the eyes. "They shot clear through that beef they just took down."

David rested his hands on his saddle horn. "Near as Eduardo can tell, they're on the warpath against another tribe. They said they talked peace with the White Father last year and won't hurt us."

"I don't like takin' a savage's word for nothin'. Except it don't look like we got any choice but to sit tight." Jessup looked around at the other men.

"Mr. Grimes and I figure we'll let them get their fill of meat. Then we'll move on as soon as possible."

"Sounds good to me," Jessup said.

Keeping the small group of cowboys surrounded, the Comanches spent the afternoon circling the herd and killing cattle at random. The hands dismounted but kept their horses saddled and ready for whenever they could get the herd moving again.

"*Amigos*, we maybe be here some time." Eduardo seated himself near the ashes of the noon cook fire.

Charlotte took her usual spot next to the cook. Maybe sitting on the ground would make her less conspicuous. Like Eduardo, David hadn't left her side most of the afternoon. *Mr. Shepherd.* She had to keep thinking of him like that since he still refused to honestly tell her what he thought of her. Plus, she hoped his actions didn't draw unnecessary attention to her from the other men.

"Rest while you can, fellas. I hope these hungry Indians get their stomachs filled soon, and we can move on." Mr. Shepherd stretched out on the ground much too close to her, causing her heart to speed up for a different reason.

Arms folded across his chest, Toby paced. He glared down at Charlotte as he paused not far from her and her protectors. She scowled up at him.

Her brother had no good reason to resent a good man like Mr. Shepherd watching over her. If that's how he felt, he should be the one guarding her. Maybe she'd ask him why after they got to Abilene.

If he'd speak to her once he realized she intended to be as much a part of selling the herd as he'd be. She shoved such worrisome thoughts aside. No use borrowing more trouble than she already had.

"I hate to say it, but I don't believe I've ever seen a finer bunch of riders." Schmidt kept his voice low as he joined the group on the ground. "They're riding bareback all over their horses, off one side or the other, then standing up or laying down and still getting off good enough shots to kill a longhorn."

"They look more like hungry dogs to me, skinning cattle and eating the meat raw." Tyler's lip curled as he looked toward the braves enjoying their feast.

The sun dragged itself to the west. Charlotte longed to leave the circle of men the way she usually did at night. Stretching her stiff limbs, she judged it to be close to four o'clock.

"They've scattered out and quietened down some. Grimes, what do you say to trying to move out?" Mr. Shepherd rose.

Toby nodded. "Let's see what happens."

The foreman looked the group over. "Everybody quietly on your feet. Don't rush to your horses. Keep your hands away from your guns. Wranglers, keep the *remudas* close to the rest of us."

The men did as ordered. Charlotte pulled her hat as low as she could and still see to work. Being sure to keep Schmidt and the rest of the men in sight, she urged Red toward the horses grazing not far away.

The men got the lead cows started. The Comanches regrouped and again surrounded the herd. When the fierce-looking renegades raised their bows, the cowboys retreated.

"What do we do now?" Wilson kicked at a rock as the men again gathered near the wagon.

"Bide our time and try again later. If they're on the warpath the way they look to be, they'll move on soon." Mr. Shepherd wiped the sweat from his face with his bandana. "Eduardo, fix us an early supper."

"*Sí, señor.*"

Charlotte welcomed having something to do as she helped Eduardo with a simple meal. They wouldn't take time to soak beans or bake biscuits. Under the circumstances, salt pork and cornbread would do.

No lively conversation accompanied this meal. She guessed they had about two hours of daylight left by the time she collected the dirty plates and utensils. They'd stack everything in the wagon and worry about washing things tomorrow.

She hoped.

A half-hour or so later, they tried once more to move the herd. The Comanches again refused to let them go.

"Got another plan?" Wilson looked straight at Mr. Shepherd and Toby as they all returned to the fire.

Toby scowled at the man. "No. The rest of us would like to keep our scalps, and I imagine you would too."

"Just wondering out loud." Wilson held his hands out palms up as the others glared at him.

Toby shook his head at the whining cowboy. "We need a plan for spending the night here in case we can't do a little night trailing. Right, Shepherd?"

"Right. Saddle your night horses so we can be ready to leave whenever these renegades let us go. No campfire, so we can save wood or leave in a hurry if we get the chance."

The hands took their time getting their night mounts ready. Charlotte saddled Jumper. If they had to get out of here quickly, she wanted her best horse. If they didn't leave soon, she had no idea how she'd manage the close sleeping arrangements necessary for her safety.

The stars came out, and still the Comanches kept them pinned down. Charlotte tried not to listen to the guttural chants drifting toward the almost silent cowboy camp.

"We'll sleep in shifts, half at a time, so we have plenty of men on watch." Mr. Shepherd paused and looked down at her, standing a couple of feet from him. "Charlie, figure out how to sleep with your hat on and keep hiding that red hair. Schmidt, you might want to do the same as yellow blond as your hair is."

"I hadn't thought of that." Schmidt pulled his hat lower.

Grateful David had thought of a way to keep her from removing her hat, Charlotte shook out her quilts. She'd leave her boots on too. She wouldn't sleep anyway.

QUIET NEARBY VOICES talking in Spanish jerked David awake. Eduardo and Charlie had started breakfast. He squinted toward the predawn horizon. Shadowy, sleeping Comanches still lay all around the herd. Even though he'd taken the first watch, he'd lain down and stared up at the Big Dipper circling the North Star until after two.

"*Buenas días.*" Eduardo greeted him when he walked over to the fire.

"What are you two doing up already?"

Charlie shrugged. "We couldn't sleep and figured everybody would rather travel on a full stomach."

"Yeah. Eduardo's cooking will smell a lot better than the dead cows once the sun comes up." He prayed they could leave soon.

"I don't want to think about any of that." Charlie wrinkled her nose.

Oh, she was cute when she did that, especially with the way the firelight danced across her face. Someone should kick him. People's lives were at risk. His heart was at risk.

The smell of bacon and coffee soon woke the sleeping men. The ones on watch wandered over to join everyone else near the fire. By the time they finished breakfast, the sun was up.

Tyler glanced toward the Indians as he handed his empty plate to Charlie. "I seen them savages stirring. Got any idea what they're up to?"

"No." David rose to get a better view of the renegades still camped too close for them to make an escape unless the savages wanted to allow the cowboys to leave. He shifted then looked toward his men. "As soon as Eduardo and Charlie get the wagon loaded, we'll try getting out of here again."

The Comanches still didn't look to be in any kind of hurry. Some sat around their own fire. Others gestured and pointed toward the cowboys as they talked.

None of the renegades had paid that much attention to them yesterday. A group of about twenty braves headed toward the camp. He prayed for guidance and safety.

"Fellas, we got company coming. Hands off your guns. Act as normal as you can."

"I don't see 'em carrying bows and arrows." Wilson spoke just above a whisper.

"Every Comanche's good with a knife. The others are close

enough to shoot us clear through faster than you can think about it." Jessup glared at Wilson.

As the Indians approached, David raised his hand in greeting.

A brave grunted something he couldn't understand. Looking like curious children inspecting new and strange things, the others walked through the camp, running their hands over saddles and such. Surely they'd seen all this before. What were their real intentions?

The men who smoked had the strings from their tobacco pouches hanging out of their vest pockets. He'd heard Indians liked tobacco. While Charlie and Eduardo continued cleaning up from breakfast, David stayed close to the wagon where he could keep her in sight.

A Comanche reached for the skillet Charlie was about to put in the back of the wagon. She froze. David sucked in his breath. The powerfully built Indian towered over her as he stared down into her terrified eyes. His hand went from the skillet to her hair beneath her hat. Charlie gripped the handle with both hands.

Praying she wouldn't do anything foolhardy, David swallowed the words of caution he wanted to shout to her. The Comanche reached for Charlie's hat as if to pull it off. She jerked away. He clamped a large hand onto her slim shoulder.

"No!" David jumped between the savage and Charlie.

The brave dropped his hand as he looked straight into David's eyes. No emotions showed on his stoic features. The Indian's dark eyes hardened.

Hoping he looked as stern as the man he was facing off with, David stared back. Unflinching.

The other Indians circled around them. The cowboys watched but remained as still as if they were rooted to their respective spots. David kept praying as he continued looking into the brave's eyes. Was the man testing his resolve or getting ready to attack him? The staring match continued. He hoped he was doing as well at hiding his true feelings as the man in front of him was.

The Comanche spoke in a low voice. David stood his ground. What felt like an eternity later, the Indian waved a hand, yelled something to the other braves, and walked away. They followed. David didn't move until all of them were back with the main group.

"Thank you, David." Charlie let out a long breath from behind him. The way she whispered his given name made him almost forget everything else around him.

"You're welcome." He kept his voice soft as he turned to face her, unable to resist looking into those beautiful brown eyes for just a moment. "Tonight, I can answer that question you asked me a while back."

She nodded as she put the skillet in the bottom of the chuck box.

He just stopped himself from tipping his hat to her before walking away. Charlie wasn't the only one who had to be more careful about giving away her secret, especially since her brother was watching them both much too closely.

"Let's try again to throw these moss heads on the trail." Grimes broke the silence as David headed toward him.

A few minutes later, Eduardo hopped onto the wagon seat. The men mounted their horses and turned the cattle onto the trail while Charlie and Schmidt started the *remudas* moving.

"Let's go, boys." David led the way.

The Comanches didn't stop them. He and Grimes would count the herd later to see how many beeves they'd lost. For now, they'd move out as quickly as possible.

"I've heard those savages respect a show of real courage, boss. I think you proved that." Jessup's voice was tinged with awe as he turned his horse to take his spot at flank.

David shrugged. "Thank God we've still got our scalps." He headed his bay north.

Despite the need for extra caution, thoughts of a pretty

wrangler kept turning his attention from scouting or watching for more stray Comanches the rest of the day. He'd risked his life for her. Again.

Just as he'd told her the other night, he definitely did *not* dislike her. She deserved to know that. He'd put her mind at ease. Tell her how much he admired her loyalty to her father, her courage and determination to see things through no matter what.

A hawk screeched overhead as if it were mocking him. Who was he trying to fool? No matter what he'd promised himself about never loving someone again, he longed to do more than just put Charlie at ease. He didn't care if she never wore a dress. He loved that woman—trousers, boots, and all.

Except that created a worrisome different set of reasons not to love her. Charlie only liked him and wanted his approval. Unlike his late wife, who couldn't be with him enough, Charlie didn't behave like a woman in love.

He shook his head at his crazy thoughts. Since she didn't love him, he should have no problem putting a female friend's mind at ease tonight. He couldn't love her for so many reasons, which meant he had no intention of telling her more than what he admired about her. And he couldn't truly tell her everything along those lines either, since he admired more about her every day.

He'd demanded the whole truth from Charlie. Yet he'd tell her only part of the truth and do his best to keep her from guessing what he'd leave unsaid.

14

S weat trickled down Charlotte's back as the hot May sun
beat down on her shoulders. She kicked at a buffalo chip to
check for scorpions before picking up the disgusting thing. But
thank God they'd survived being waylaid by Comanches, and she
could be bothered by nothing more than buffalo chips.

Still, she hoped and prayed David found a creek this
afternoon with enough trees around to gather firewood for
supper.

Now he wanted to tell her what he really thought of her. But
only after saving her life for the second time in a week. Except
for staring at her whenever he thought she wasn't looking, he'd
ignored her for days until the Indians rode up. Then he'd stuck
so close they might as well have been tied together. Acting as if
he didn't care how mad he'd made Toby, or what any of the other
men might think about how obvious he'd been while protecting
her.

She dumped the buffalo chips next to the fire Eduardo had
just started. "I might burn these gloves once we make Abilene.
Never thought I'd need to stoke a fire with something so awful."
She wrinkled her nose at the thought of what fueled the flames
crackling in front of her.

David chuckled from off to her side. "You look like a rabbit when you do that."

She jumped. When had he headed closer to the fire, close enough to watch her so carefully? He was supposed to be keeping an eye on the herd approaching and checking for signs of unwanted stray Indians.

As if he could hear her thoughts, he pivoted then walked to the edge of camp, staring south with his back to her. His stance was so rigid and exaggerated she might have laughed at him if she could figure out why he was so intent on protecting a woman he didn't consider a true lady. The man made less sense every day. Every hour.

Eduardo grinned. While placing the biscuits in the Dutch oven, he reminded her in Spanish how sure he was David cared for her. He heaped coals over the lid as he assured her God had wonderful things planned for her and the foreman once they reached Kansas.

As she stirred the simmering beans, Charlotte suppressed a groan. God had given her peace about keeping her promise to Pa, but not a moment of peace concerning the foreman.

The cook insisted David looked at her like a man in love whenever he thought no one was paying any attention to him. The best she could hope for was to have him truly not dislike her as he'd said. The pain of what he wouldn't say still made her chest tighten if she thought about that night. Whatever he intended to tell her must be harsh enough he wanted to spare her.

Yet he'd risked his life for her. Twice. The lid for the beans almost slipped from the pothook. She had to rein in her hopes. Getting stuck in quicksand might be less treacherous for her heart.

Maybe she should pretend to be more tired than she was and not give Mr. Shepherd a chance to speak his mind tonight. Maybe they should end all this uncertainty, get things out in the open so she could deal with the truth, however painful that might be. She had no idea what to do about David Shepherd.

But God did, and the sooner he shared His answer with her, the better.

———————

SITTING around the fire with the other hands, David tried to be discreet while watching Charlie and Eduardo clean up from supper. With no Indians around, he had no excuse for openly keeping a close eye on the pretty wrangler.

She yawned more than once as she worked. Of course, she was exhausted. So was he. But the need to set things as right as possible between him and Charlie gnawed at him like a persistent untrained pup.

"I hear my bedroll calling me." Tyler stood and stretched.

The other men soon gathered up their quilts. Since Grimes had just started his watch, David followed Charlie behind the wagon. The cook picked up his bedroll and walked away. His lantern still shone from its spot on the chuck box shelf. Maybe Charlie wouldn't turn the wick down. A light shining up onto her face would keep her hat from casting shadows on her pretty features.

"Could we talk?"

"I should douse this light first." She looked toward the herd.

Yes, she should. The harder it was to see her, the better off he'd be.

"Please, don't. I can pronounce Spanish words better if I can see your lips when you say them."

If only he could take his words back. Rein in his wayward thoughts. He had to quit thinking such dangerous things. Especially when the reason he wanted to watch her lips had nothing to do with helping him pronounce Spanish words better.

She stared at him a moment as if studying him. Hopefully, she had no idea why he truly wanted a light. "Toby doesn't need any help seeing us better. I don't put anything past him anymore."

Neither did he, especially since he'd been the one to guard Charlie from the Comanches instead of her brother. "The moon and stars are so bright Tobias can see us even if we don't have the lantern."

"No. I ... I need less light."

She needed less light. She didn't want to see him better, and he couldn't get enough of watching her no matter how much he shouldn't. As she turned the wick down, he dared not protest again. He'd already said more than he should if he wanted to continue holding in his true feelings. Saying anything else about her lips would be too much, and she'd figure out how much he longed to kiss her.

"Just say a few words in Spanish once in a while in case your brother tries to slip up on us."

"All right. We can talk and work on telling time."

"Sounds good to me." He slipped his hands into his pockets. He'd like to do more than talk. *Careful with your words, man.* He was about to dig himself into a hole too deep to dig out of. "I can answer your question now."

"*¿De veras?*"

"De what? You didn't teach me that one yet."

"It means—"

"It means I'm past tired of telling you to leave Charlie alone." Grimes's low growl emphasized his threatening tone as he stepped from around the side of the wagon.

How long had he been there, and how much had the man heard? He shouldn't have been concentrating on the woman in front of him so much that he hadn't heard his partner quit singing to the cows.

David stepped in front of Charlie and faced Grimes. "And I'm tired of you putting us all in danger by neglecting your watch, especially in Indian Territory."

Charlie moved from behind him. Hands on her hips, she

looked straight up at her brother. "I can teach this man Spanish any time I please."

"And what else?"

The shadows from his hat hid his face, but David couldn't miss the sneer in the man's voice. Or keep from wondering why he'd said such a thing. Did he suspect David had discovered Charlie's secret? He balled his hands into fists and wished he could do more than glare in the dark at the man in front of him.

"I have no idea what you're insinuating, but your brother is only doing me a favor."

"Sure, *partner*. We'll settle all this in Abilene." He stalked off.

CHARLOTTE WANTED to scream at Toby's retreating back. How dare he say such things in front of David, who already thought so little of her? She'd tell her brother exactly what she thought as soon as she got a chance.

In the meantime, she needed to think of something to say to the man next to her. But the only words that came to mind she couldn't say. He must never know how much she was beginning to care for him.

"Some of us want to get some sleep instead of listening to y'all jawing," Wilson complained from his spot not far from the embers of the fire.

"Sorry." David turned toward her. "Guess I got a little louder than I realized telling your brother what I think." He kept his last comments soft enough for only her ears.

She shrugged. "He needed to hear that and more. Goodnight, Mr. Shepherd."

"Goodnight." He grabbed his bedroll and walked off.

Making as little noise as possible, she stowed the lantern in the wagon. After shaking out her bedroll, she lay down and stared up at the stars. Her exhausted body needed a good night's rest, but her brother's words taunted her every time she shut her eyes.

The things he'd insinuated about her were bad enough. His veiled threat to David made her shiver. He had every reason to be upset with her, but no reason to be so angry with his partner who had done nothing but befriend her and save her life. Because of David, she was still around to get in Toby's way. Her skin prickled. Maybe that was why he was so mad at her and David.

The next morning, dawn tinted the sky with wispy orange and pink clouds. Charlotte stifled yet another yawn as she ground the breakfast coffee. She wasn't sure how long she'd prayed before finally falling asleep last night.

Eduardo grinned as he grabbed a skillet then peppered her with questions in Spanish about how well her time with David must have gone.

She closed her eyes.

His eyebrows knitted together. Rather than risk anyone figuring out what she thought about her brother, she'd wait until they were alone to give him an explanation.

By the time Charlotte roped the afternoon horses, her arms moved as if weighted with lead. Clouds the color of a cast iron pot loomed to the north. She tried to ignore the darkening sky as she worked.

"Hope we're not fixin' to ride into more bad luck. We don't need a storm with lightning and skittish cows on top of what we just left behind." Tyler glanced toward the horizon while Charlotte's lasso went over the head of his mount.

"God kept us safe from Comanches. He'll handle everything else." David clapped his hand on the doubtful man's shoulder.

Tyler shrugged as he led his horse off. "If you say so."

"No use borrowing trouble before it's here." David grinned at Charlotte.

Afraid to trust herself to say anything sensible, she settled for a nod. She had to find a way to keep this man from affecting her like this every time he got so near.

Toby inserted himself between her and the foreman while she roped Toby's roan. Hopefully, the other men were too busy saddling horses to notice her brother's obvious actions. He made a show of throwing on his saddle blanket, staying within earshot of her and David.

When David lowered his head toward her ear, her lasso almost missed her bay. "Remember my orders and your promise in case we have problems later."

For all the wrong reasons, his husky whisper sent chills down her back. If he kept standing so close, she'd forget about storms, stampedes, and everything else. She glanced up into those incredible blue eyes focused on her and her alone. All she wanted to do was keep staring at him. He expected an answer. She couldn't think straight.

Toby coughed.

"Yes, sir, Mr. Shepherd." She bent to untie the corral ropes.

David led his horse away.

By the time Charlotte guided the *remuda* toward the wagon that evening, thunder rumbled overhead. Lightning crackled across the sky. She'd gathered extra dry wood after breakfast. She'd get more before helping Eduardo with supper. Just in case, she picketed Jumper not far from the wagon. Maybe he wouldn't break loose if the weather caused a stampede.

She smelled the rain coming about the time the men brought in the herd. While everyone else scrambled into their jackets, Eduardo finished setting up his makeshift tarp awning over the fire. A jagged lightning bolt crashed to the ground a few feet from the lead cattle. The beeves took off.

As the rain started, Charlotte dashed to the wagon and hopped up on the seat. Eduardo jumped up beside her. "Won't the men want your help?"

"*El jefe* say not leave you alone while in Indian Territory. He not want you finding horses without help."

"I hadn't planned on doing that."

"*Bueno, señorita.*"

Soon the rain came down so hard they could barely see twenty feet in front of them. Charlotte scrambled inside the wagon. Eduardo followed. The men got the herd under control a couple of hours later. By the time the hands wandered back to camp two or three at a time, Charlotte and Eduardo were finishing up the delayed supper.

Toby stomped over to her. "Why aren't you out rounding up our horses? It's not raining now."

"I don't cotton to coming across some Indian who likes my hair while I'm riding alone."

"I'll go with you if you can find one of your horses."

"Jumper's behind the wagon."

As she headed toward her roan, Eduardo shot her a warning look. But she had no choice. Red hair or not, the wrangler was expected to take care of the *remuda*. She'd had too much special attention lately and didn't need more.

How awful to pray silently for protection as she rode off with her brother. The clouds obscuring the moon broke just as they reached the edge of camp. God would not forsake her. He wanted her here.

"I saw you hightail it for the wagon like a coward when the stampede started." Shadows from Toby's hat hid his face, but his harsh tone of voice left no doubt he was glaring at her as usual.

She wasn't about to tell him she'd followed David's orders. "I'm not riding off alone 'til we're in Kansas."

" 'Cept you'd ride off anytime, anywhere alone with a scoundrel like Shepherd."

"Why do you despise a good man like David?" *Oh, she shouldn't have called him that.*

"*David?* You're calling him by his first name now?"

"We're friends."

"None of the other men line up for Spanish lessons after dark."

Spying a small group of horses up ahead, she urged Jumper into a canter. Toby followed. They stayed busy enough finding the rest of the *remuda* to prevent conversation.

Stars twinkled in an almost clear sky by the time they headed back toward camp. Charlotte prayed as she braced herself for another verbal attack from Toby.

"So, are you and *David* both on a first name basis now?"

"You know he's called me Charlie since the first day. He doesn't have any idea who I really am, remember?" Since he knew the answer to his ridiculous question before he asked, she wished she knew what he was actually trying to discover.

Toby's derisive snort said too much. If he didn't yet know David had discovered her secret, he was all too sure that would happen.

"You dodged my question. Why do you so despise a good man neither of us will ever see again after we sell our herd?" She tightened her grip on the reins.

"I got my reasons."

"Really? They can't be good ones."

Grabbing Jumper's bridle, he halted both horses. "I'm trying to protect you, protect us."

"From what?"

"I won't let Shepherd take our ranch away. You and I are the ones who've sweated and bled for what's ours. Not him." His eerily calm voice sent shivers running up and down her spine.

"You're crazy. David wouldn't take anything from us even if he could."

He jerked his hand from Jumper's bridle. "How can you be so blind?" He spurred his horse and galloped toward the distant fire signaling the way back to camp.

She stared at her foolhardy brother until the shadows swallowed him up. He knew better than to gallop a horse in the dark when he couldn't see gopher holes his horse could trip in. He knew better about a lot of things.

Only a crazy man imagined things that could never happen

while ignoring the danger he was putting himself in now. He couldn't possibly have good reasons for despising David. The bad ones he'd hinted at made no sense.

DAVID FORCED himself to remain by the fire with the rest of the men instead of watching for Charlie to return. He jumped to his feet the moment he spotted a lone rider cantering toward them.

"Where's Charlie?" He didn't bother disguising his angry tone at the sight of Tobias coming back alone.

"Not far." Grimes dismounted. "Missing my watch wouldn't be fair to the other men."

Despite his glib tone, David recognized the sarcasm dripping from Grimes's voice. He resisted the urge to pummel the cad standing in front of him.

"No Indian can see that red hair in the dark, but if you're so worried, you can ride out to meet the kid."

"I'll do that since you don't care." He kept his voice too low for anyone else to hear.

"Right." Even in the starlight, Grimes's stiff stance signaled he understood every word David said and didn't say. "Charlie should be back with the horses by the time I finish whatever's left from supper."

David nodded, sure Eduardo would see that the man didn't gobble every bite and keep Charlie from getting anything to eat. He headed toward his roan. If not for their cowboy audience, he doubted Grimes would have been so agreeable to the idea of David riding off to see about Charlie.

Not wrapping his hands around his partner's throat got harder every day.

A short time later, he spotted Charlie and the Tumbling G *remuda*. The sliver of a moon illuminated her slim silhouette, the waist he could probably span with his hands if he dared. More thoughts he should not allow himself to entertain.

"Charlie." He called her name to keep from scaring her.

"Why did you come out here?" She looked over at him when he reached her side.

Because I care. "Because I don't want you alone as long as we have to worry about Indians spooking horses."

He'd bit his tongue to hold back the words he couldn't say out loud and hoped she didn't notice how quickly the words he did say tumbled out of his mouth. He had to figure out how to control his contrary heart that refused to listen to his head and quit loving the woman riding next to him.

"Thanks, but don't do something like this again." She sucked in her breath. "My brother doesn't just not like you. He hates you."

A chuckle slipped out despite how serious, almost frantic she sounded. "I figured that out already."

"He thinks you want to take our ranch away."

"Why when I have one of my own?"

She reined in her horse. He halted beside her. "How can you have a ranch when you keep talking about your boss?"

"If this drive is as successful as last year's, I'll have the money to finish buying out Mr. Bentley."

"Oh."

"I told Tobias my plans when we talked in San Antonio."

"Then what he told me makes even less sense if he knows you'll soon have your own land."

David could think of only one way he'd have a say about her land, but he couldn't allow himself to entertain the idea of becoming her husband and having any kind of claim on her or her ranch. Keeping the promise to himself to never love anyone again was the only way to avoid the kind of agony he'd experienced losing a wife and child while away fighting a war.

Since Charlie didn't seem to want to say more, either, they rode the rest of the way in silence. He'd hoped to use this time alone to reassure her as best he could that he didn't dislike her. He respected her.

He truly admired her gritty courage and determination. Except such unswerving determination told him how much she loved that ranch instead of him. He couldn't bridge an eight-hundred-acre gap half-owned by an angry madman who'd probably just as soon see him dead.

Even more reason he should stop loving her and quit spending time alone with her. Tonight would be a good time to start being sensible.

15

As the sun came up, Charlotte stole covert glances at David while grinding the coffee. He hadn't come to talk to her about Spanish or anything else the last couple of nights. Why, she had no idea, since he'd said he wanted to finally answer her question about what he thought of her. *Men.* They accused women of being flighty when David made Jumper look as calm and predictable as a lady-broke mare.

"Coffee is all ground."

She jumped as Eduardo walked up behind her. "Sorry. I was woolgathering."

The cook placed a hand on her shoulder. "You and *el jefe* no talk again *anoche.*" He whispered as he took the coffee from her.

Her thoughts spilled out to him in Spanish about why she and David hadn't talked again last night.

Eduardo repeated how sure he was God had told him David cared for her. The trail boss had to have a good reason for not meeting with her lately.

"We pray more, *mi chiquita.*" He spoke close to her ear before carrying the coffee pot over to the fire.

Prayer. She couldn't survive any of this without God. He wanted her here. Troubles or no troubles, she'd do what she was supposed to do. She finished her chores without another glance in David's direction. Let the Lord take care of him too.

And then he took the spot by the fire closest to where she and Eduardo usually sat to eat. He grinned at her as he sipped his coffee before turning his gaze toward the others.

"We'll cross the Washita this afternoon, boys. Unless they've had more rain upstream than around here, we shouldn't have any problems."

"Sounds good, boss." Jessup popped a bite of bacon in his mouth, looking as if the foreman's words settled everything.

Since David had sounded so sure the Washita River would be no trouble, Charlotte spent a blessedly uneventful morning herding horses. Toby was riding point and well ahead of her. The horizon looked to be clear of Indians every time she checked.

If only her thoughts about a blue-eyed man would leave her alone. She couldn't think of a good excuse for why David had ignored her lately. Maybe the foreman had simply lost his courage to say whatever bad things he intended to say. Strange how he could back down a Comanche but not talk with her.

Lifting her canteen to get a drink, her nose wrinkled in disgust as she wiped the sweat and dust from her face with her bandana. Even if David liked her, they'd never be more than friends. No man she knew anything about preferred a woman who smelled more like a horse than a human being.

Despite all her warnings to herself, she'd fallen in love with David Shepherd. She needed to get over her silly notions about him. He'd never understand her wish to keep working a ranch. If only she could stop her heart from wishing for a way to work things out with him.

The sun was almost straight overhead—time to gather up the horses and head toward where Eduardo had probably stopped over the next ridge. Maybe the noon meal would be as uneventful as breakfast. Only if a certain man kept his distance.

The object of her bewilderment stayed away from her and

Eduardo until everyone else headed toward the fire to eat. He grinned at her when she put a biscuit on his plate.

"Thanks."

"You're welcome."

He walked away without another word. After everyone had their food, she took her usual spot next to Eduardo.

David seated himself across from her. "I scouted the Washita. We'll be across in no time."

"We deserve one easy river." Miller sopped up his beans with a biscuit.

Conversation soon turned to the unusually warm May weather and other mundane subjects. David said little and looked Charlotte's way even less. She should welcome his lack of attention, not be bothered by it.

Later that afternoon, Charlotte could have dismounted and kissed the dry bank of the gently flowing, muddy Washita River as she looked across to the other side. The men removed nothing more than their socks and boots then rolled up their trouser legs before getting ready to cross the herd.

DAVID KEPT an eye on Charlie as she finished putting the dishes in the chuck box after supper. She took her time walking back to the fire where he and the other men sat. If she slipped off the way she did almost every night, he should be man enough to follow her. Man enough to answer the questions she deserved answers to after she'd braved telling him so much about herself.

No. He shouldn't. No matter how miserable he was from not speaking to her the last couple of days, he should continue being sensible and stay away from her. He'd be worse than miserable if he didn't keep his heart at a safe distance.

But only a coward dodged telling someone the truth. Except he still wasn't sure how to say what he could. While being sure he didn't say what he shouldn't. Keeping his head clear and watching his words around her got more difficult every time they were alone.

The clouds coming in might do him a favor if they'd block out the moon by the time she headed to her usual spot at the back of the wagon. He wouldn't ask her to leave the lantern burning. The darker it got tonight, the safer he'd be from the effects of looking down into her expressive brown eyes.

Not really. Safe was staying right here where he was.

Charlie took her place around the fire without even a glance in his direction. Usually, she gave him some sort of notice and, once in a while, a slight smile. But she'd smiled precious little since the last time he'd talked to her.

As soon as the men switched from discussing the hot weather to talking about women, Charlie got to her feet. She headed away from where the herd was bedded down, away from her brother, who was supposed to be on watch. But she kept walking too far past the back of the wagon.

Heartache or no heartache, a decent man wouldn't allow a woman to put herself at such risk in Indian Territory, where even peaceful Indians stampeded horses to steal cattle. Especially on dark, cloudy nights. He forced himself to take his time standing instead of running after her.

"Looks like my Spanish teacher is ready to try to drum something else into my thick head." His heart raced while he sauntered off as if he didn't have a care in the world.

She halted a good forty feet away from where he wished she had, then turned his direction as if waiting for him to catch up to her. His crazy emotions wished he could run to her. His head told him to go the other way faster than he was heading her way.

"I'd rather you stay closer to camp." He looked down at her, regretting he'd gotten his wish for the clouds to obscure the moon.

"I figured you'd eventually talk to me again. I'd rather the whole camp doesn't hear whatever it is you plan to chew me out for." She shrugged.

"What?"

"Why else did you decide not to talk to me the last few nights? And you haven't said two words to me today."

"I'm not mad at you."

"Then why won't you talk to me?"

He kicked at a clump of prairie grass. "It's hard ... hard to explain." He'd had the best of intentions the other night. Except the best intentions for his heart would have been to stay by the fire again.

"You demanded the truth from me. Give me the same courtesy even if the truth isn't pretty or nice." Her voice cracked.

"I think you're pretty and nice." Too bad a tornado couldn't swallow him up and carry him far away. *Think before you say another word, man.*

"I am?" Her breathy tone confirmed his remorse over his blunder.

"Uh, I mean I admire your courage. I respect you for keeping your word to your father, and I ..." He wiped his clammy hands on his trousers.

He'd better stop before he got himself in deeper trouble. Even if it were so pitch black he couldn't see his hand in front of him, a woman as sharp as Charlie would see through him.

"And what, David? Please tell me the whole truth." She folded her arms across her chest.

The whole truth? Not on his life. He swallowed hard. She'd called him David. Again. She kept looking at him for what felt like an eternity. Even with the edge to her tone and the rigid stance she'd assumed as soon as he'd told her what he admired about her.

Good thing it was so dark she couldn't see his face well enough to guess his crazy thoughts. The ridiculous urge to wrap her in his arms and kiss her until she had no doubts about the truth she demanded almost overwhelmed him. He couldn't do such a thing. Ever. She didn't love him, and he couldn't risk loving her even if she cared for him.

"When we get to Abilene."

His heart couldn't have picked a worse time to take over his mouth and outrun what little common sense he had left. But it had, and Charlie would probably take his words as another promise he had to keep.

Spinning on his heel, he trotted to get his bedroll.

———

CHARLOTTE SUCKED in several shaky breaths as she stared through the darkness at David's retreating back. Again. The reasons for his abrupt departure eluded her. But this time, his stumbling yet crystal clear words left no delusions for her to cling to.

She bit her trembling lip. Tears wouldn't do her any good. So much for Eduardo insisting David loved her. She would have enjoyed his compliments if he hadn't apologized for them in the next breath by talking to her as if she were a man he thought well of.

Whatever truth he'd withheld, she doubted she wanted to hear. Especially if it was just more masculine traits he admired. Except she couldn't figure out why he refused to finish whatever he wanted to say until they got to Abilene. She'd never met a more befuddling man.

But she still loved him. Her stubborn heart refused to listen to her mind. She sighed. The foreman had had enough time to reach the vicinity of the fire. She'd better be sensible and head closer to the others.

Sensible. Not many people around here understood the meaning of that word, much less put it into practice. She ignored the laughing men as she walked to the back of the wagon to grab her bedroll.

She shook out her quilts. Her saddle pillow felt normal now.

As did staring up at the night sky, trying to once more figure out what David had meant.

God understood everything. And the One who made the sky wanted her here and would help her keep her promise to Pa. The peace that truly did pass understanding washed over her. She yawned. Maybe tonight, thoughts of a confusing blue-eyed man wouldn't rob her of sleep.

16

While the rising sun peeked over the horizon, Charlotte stared into the fire. No matter how much she tried, David's words from last night still didn't make sense. Eduardo placed the coffee pot on the grate and asked in Spanish about her talk with the trail boss last night.

Before she could say anything, the subject of their conversation walked over to them. He yawned. "Looks like we'll have good weather."

"I wouldn't mind that." Charlotte watched him from the corner of her eye while pretending to keep her attention on the flames.

David covered another yawn. Eduardo grinned. As soon as the foreman was out of earshot, she'd set the cook straight.

Judging by the dark circles under David's eyes, anyone would think he'd spent the whole night on watch. She was the one he'd frustrated and hurt last night, but he appeared to be the one who'd lost sleep over their conversation. Strange didn't begin to describe this man.

She was wasting her time and breath telling Eduardo again that his hopes for romance between her and David. But she had to at least keep trying to set him straight.

"Boss, I got bad news." Schmidt galloped their direction.

Tucking his shirt into his trousers as he approached, Toby ran around the wagon from somewhere. "What's wrong?"

"All I can find of both *remudas* is signs they're heading south."

"Indians, you think?" Toby looked at David.

"Maybe. Could be a straggling buffalo or two. At least we've got our night horses."

"Guess the boy and I'll go find the rest while you get the herd moving." Schmidt motioned toward Charlotte.

"No. I'll go with Charlie." Looking past her as if she weren't there, Toby stared straight into David's eyes. "The kid's no good at following a trail."

Several cowboys looked doubtful about Toby's statement, but no one challenged him. Charlotte's heart raced at the thought of spending so much time alone with her brother, but she didn't dare voice her fears.

Shifting his weight from one boot to the other, David didn't look any happier than she felt. "We could spare two wranglers better."

"Schmidt can ride swing for me." Toby turned his attention to Charlotte. "Saddle that jumping jughead you like so well, and let's go find the rest of the mustangs."

She trudged toward Jumper, picketed not far away. Before she and Toby rode off, David caught her eye. He still looked uneasy. She hoped her brother wouldn't notice the silent exchange between her and the foreman.

Not far from camp, Toby dismounted and knelt to check for signs of the *remudas*. "The trail is fresh. They're running south like Schmidt said."

Since she could safely use her tracking skills now that the other men couldn't hear or see her, Charlotte studied the signs from her saddle. "I don't see any traces of unshod Indian ponies. Wonder what scared them?"

Her brother shrugged. They rode in silence over the next ridge. He paused again to be certain of the trail. "Since Shepherd keeps calling you a boy and thinks you could ride out alone with Schmidt, maybe you're telling me the truth about what my partner knows about you."

To hide her face from him, she shaded her eyes as she looked toward the horizon. "I don't like lies." Which was true. If only things were right between her and Toby, and she could be completely honest with him.

"You think *I* lie?"

"I didn't say that."

"You sound like you think I'm lying."

"If your conscience is bothering you that bad, tell me how much you really got for those horses." She twisted in her saddle to look him in the eyes.

He looked away from her. "I got a good price."

"How much, Toby? It's my money too."

Staring straight ahead, he clenched his jaw. "Enough to pay for this drive, just like I said."

"No. You couldn't afford to hire a wrangler or another hand to cover the watch." Since she probably wasn't supposed to know, she didn't mention how much they must owe David for supplies.

Horses whinnied in the distance. "You want to find the *remudas* or jabber?" He spurred his bay in the direction of the sound.

Both. Trying to discover the truth wasn't jabbering unless someone wanted to continue hiding the facts. But she kept quiet as she urged Jumper into a gallop to catch up to Toby.

He halted as soon as they caught sight of the missing herd. Charlotte reigned in her roan. Cautiously sniffing the warm, humid air as if danger still lurked nearby, the animals stood at attention.

"Something's still scaring them." She spoke softly to keep from startling the uneasy horses or maybe alerting whatever might be close by.

"No Indian signs, so I'd like to see what's making them so skittish." He urged his horse forward.

Her curiosity didn't match his, but they did need to be sure they and the horses could safely turn their backs on whatever or whoever was out there. So she followed him, praying they wouldn't need more than the revolvers they each carried.

They rounded the edge of a hill and spotted a small band of about twenty buffalo some two hundred yards away. At her first sight of the huge animals, Charlotte sucked in her breath.

"If we drop back and stay close to the hill, maybe we can keep them from seeing or hearing us." Toby's whisper sounded more like a boy in awe of receiving his first gun.

Afraid to ruin this unexpected moment, she nodded. Her brother hadn't looked or sounded this cheerful in years. A few moments later they dismounted, careful to keep the hill between them and the fascinating animals. Climbing to the summit of the small hill gave them a magnificent view of the buffalo below.

While lying flat on their stomachs, Charlotte marveled at more than the sights around her as they spent several idyllic minutes watching the shaggy brutes. They hadn't done anything like this together since they were kids.

Maybe the old Toby still existed somewhere deep inside the angry man who had taken his place. If only her brother would let his guard down more often, let go of whatever still haunted him from the war. Let go of his unwarranted hatred of David.

Toby shifted. "We've spent more than enough time lollygagging." He rose, his expression back to a thin-lipped frown.

Charlotte followed him down the hill. For the first time in years, she dared hope he'd someday go back to the man she'd glimpsed just now. Maybe the Lord had given her these last few minutes to tell her not to give up on her brother. To give her hope for running the ranch with him.

THE MORNING CRAWLED by as David scouted the trail for Indians and stray buffalo while his mind wandered to a pretty redhead riding alone with a brother neither of them trusted. He prayed buffalo had spooked the horses instead of Indians. Charlie and Grimes wouldn't stand a chance running up against unfriendly renegades with just the two of them.

Too bad he'd had no choice but to get the herd moving while she rode off with her brother. Every hand in the outfit would have thought he'd gone crazy if he'd wasted good daylight to wait for scattered horses. No use letting every cowboy know just how close to crazy their foreman was when it came to a certain wrangler.

Leaving Charlie in the Lord's hands was the best he could do. Not just for reasons concerning her safety. He groaned. Last night he'd come much too close to saying even more that he shouldn't have said.

Thunder rumbled in the distance. Dark clouds obscured the sun. He pulled his watch from his vest pocket for the fourth or fifth time this morning, running his fingers over the intricate engravings of a buck in the forest before opening the case.

The way Mr. Bentley had taken him in still amazed him. Such a fine man would like Charlie, but it was no use even thinking along those lines. He refocused his attention on the watch and the job he should be doing. Almost eleven o'clock.

With rain threatening, Eduardo had probably stopped early to begin cooking the noon meal. So he could turn back and not look like a fool heading toward the wagon this soon.

Half an hour later, he'd found the cook. He strained to be sure he could see two people herding the *remudas* his direction. The tallest rider sat his saddle like Grimes. No mistaking the identity of the smaller rider.

Eduardo walked over to join him while also peering into the distance. "I use *Español* and find out how she is while we cook. She talk to you tonight."

"Uh, yeah." He yawned again.

Before heading for the fire, the cook flashed him an ear-to-ear grin. David grimaced at the man's back. Surely the wiry Mexican wasn't still trying to play matchmaker. The man knew Charlie like his right hand, which meant he knew the woman didn't love David.

When Charlie and Grimes brought the *remudas* to edge of camp, David forced himself to slowly put one boot in front of the other instead of running to check on the riders. He had to see Charlie up close for himself. If the woman had so much as a trace of a welt on her face, her no-account brother would be looking up at him from the ground.

The instant they halted in front of him, he looked straight up at Charlie. "What spooked the horses?" No signs of any physical abuse. She looked totally at ease as she returned his direct gaze.

"About twenty buffalo sent them running. *I* found the missing herd, so talk to me, not Charlie." If not for the harsh tone of his voice, Grimes's words would have sounded like an ignored, spoiled child.

David kept his eyes focused on the woman he had to quit caring about. "Over half those horses are mine. I will inquire all I want about my livestock."

"As long as you talk to me. You have no business *inquiring* about anything alone in the dark with Charlie."

"*Callate su boca grande.*" Charlie spoke almost under her breath, but the sharp sound of her voice signaled whatever she told her brother was no blessing.

David grinned up at her. *Grande* meant big, but he had no idea about the rest. "You got something against the boy telling me about the big buffalo y'all saw?"

"I'm not the fool the two of you think I am."

No, you're at least twice the fool you think you aren't. His tongue itched to speak his thoughts out loud.

"I have all kinds of things to tell you tonight about the buffalo we saw, David." Charlie tossed David a jaunty smile.

Grimes's contemptuous glare went from her to David the

instant she used his first name. The man hadn't missed one syllable of his sister's spoken or unspoken challenge. Thankfully the scoundrel rode off without another word.

Throwing him a breath-stopping grin, Charlie dismounted. "Want to know what I told him?" Her playful whisper made his pulse pound in his ears.

David nodded. He hoped the flirtatious gleam in those big eyes wasn't aimed at him but meant instead to defy her brother. Admiring more than her spunk and courage was something he dared not do.

"I told him to shut his big mouth."

"Good thing he didn't understand you." He kept his voice low, hoping his partner wouldn't realize he and Charlie were whispering together like a couple of kids with a secret. Which, of course, they were. But Grimes couldn't know that.

"Toby understood everything I wanted him to."

"I hope you know what you're doing."

"I do." She laughed.

A wonderfully sweet sound he'd seldom heard from her. If only he could hold her close, keep her safe, and make her feel like laughing for the right reasons every day. If only he could stop himself from thinking such dangerous things.

Her smile faded from her tempting, kissable lips. "I'd better help Eduardo. Schmidt and I can separate the *remudas* later."

"Later will be fine." *Good and later.* He needed time to rein in his crazy thoughts. She could be in danger the way she openly mocked and defied her brother. His heart definitely was. His promise to avoid loving anyone again got more difficult to keep every day.

So he kept an eye on his partner during the noon meal instead of the pretty wrangler he'd rather watch. Keeping her safe was all right. More would be all wrong for him. Grimes's scowls at his sister made David wonder what the man might do. He should quit talking to her at night for her own sake. Do what was best for her the way any gentleman should.

Who was he fooling? He needed to stop visiting with her for his sake. Loving a woman who didn't love him would only get more painful. Grimes's temper and threats should give him the perfect excuse to try again to end their Spanish lessons without hurting her feelings.

He'd tell her tonight he could no longer allow her to risk Tobias's wrath by teaching him Spanish. Caring about someone, even as a friend, meant being willing to sacrifice to keep them safe. Tonight really would be the last time he'd talk to her alone. It had to be.

THE RAIN CAME DOWN with a vengeance not long after Charlotte got the *remuda* moving for the afternoon. She'd had to scramble into her jacket to keep from getting soaked. So far, the lightning and thunder weren't bad. But thinking about smelling like a wet horse didn't help her mood.

Only God knew how she and her brother were going to run the ranch together after they got back home. Glimpsing the old Toby this morning gave her some hope, but she still needed to be careful until he let go of his crazy notions about David. Since God wanted to use her to save the Tumbling G, He must have something in mind for her brother. The Lord could show her what that something was sooner rather than later.

The rain stayed steady the rest of the day. Charlotte helped Eduardo stretch a tarp over four branch poles so they could start a fire that evening.

"Is good you always bring in extra wood." The cook grinned as he added kindling to the beginning of the flames.

She nodded.

Eduardo studied her before asking in Spanish for reassurances that Toby hadn't tried to hurt her when they'd gone off after the *remuda*.

She told him of the unexpected moments they'd spent watching buffalo.

Like her, Eduardo hoped the old Toby would return one day.

The men's glum expressions matched their mood when they rode into camp. Unable to enjoy stretching out in front of a fire, they cursed and complained while they stood in the rain to eat.

"I think I see a patch of blue sky to the north." Fork in hand, David gestured toward the horizon.

"Maybe so." Jessup turned his attention to where the foreman pointed.

Charlotte looked too. If only the clouds would clear in time for her to see David's face better in the starlight after a while. If after a while came.

It shouldn't. And probably wouldn't, judging from the way he kept walking away from her whenever she insisted he should be truthful with her. She had to stop daydreaming like a silly girl about a man who thought of her more like another cowboy than a woman.

Except he'd said she was pretty and nice. Then talked to her as if she were another male he thought well of. Which of his words were the honest truth, she couldn't tell.

After loading the clean plates and utensils into the chuck box, Charlotte stayed behind the wagon.

"Nice to see a few stars, but I'm glad there's not too many yet."

Charlotte jumped at the sound of David's voice as he came around the wagon.

"Sorry, I didn't mean to startle you." He halted in front of her.

Looking up at him, she couldn't stop herself from wishing for a full moon. "A clear sky full of stars is better than clouds and rain any time."

"I hope it keeps your brother from seeing us." He rubbed his palms along his trousers as he stared at her.

She shrugged. "I told him I'd talk to you any time I wanted. So he knows, and I don't care that he knows."

"I care. Uh ... I care if he knows." He looked away toward the herd.

He cares? Surely not for her. With what he'd said last night, he couldn't.

"You should take your brother seriously when he says he doesn't want us together like this."

"No. I can't. I mean—I won't."

He continued staring off in the distance. "We shouldn't do more Spanish lessons or have any conversations alone."

Her mind screamed she should agree and let him walk away for good, while her heart prayed for something to say to get him to stay.

"Giving in to Toby will make him worse. I have to stand up to him now, or I'll never be able to run the ranch with him later. Help me. Please." Her heart had once more won out over her mind. How she longed for his help forever.

"Help you?" He shoved his hands into his pockets as he returned his attention to her. "I ... I don't know."

"Please, David."

He sucked in several breaths as he continued looking down at her. If only she could guess what he was thinking, why he acted so nervous, as if he might have other reasons for not talking to her alone.

"All right. If you're sure I'm really helping you."

"I'm sure."

Sure she was setting herself up for even more pain by continuing to pretend he was only a friend. And pure agony once they reached Abilene and she had to tell him goodbye.

17

Threatening rain clouds again obscured the sky as David tried not to watch Charlie help Eduardo cook breakfast the next morning. Another gray day matched his mood. He shouldn't have let a certain lady talk him into continuing their Spanish lessons.

But every time she said his first name, it sounded like a caress to his hungry heart. The way she'd begged for his assistance made him want to fight a war for her if needed. So he'd help her battle her brother as long as he could.

Such ridiculous thoughts. Such dangerous ideas. He'd lost one woman. Wouldn't risk losing another one.

What happened to Charlie was up to God. Only God knew how, or if, things would work out for her—or for him. David himself couldn't figure out much of anything lately. The more he tried not to love the woman, the more his heart rebelled against his common sense. Good thing he had only a few short-but-long weeks until they'd reach Abilene and the end of the trail.

The rain started again about the time everyone finished saddling their morning horses. David mounted his black and surveyed the men. "I'll see y'all at noon with a report on the Canadian River."

"Might not be a good one with all this rain" Jessup spoke before riding toward the herd.

A sidelong glance at Charlie's pale face made David want to throw a hand full of rocks at the retreating cowboy and tell him to quit scaring the wrangler who couldn't swim.

But he had no reassuring words to leave behind. He grinned Charlie's direction, barely stopping himself from tipping his hat to her before riding off. Too bad he couldn't set her in front of him and carry her across on his horse, or—

Stop it, man. He spurred his mustang.

CHARLOTTE TRAILED along with the *remuda* and tried to think of something besides another river in her way. David's whisker-covered-lone-dimpled grin had not been as comforting as he might have meant it to be. If only his beaming smiles did mean more.

No use wishing about that. But daydreams of the foreman were so much more pleasant than thinking about river crossings, or the light rain soaking everything around, or her problems with Toby.

Even though no one in sight was paying her one bit of attention, she squared her shoulders and sat as tall in her saddle as she could. Toby would not win. With God's help, she'd keep her promise to Pa. The Tumbling G would be safe.

No carpetbagger would ever buy them out cheap as one had offered just before Pa died. She closed her eyes, trying to banish the awful memories of the Yankee's gall. Badgering a sick man, hoping to take advantage of him. Lord willing, the Grimes family's finances would never be in such bad shape again.

The rain continued off and on through most of the afternoon. The men griped their way through the noon meal. No matter how all this rain might raise the waters of the Canadian, Charlotte had to remind herself more than once that God hadn't deserted her. After returning to the trail, she welcomed the solitude. Horses didn't curse, no matter the weather.

The sun came out in the late afternoon. The most wondrous rainbow she'd ever seen arched across the whole sky ahead of her. If God were trying to tell her to keep pressing on, He couldn't have picked a more magnificent way to say it. She let the reins go slack in her hand as she marveled at the vivid shades of pink, white, yellow, and green.

She should teach David the names for colors the next time they worked on Spanish. Beautiful colors and pleasant words instead of his stumbling phrases comparing her to a man.

Topping the next ridge, she spotted Eduardo's wagon already stopped a mile or so ahead.

A couple of the men mentioned seeing the rainbow as they stood around the fire finishing supper a while later.

"It was pretty, but all this rain means the Canadian ain't gonna be so pretty. What about that river, boss?" Jessup took a large gulp of his coffee.

David finished chewing a bite of biscuit. "The footing's bad. We'll have to watch for quicksand."

The only sound in camp came from someone clinking a metal cup against their tin plate.

"We'll get an early start in the morning. Then water the herd well before we get to the river, so the beeves aren't thirsty and stopping while they cross."

The foreman's calm tone didn't untie a single knot in Charlotte's shoulders. Knots that chased away all thoughts of rainbow colors. Rather than join the men around the fire after cleaning up, she took her time loading things into the chuck box.

She stared up at the brilliant stars shining in the darkening, rain-washed sky. Strange how the same God who made rainbows and beautiful night skies had also made the raging rivers she'd come to fear.

"Are you already talking to the Lord about tomorrow?"

At the sound of David's voice behind her, she almost

dropped the forks she had yet to put into the drawer. His hand steadied hers for just a moment as he took the utensils and placed them where they belonged.

"Let's talk." He gazed down at her.

His gentle husky voice gave her visions of laying her head against his chest and feeling his comforting arms wrap around her.

"About what?"

"Tomorrow. We'll have to cross a couple hundred beeves at a time. I'd like to leave you, Schmidt, and Eduardo with the rest of the herd. We'll cross the horses and wagon last."

"I can do that."

He let out a long breath. "I won't be able to look out for you the way I did at the Red River."

His wanting to protect her sent delicious, tingling chills all through her. If only she knew his real reasons. "Why, David?'

Oh, she shouldn't have blurted her thoughts out loud like that. She had to quit using his first name.

"Why what?"

She looked up at him. If she had a better view of those blue eyes shrouded by the shadows from his hat, maybe she could tell if she should risk explaining. Especially since she doubted he'd give her the answer she longed to hear.

"Why do you watch out for me?"

Shifting from one foot to the other, he looked away. "Because ... uh ... friends do that for each other."

Wrong answer. She closed her eyes and forced herself to take a couple of deep breaths. She must close her heart to this man, especially since she wanted more from him than he wanted from her.

"Charlie? Are you all right?"

Her eyes jerked open to find him looking straight at her. She stared back at him. "Um, I'm fine." *Such a lie.*

"I promise I'll do my best to keep you safe."

"I know."

He kept his gaze fixed on her. "Uh, we should both get some extra rest before our long day tomorrow."

She nodded.

"Goodnight." Stopping just short of tipping his hat to her, he touched his fingers to the brim of it before walking away.

Such a gentlemanly gesture. "Goodnight." She whispered to his back.

Eduardo might be right. Maybe David did care for her, love her. Or maybe she'd grow wings and fly the rest of the way to Abilene. *Silly goose.* He'd called her his friend again.

She had to quit loving him. Accept how he felt about her.

Which was probably why he wouldn't answer her questions until they got to Abilene, where he'd politely tell her goodbye and part ways with someone so unlike the hoop-skirted ladies he was used to.

AROUND NINE O'CLOCK THE next morning, David had the men turn the herd off the trail to a creek about three miles from the river. "See they get their fill of water. Any cow stopping for a drink in the Canadian will sink in the quicksand."

Grimes rode up next to him. "You sure your plan will work?"

"No, but God still works miracles."

"God and I gave up on each other during the war." Grimes snorted.

David looked straight into the man's eyes. "You gave up on God."

A derisive-looking sneer curled Grimes's lip. "No, it was mutual." He cantered off toward the lead steers.

Unexpected sympathy for his partner welled up inside. No wonder he was so bitter. David had learned the hard way not to turn his back on God after losing everyone and everything he'd had in Georgia. If not for Mr. Bentley's patience and prayers, he might have become as cynical as Grimes. Maybe he'd been too hard on the man.

Except that still left his problems with Charlie and the way Grimes treated her. But the Lord said to pray for his enemies. So he prayed for Grimes along with asking the Lord to help them all cross the Canadian safely.

David waited until every straggler had all the water he wanted before throwing the herd back on the trail. About a half-mile from the Canadian, he halted them again.

"All right, boys. Cut the leaders out." He rode back toward the side of the herd Charlie was holding. She and Schmidt already had those beeves milling.

"You make a good cowhand too." He grinned at her.

No return smile curved her pretty lips.

"You'll be fine. I'm praying for you, and I'll watch out for you."

She nodded. He started his horse toward the river and away from her and the temptation to set her in front of him on his horse. He had to stop thinking such a thing every time they crossed a river.

"I'm praying for you. *Vaya con Dios, David*." She used the Spanish pronunciation of his name before saying more Spanish words in a voice too low for him to hear with his back to her.

God be with you, he remembered. But the soft, musical way she added whatever else she said sounded like something special meant just for him. He used every ounce of willpower he could muster to keep from returning to her no matter how it would look to Schmidt or Eduardo who were so close by.

He had to be the world's biggest fool. Charlie loved her land, not him. Her willingness to sacrifice so much proved that beyond any doubt. He returned his attention to the Canadian where it belonged. Facing a river with quicksand was less dangerous than going back on his promise to himself and loving anyone ever again.

Before David reached the first group of beeves they'd cut

out, Grimes was already driving them into the water with as much fury as the swift current would allow.

"Keep holding the others here," Grimes yelled over his shoulder to the wranglers as he spurred his horse toward the river.

David did his best to help the men keep the longhorns moving. Jessup cursed at a dun steer while cracking his whip over the beast's head. As soon as the stubborn animal dodged him, it started sinking into the quagmire. Several other beeves soon met with the same problem.

"Grimes, hold up!" David might as well have yelled into a tornado. Oblivious to anyone's shouts about bogged cattle, his partner kept riding toward the other bank.

The man scaled the opposite bank before looking back to the rest of the herd. His mouth dropped as he surveyed what looked to be nearly twenty beeves stuck in the quicksand. The hands let the other cows head back to the main herd.

By the time they freed the last bogged cow, the men had missed their noon meal by several hours. Eduardo started an early supper on the same side of the river they'd been on this morning.

"The cows will be the only ones with meat on their bones if we keep missing meals." Tyler stood with the other hungry men eagerly watching the cook and Charlie.

"Early tomorrow, I'll scout for a better spot." David ignored his nearby, glaring partner, hoping the man still had sense enough to be quiet while he had such a big audience.

"I'll find a ford tomorrow." Grimes folded his arms across his chest.

"Sounds good to me." Hoping to defuse the tension as the men looked from one partner to the other, David shrugged as he forced a grin. "I'll go one way on the river. You go the other."

Tobias let his arms go slack at his side. "We'll have a better day tomorrow."

"I hope and pray so." David made sure his pretend smile included his partner and the rest of the men.

The hands made themselves comfortable close to the fire and the smells of supper cooking. Talk turned to the river itself.

David grabbed his Bible and slipped off to pray. Dealing with bogged cattle all day was bad. Thinking about what could happen to the pretty redhead who couldn't swim if her horse got stuck was worse. Much worse.

Wishing the Canadian was flowing as placidly as the creek in front of him, he seated himself on a fallen log. He rubbed the back of his neck, trying to ease the tension in his tired muscles.

His Bible fell open to one of his favorite verses in Matthew. "Come unto me, all ye that labour and are heavy laden ..." He closed his eyes to speak the remainder from memory. "And I will give you rest."

Rest. His body ached from exhaustion. His mind and heart ached from confusion. Only God knew where to cross the Canadian. Only God knew what he should do about Charlie. Only God knew how ...

His chest tightened as if a giant hand were trying to twist not just his body but mind and heart in two. He prayed for help. God alone had the answers to all his questions.

The next morning, David rode downriver with Miller. Grimes went upstream, taking Jessup with him. Three or four miles downstream, David and Miller came upon a swift, narrow channel with a large sandbar in the middle. They crossed and recrossed the river with no problems.

As they scaled the bank for the last time, David grinned. "Let's go tell the others what we found."

When they caught up to the herd, David said a silent prayer of thanks at the sight of longhorns still grazing. Grimes must not have found a good ford, or the prideful man would have probably started the cattle toward whatever spot he'd found without waiting for David to return.

"Find anything?" Tyler called to David.

"Yeah. Mr. Grimes isn't back yet?"

"Haven't seen him yet."

David's heart urged him to ride toward Charlie. Instead, he went in the direction of Eduardo and the wagon. He'd have to tell the wranglers his plans, but the less time he spent with the red-headed one, the better.

"We found a good spot. I'll tell Charlie and Schmidt to hold the herd the way they did yesterday so we can cross the beeves in bunches. Lord willing, we'll get our noon meal close to on time today."

"*Sí, señor*. I pray for better day."

The man's grin lit up his entire face. Grandmother would have loved this kind man with such similar ideas for her grandson.

But he had to keep reminding himself of the promise he'd made to keep his heart safe.

Charlie's eyes sparkled the instant he rode up to her. He had to concentrate on crossing the river that had caused them so many problems the day before.

"Downriver, there's a place with a sandbar in the middle where the water's not as deep. I want you and Schmidt to hold the beeves again, so we can cross them in small bunches the way we intended yesterday."

"Sure."

Her tense posture signaled how unsure she was. He had to quit thinking how he'd like to set her in front of him and ease all her worries.

Horses galloping their direction interrupted his thoughts. For the first time since they'd started this drive, David didn't mind seeing his partner coming in.

Tobias reined in his mustang next to his sister. He scowled over at David. "You must not have found a spot, either, since you beat us back."

"Miller and I found a good place. Miracles still happen."

"Yeah, preacher." Sarcasm dripped from Grime's voice. "We all need help from someone else after what you tried yesterday."

"Yes, we do. The day's wasting. We've got longhorns to cross." David headed his horse toward the hands and the herd.

Without another scornful word, Grimes followed. Another unexpected wonder. But David wouldn't say such a thing to his partner.

CHARLOTTE CHECKED the sun's progress across the clear sky. About ten o'clock. Lord willing, she could soon help Eduardo start the noon meal on the other bank of this treacherous river.

Her prayer was partly answered when the men returned to cut a third bunch of beeves from the herd she and Schmidt were holding.

"We bogged two or three, but they're in shallow enough water to safely leave them there and cross the rest." David grinned as he rode up to her.

"Good." His smile lifted her spirits considerably.

"Don't cross the *remudas* until I get back to help you." His expression sobered.

"Thanks."

Instead of dwelling on swimming another river, she concentrated on holding the dwindling longhorns together. David's concern for her thrilled her heart. Until thoughts of how crossing the Red River had gone.

About an hour later, the men herded the last group of beeves toward the river. Charlotte did her best not to look at the shirtless cowboys. Heat flooded her face when David, minus his shirt, returned to help with the horses as promised. She forced her gaze toward the horizon. Ma would be appalled at her daughter's unladylike wish to admire the muscular foreman's broad shoulders.

"We'll cross the horses and wagon upstream from the cattle.

The men are still digging out six or seven longhorns. But we shouldn't miss our noon meal today."

Charlotte nodded. She forced her gaze away from David and busied herself pulling off her boots and wrapping them in her jacket along with her leather vest. Pete had been so proud when Pa had given it to him. Her father would have never dreamed how glad she was to own the treasured vest that helped disguise her femininity so well.

Once the horses plunged into the river, David stayed within four or five feet of her. Charlotte gripped the saddle horn the instant Red started swimming. Her trousers were soon soaked almost to her thighs. A nearby horse splashed water on her shirt. She focused her attention on the opposite bank now less than a hundred feet away, glad that so many swimming mustangs helped block Schmidt's view of her.

Red and the rest of the *remuda* soon scrambled onto dry land. Charlotte sucked in a couple of deep breaths as David looked over at her. Gentleman that he was, he kept his gaze fixed on her face instead of her clinging, wet apparel. Somehow she managed to study only his lone-dimpled smile that refused to be completely hidden by his light beard. How nice he took the time to shave occasionally instead of looking as wooly as the other men.

"The wagon made it just fine." David motioned to where the cook was unhitching the mules.

She jerked her attention back to where it should be. "Uh, yeah. Eduardo will need my help as soon as we settle the horses."

"Schmidt can handle both *remudas*. The men need to eat as close to noon as y'all can manage."

"Sure." She turned Red toward the wagon.

"One more thing, Charlie."

She halted her bay.

"We've got the wagon a ways from the herd on purpose since these bogged moss heads are angry enough to charge once they're freed. Keep an eye out until all the beeves are back with the herd."

"All right."

"I wouldn't mind a Spanish lesson tonight." He grinned.

Looking into his shining eyes made her heart race as if she'd fallen back into the river. She nodded rather than say something that might give away her true feelings.

He rode toward the nearest group of men working on digging out a cow. She headed Red to the wagon.

While helping cook, Charlotte discovered a definite advantage to having to be watchful of the angry beeves. She had a perfect excuse to observe the handsome foreman helping free the bogged brutes. And Toby was so busy he didn't have time to notice how much attention she was paying to David.

"We no have biscuits if you no cook them soon." Eduardo chuckled.

Her cheeks must be almost as warm as the flames dancing a few feet away from her. She plopped the last biscuit into the Dutch oven and carried it to the fire.

"*Es un hombre muy bueno.*"

"*Sí.*" But she quickly added in Spanish no matter how good the man was, David didn't love her the way Eduardo thought.

"Ah, *chiquita mia*—"

"Shepherd, watch out!" Miller's shout riveted Charlotte and Eduardo's attention to the river bank.

As a huge longhorn pawed the ground and charged the foreman's direction, the men ran for their horses. David stumbled and fell.

"No!" Charlotte clamped both hands over her mouth to stifle her scream.

Eduardo grabbed her upper arms to prevent her from running to David.

Tyler's lasso missed the brute. David scrambled to his feet, but he couldn't possibly outrun the powerful longhorn. Toby was closest to the animal, but he still held his lariat in his hand.

"Oh, God ..." The rest of her prayer stuck in her throat. Surely her brother wouldn't allow the raging beast to gore David.

She shook uncontrollably as Toby finally made his cast. His rope caught the animal by his two front feet, throwing him hard to the ground, allowing David to jump into his saddle.

She caught her breath once her heart slowed enough to allow her to take in air again. Eduardo patted her shoulder. He whispered in Spanish that God had kept her sweetheart safe for her.

She didn't have the strength to argue with the cook. All she could think about was how close she'd come to losing David and how close her brother had come to allowing it to happen.

18

Taking in several ragged breaths to try to slow his pounding heart, David gripped his saddle horn. Thank God he was here to breathe. Maybe Grimes wasn't all bad.

Several of the men had jumped on the steer to hold him down. Once they released the subdued brute, he ambled of his own accord back to the herd.

David rode to meet his partner. "Thanks. I owe you."

"We're even. You saved Charlie." The man turned his horse in the direction of the wagon.

The other hands also drifted toward the smell of the food, gathering around Grimes. No doubt the man was basking in their praise. But for once, he'd earned it. David had never thought he'd have a reason to be thankful for his partner.

After tending to his horse, David joined the others by the fire. He tossed a grin at Charlie as she stirred the beans, hoping to reassure her that he was all right. She didn't give him her usual smile. Her expressive eyes looked too big for her face as she studied him. Something looked to be bothering her, but he couldn't act as if he noticed in front of her brother or the other men.

"Glad you didn't meet your maker today." Schmidt clapped him on the back.

"Good thing my partner can rope so well."

Charlie dropped the lid onto the simmering beans with such a clatter that David and several hands jumped. She scurried toward the wagon like a scared rabbit. Something was definitely wrong, but he'd have to wait until tonight to talk to her no matter how much he wished otherwise.

They had to get the herd back on the trail and start making up the time they'd lost.

Which should be what he focused his mind on this afternoon instead of a pretty redhead. Loving a woman who didn't love him had its downsides. Even if by some miracle she loved him, her hotheaded brother and eight hundred acres still stood between them.

Stop it, man. Keep your promise to yourself. Keep your heart safe.

CHARLOTTE SNATCHED the plates and cups from the drawer. Every time someone complimented her brother for saving David, she wanted to scream. She and Eduardo couldn't have been the only ones who saw Toby hesitate as if he had to think about saving his partner's life.

Too bad she couldn't slam her fist between Toby's eyes, or shove him to the ground with the pothook, or ...

Vengeance is mine.

The powerful but still small voice jolted her to the toes of her boots, and she closed her eyes. She'd never hated anyone in her life. But now, without God's help, she could hate her brother. She bowed her head. Forgiving Toby would take strength she didn't have. *Help me, Lord.*

"Food is ready." Eduardo gently touched her arm. "God still good. He take care of everything and everyone."

She nodded before following him back to the hungry men.

While she stood next to him with the biscuits, Eduardo ladled out the beans and salt pork. David was the last man to get his plate. Those blue eyes she could lose herself in told her he'd have questions tonight about her crazy behavior. And she'd have answers along with a warning about her brother.

The rest of the afternoon crawled by slower than a worn-out dog on a hot August day. All she wanted was time alone with David. What felt like a year later, the sun finally showed it to be close to four. Time to urge the *remuda* forward toward wherever the foreman had picked for them to camp tonight.

Her heart skipped several beats as she spotted a certain sandy-haired cowboy talking to Eduardo while they stacked wood for a fire. *Charlotte Grimes, you mustn't*. He wanted to learn Spanish from her, nothing more. The sooner she could convince her heart of that, the better off she'd be.

"*Buenas tardes.*" David waved to her as she rode into camp.

Eduardo's lips twitched into an indulgent grin that shouted to her *I told you he loves you*.

Charlotte busied herself grinding coffee. Keeping to his usual routine, David walked off to watch for the herd still about two miles or so away.

Her dear friend kept up a barrage in Spanish, telling her how pleased he was that she and David had found love. Charlotte didn't waste her breath arguing with him. In a few short weeks, she and Eduardo would both be disappointed.

Much sooner than she wished, Toby and the others came in.

"I can't believe how much y'all jabber about every day." He walked over to her and Eduardo as she stooped to cover the top of the Dutch oven with coals.

"I enjoy talking with someone who isn't criticizing me and actually cares." She kept her comments too soft for anyone else to hear, not bothering to look at him.

"You don't think I care about you?"

She stood to look him in the eyes. "If you were me, would you?"

He flinched. "We'll talk before I start my watch tonight."

"I haven't got anything to talk to you about." She whirled then trotted to the back of the wagon.

To her surprise, he didn't follow. Maybe forcing him to face the truth had made him uncomfortable enough that he wouldn't bother her after supper.

How sad she didn't want to be with her brother. How were they going to run a ranch together after they got home? Another question only God could answer. Yet the more she prayed, the more certain she was God wanted her on this drive and wanted her to keep her promise to Pa.

Except that got harder by the day. No matter how many times she'd asked, God hadn't taken away her love for David. She couldn't see anything but heartbreak ahead. She dreaded reaching Abilene as much as she longed to get there.

Toby didn't say a cross word to her during supper. The way he watched her every move after she took her spot close to Eduardo, he didn't need to. David had seated himself across the fire from her. Toby positioned himself where he could see her and his partner.

The talk turned back to the Canadian. Charlotte wished they'd think of a more pleasant topic. No river would ever look the same to her again.

David gave her a glance that made her wonder if he'd guessed her thoughts and wanted to reassure her. The way he looked down at his food so quickly she couldn't tell what he'd really meant or if it had been wishful thinking on her part. Until she saw her brother's unmistakable scowl. David's look *had* been just for her.

She finished her stew, wishing her brother's glares and the men's conversation hadn't all but ruined the taste. For once, she looked forward to cleaning up. She rose and carried her dirty plate to the tin tub they used for dishwashing.

Eduardo soon followed.

Within minutes after they stacked the plates to dry, Toby

showed up. "Eduardo can put everything up." He laid his hand on her arm.

She tried to jerk away. His grip tightened. If she protested too loudly, she'd cause a scene. That would bring David on the run. Not wanting to risk another fight between the two partners, she allowed Toby to guide her to the far edge of camp.

The wagon blocked David's view from the fire. Only Eduardo would be able to watch her. Now she wished the sun would set a little later. She glanced over her shoulder as they halted.

"Shepherd's watching. He never takes his eyes off you." The sneering tone of his voice made her shiver.

"It's not like you're the most trustworthy man."

Looking as if she'd just slapped him, he stepped back. "How can you not see you've got everything wrong? I'm the one you should trust, not him. Please, believe me."

Please? She couldn't remember the last time he'd said the word to her. If only his hard heart would soften again, and things could be like they were before the war, or the few minutes they'd watched buffalo.

But the harsh reality of how he'd hesitated to help David chased away the scraps of sympathy she had for him. "How can you have to stop and think before saving a man's life?"

"What?"

"I saw you hesitate to save David. You're more of a brute than the beast that charged him."

"Except I did save him, despite what he'd like to do to you. To us." He held his hands out, palms up. "That man will take the ranch from you if you let him. We'll lose everything we've worked so hard for if you don't wake up. Wait till we get to Abilene. Everything I'm saying will make sense then."

She shook her head. "I doubt that."

Shoulders slumped as if he'd lost a major battle, he walked away. Toby confused her more every day. If only everything would make sense when she got to Abilene. Toby and David were both convinced that would happen.

She wasn't.

WHILE CHARLIE and her brother talked, David joined Eduardo to watch. David balled his hands into fists. The cook gripped his arm, ready to again prevent him from running to the woman's aid.

"If he had touched her, my partner would be missing a few teeth."

"*Sí*, but he no do that."

"How can you be sure?"

"Too many people here he want thinking he is good man."

"Yeah." The kinks in David's neck loosened up. "How can a man save someone's life and then act the way he does toward his own flesh and blood?"

The cook shrugged. "He need God."

David nodded. He could pray for his partner more easily after what the man had done for him. Without Mr. Bentley's prayers and concern, he'd probably be in as sad a state as Tobias, or worse.

Charlie walked in closer but didn't join him and Eduardo until after her brother rode toward the herd. "You were watching out for me, weren't you?"

"Yes. I saw it all."

Eduardo turned down the lantern. "*Buenas noches, mis niños.*" He grabbed his bedroll and walked away.

"Goodnight." David chuckled. Charlie had told him *niños* meant children. Just as he did with Charlie, Eduardo now considered David part his. The cook's acceptance warmed him from head to toe. Mr. Bentley would like Eduardo.

But what about Charlie? Such an unladylike woman would probably confuse his boss as much as she confused him.

"We have to talk." She turned to face him.

"What's wrong? You've acted like a filly with a burr under your saddle blanket since noon."

She stepped back and looked up at him.

Oh, she is gorgeous in the starlight. If only he could take her hat off and see her face better. Just touching her hair—

"Do you think you can trust Toby now?"

"Huh? Well, maybe he's not as bad as I thought."

"You didn't see him stop and think about it before lassoing that longhorn and saving you."

"No, but I'm the enemy he thinks wants to take his ranch away. A man who can save an adversary like that must still have some good buried deep inside somewhere."

"How can you have any sympathy for someone like Toby when I'm not sure I do anymore?" Her voice cracked.

"I could have become your brother after the war if not for my boss helping me return to God."

"But you didn't. That still doesn't excuse Toby and what he's become."

"Maybe, but after today I can probably pray for him easier and understand him better than a lot of other people."

"No! Even a poisonous copperhead looks shiny and pretty sunning itself on a rock." The venom in her voice matched the snake she'd described.

"So you're saying I don't really know Tobias even though he saved my life?"

"Don't let him fool you. I can't have anything happen to you. I mean, you're the best friend I have on this drive, and ..." She clamped both hands over her mouth.

And what? Her words tumbled out one over the other as if she'd meant to say something more. Something different than that explanation.

"Toby won't let go of his wild idea that you're trying to take the ranch away from me."

"Just from you? That doesn't make sense."

"His greed makes him crazy. *You* can't trust him. *I* can't trust him."

"Then how are you going to run a ranch with a man you just compared to a snake?" He fought to keep his voice low. He had to hide his true feelings from her as much as he did from her brother.

"I ... I don't know." Her trembling voice emphasized her anguish.

As if it had a mind of its own, his hand rested itself on her narrow shoulder. She looked up at him but didn't back away.

He forced himself to slide his fingers off her and let his arm hang at his side, hoping she wouldn't guess how much he wanted to ease her mind. To take her in his arms and shelter her for the rest of his life. "We'll pray. That's all I know to do."

All he could do. For her and for him. He was getting much too close to breaking the promise he'd made to himself standing in the family graveyard.

"Thank you."

He swallowed hard. He had to be more careful. "Um, it's been a long day. We should both get some sleep."

She nodded.

"Goodnight. *Vaya con Dios.*" He grabbed his bedroll from its spot next to the wagon wheel.

"God be with you too." She snatched up her quilts and marched away.

As quickly as she turned to leave, he'd probably said too much about a lot of things. But she needed to face the hard, troubling facts about how she'd run a ranch with a brother she didn't trust. If only he could convince her to walk away from what was only a piece of land. Walk away hand in hand with him.

A low groan escaped. She'd have to love him for that to happen. He had to stop wishing she considered him more than a friend. So many good reasons to be only friends with her. But his heart got less reasonable every day.

19

Even with the hot afternoon sun beating down on her shoulders, Charlotte welcomed her solitary job of herding horses. Cows didn't make much noise on the trail, and she was far enough from them not to be bothered by the men's choice words. So much tranquility might lull her to sleep.

Maybe the sweat dripping down her back would keep her from napping in the saddle. Last night, she'd prayed until the Big Dipper was well on its journey around the North Star. She still had no answers concerning her dilemma with David or Toby.

David. She'd almost given away a bigger secret than her true identity when she'd told him she couldn't have anything happen to him. Instead of backing away from his quick touch, she'd soaked in every moment of feeling his hand on her shoulder.

She needed to quit thinking about him. Quit talking to him. Her crazy emotions were more twisted and tangled than a dropped ball of yarn rolling clear across the room.

Toby. David's talk of understanding and praying for Toby frightened her in more ways than one. Letting his guard down like that could be dangerous, as much as her brother hated him.

Yet she was walking into a different kind of danger if she completely let go of ever hoping Toby could change. Her brother was a walking example of what bitterness could do to someone. She couldn't allow herself to become like that. So she'd have to find a way to forgive Toby. To keep praying for him. Whether he wanted her forgiveness and prayers or not.

If she couldn't do either of those things, she couldn't work the ranch with her brother. If Toby kept running from God and didn't change, she probably couldn't work with him, either.

Yet God wanted her on this drive. Wanted to use her to save the Tumbling G. Those two things were about the only things she was sure of now. She'd never been so uncertain of following God's will in all her life.

Ma and Pa had always talked about walking by faith. She was stumbling by faith and didn't know where she might land.

A hawk screeching overhead reminded her she'd best keep her mind on her job. No one had spotted any Indians for the last few days, but she scanned the horizon just in case. David kept expecting Seminoles to show up asking for beeves.

By the time the sun indicated about four o'clock, the gentle, rolling plain had almost lulled Charlotte to sleep. David would soon be signaling Eduardo he'd found a good spot for the night. She rounded up the horses and urged them ahead at a faster pace.

As she topped the next ridge, she spied the wagon about two miles away. A good-sized stand of trees indicated a decent creek not far from where Eduardo was setting up camp. As usual, a second man worked beside the cook.

She waved her greeting as she rode into camp a while later. Eduardo's welcoming grin eased her restlessness. He didn't have answers for her, but he cared. "I'll ride to the creek and look for firewood."

"*Con cuidado.*"

"I'll be careful." She'd stay good and close to camp as long as they were in Indian Territory.

The cool shade refreshed her body and spirit as she rode along the bank, hunting for fallen branches. She halted behind a thick stand of cottonwoods and removed her hat. Untying her bandana, she dampened it with water from her canteen then wiped the sweat and grime from her face and neck. What she wouldn't give for a bath in the babbling creek. But such a luxury was hard to arrange since she needed Eduardo to stand guard for her even if she could find a suitably hidden spot.

Something rustled behind her. She twisted in her saddle but didn't see anything unusual. She put her hat on and repinned it. The men weren't far off with the herd. She had best concentrate on finding the wood she needed so she could get back to camp.

Twigs snapped off to her side as she lassoed a good-sized dead branch. She looked toward the sound. Two mounted Indians rode from around the other side of the cottonwoods, less than twenty feet away.

Terror stifled her scream. She dropped her rope and spurred Red. Crashing through the brush, she galloped toward camp. The two braves gave chase.

"Indians!" She yelled before she reached the edge of camp.

David ran toward her, revolver in hand. "In the wagon."

She jumped to the ground behind him, too frightened to convince her feet to move. The two intruders halted their mounts in front of the foreman. Rifle at his side, Eduardo walked from the other side of the wagon. Schmidt pulled his hat lower before fingering the handle of his holstered gun.

"Do what I said, Charlie." David kept his eyes on the men in front of him.

The oldest Indian raised his hand and pointed straight at her.

She forced her leaden feet to move and scrambled onto the seat, then into the bed of the wagon and out of sight. The Indians had to have seen her hair. Maybe they'd been close enough to see the braids coiled around her head.

A brave said something unintelligible.

As the men went back and forth, David's voice remained calm but firm.

She assumed the long silences meant each side had resorted

to sign language to communicate. What felt like two or three years later, she heard the other men bringing the herd in.

"They want a toll. The rest of you stay back and keep your hands off your guns." David called to the men.

"Where's Charlie?"

Her brother's voice carried to her hiding place. Toby wanted to know where she was. Maybe he still cared about her as much as he kept insisting he did.

"In the wagon."

David's terse answer must have satisfied her brother since she didn't hear him say anything else.

The negotiations continued a while longer before David ordered the men to cut out two of the footsore stragglers.

A few minutes later, Eduardo climbed onto the seat and stuck his head through the canvas opening. "Is safe now. We cook."

Safe wasn't what she was thinking about, considering how easily two Indians had sneaked up on her. She'd have to be more careful.

DAVID WATCHED Charlie stifle yet another yawn as she took her usual spot around the fire after she and Eduardo finished cleaning up from supper. He never knew if she was truly tired or pretending so she wouldn't have to spend too long listening to the men's rough language.

A short time later, she stretched. "I'll see y'all in the morning."

"You sleeping in the wagon tonight, boy?" Wilson's sarcastic tone signaled his question wasn't friendly teasing.

Charlie halted and stared slack-jawed at the man. "What?"

"I figured you might want to start hiding in that wagon at night too."

"The boy followed my orders. We've already had one bunch

of Indians get too curious about his red hair." David fixed the man with a glare he hoped Wilson could discern even in the firelight.

"I was only joshin'." The hand's dry chuckle didn't sound convincing.

"I wasn't." David didn't care how the men took his terse reply. Keeping Charlie safe was more important.

"Jessup says the North Fork of the Canadian's next. How long till we get there?" Tyler didn't look away from the stick he was whittling.

"We'll cross early tomorrow." He rose. "I'll see if my Spanish teacher wants to help me embarrass myself."

Hoping Charlie hadn't walked any farther away, he sauntered toward the back of the wagon. His heart raced the moment he caught sight of her, but he kept his pace slow as he walked up. She'd already put out the lantern. He could picture her smile and kissable lips if it were pitch dark, anyway. Something else he had to quit thinking about.

"No more hunting wood alone till we're in Kansas." Good thing she didn't know what else he was thinking concerning her.

She nodded. "I won't argue with you."

"That's nice for a change." He laughed.

She didn't.

"Down by the creek, I took my hat off so I could wash my face. The Indians maybe got a real good look at my hair."

Prickles of fear chased up and down his spine. "How good?"

"I splashed water from my canteen and didn't dismount, but they must have been behind me then and might have seen my braids."

"We'll all be more careful to watch for unwanted visitors. You don't go anywhere alone."

"I won't. *Nunca.*"

"What does that mean?"

"Never."

He repeated the word in Spanish. A word he should be

putting into practice now and never be alone with her again. But his crazy heart made a fool out of him every time he tried to quit spending time with Charlie.

"At least it's not another *r*-word."

This time she laughed. He'd eased her mind.

"You're getting better at them, considering your Georgia roots. Which I'd like to know more about."

He sucked in air. "Why?" He'd stalled before whenever she brought up his past. By pinning her down for a reason she was so curious about him, maybe he could continue putting off not talking about his painful history.

"Well ... because ... maybe knowing more about you would help me convince Toby you don't want his land."

The stumbling style of her words made him wonder what her real motive was for wanting to know more about someone she considered only a friend. "Tobias is the last person I want to have more information about me."

"I'd never tell him or anyone else a single word." She let out a long sigh. "The truth is *I* want to know more about you just because ... because I want to. Please."

Please. He recognized the tone of a woman trying to use her feminine wiles to get what she wanted, even a woman who roped and rode as well as he did. The strange combination of ladylike and unladylike behavior wrapped up in one redhead had his senses reeling.

He didn't like bringing up any part of his Georgia past to anyone, but he wanted to stay and soak in as much of this woman's presence as he could. He should turn and leave. Now.

"I told you what you wanted to know about me. Please, David."

If only the way she said his name didn't always sound like a caress to his hungry heart that kept refusing to listen to his mind. She tilted her head as she continued looking up at him. He had no problem picturing the expectant look in her eyes shadowed by her hat. If he weren't careful, she'd have him telling her everything about anything. He rubbed sweaty hands up and down his trouser legs.

"All right." *Anything for you.* He clamped his mouth shut to keep from saying the rest of the words out loud. "I grew up on my grandparents' plantation not far from Savannah. Grandfather died just before the war started, but ..."

He gulped in more than one unsteady breath. "Thanks to the Yankees, I came home ..." He hated the way his voice choked on his words, but he had to finish what he'd started. "Home to my wife, my infant son, and my grandmother in the family graveyard next to my grandfather and mother."

She gasped. "Oh, David. I'm so sorry."

"Yeah." He looked down as he shifted from one foot to the other. The painful memories threatened to overwhelm him. And he hadn't mentioned how his mother died giving birth to him or why he never spoke about his father.

He had to walk away from the woman in front of him. Run, if he were smart. He couldn't endure risking that kind of loss, that kind of pain again.

"Uh, no more Spanish lessons tonight." Hoping she wouldn't notice how strained his voice sounded, he stepped back to leave.

"David, please..." She grabbed his arm.

He tried to keep walking. Her grip tightened. He turned to face her.

"I shouldn't have asked about Georgia. Talking about the past hurts, and I ..." Her voice cracked. She looked away as she sucked in a shuddering breath.

As she sniffed away what he feared were tears, he caressed her slender fingers still holding tightly to his arm. Maybe his painful past dredged up her own agonizing memories of losing loved ones. Or she cried for him? He hoped not. Hurting her wasn't what he'd planned.

"Anyway, I'm sorry." She sniffed again.

Without thinking, he reached down to wipe away the moisture from her cheek.

Anyone watching would think he'd slapped her as quickly as she stepped back.

"I'm sorry. Forgive me for being so forward." He fought to control his emotions. He'd answered the questions she'd asked. But he'd ruined it all by touching her when she thought of him only as a good friend.

"I grabbed your arm. You should forgive me." Her voice still sounded thick with emotion.

"Forgive *you*? For what?"

"For ... uh ... for—I don't know." She looked away. "I—don't know."

"Let's just say goodnight, shall we?" If only he felt as chipper as his words sounded.

Grandmother would have been so pleased with his gentlemanly manners and recovery from such an awkward situation. Only if she recovered from her faint when she'd seen him caress Charlie's cheek as if they were formally engaged.

She nodded. "Um, yeah. That would be good."

He hated to wish her a good night and walk away again. But he had no choice. The more he wanted to stay, the more he should go. "Goodnight, Charlie."

She stared up at him. "Goodnight."

He snatched up his bedroll lying near the wagon wheel and forced himself to walk away. Her words meant he wouldn't have a good night. Not for sleeping as he once again tried to put a pretty redhead out of his mind.

Out of his heart.

20

Waiting for the foreman's signal to start the *remuda* toward the other side of the river, Charlotte averted her gaze from the shirtless cowboys crossing the herd downstream. Staring instead at the opposite bank of the North Fork of the Canadian. The water wasn't flowing as swiftly as the others they'd crossed. So she should feel much better.

Except David had only spoken to her if absolutely necessary since sunrise. She shouldn't have asked him about the past. Giving in to her curiosity and begging him to tell her about Georgia hadn't gone at all the way she'd wished. They'd both ended up hurting from thinking about painful memories.

Worse, he'd confirmed how he felt about her. If he wanted more than friendship, he'd willingly bare his soul to her and not have to be coaxed the way she'd done. Good thing she'd jumped backed when he'd brushed away her tears instead of pressing his fingers to her lips the way she'd almost done. She'd come much too close to following her silly heart last night.

Regardless of how he'd meant it, she'd always remember his gentle touch.

Schmidt's nearby loud whistle jarred her from her thoughts.

She jerked her head up to see David motioning them to start crossing the horses.

"Let's go, boy. You can woolgather later." Schmidt started the Double B *remuda*.

Charlotte scrambled to clear her mind and focus on her job. David hadn't come to help or see that she got across. This river must be safe since he was staying with the herd. Such thoughts gave her no comfort. As hard as he was working to avoid her, she must have hurt him deeply.

Half an hour later, Eduardo had crossed the wagon, and the last Tumbling G mustangs stood on the opposite bank. She glanced up at the sun. Only around ten o'clock. With her heart so burdened, she'd have sworn it was hours later.

Eduardo grinned from his spot on the seat as she came up. "My feet are dry enough to put my boots back on, so I'll do that while they're crossing the rest of the beeves. I'm sure David will want us to make three or four miles before we stop for noon."

"*Sí*, he tell me."

"Already? When?"

"While you get morning horses."

"I see." What she saw caused a lump in her throat. On days they had a river to cross. David had been telling her his plans. She dismounted. She'd best not waste time putting on her socks and risk someone seeing her exposed ankles.

She glanced up at Eduardo, so carefully watching her pull on her boots that if anyone had been nearby, they'd wonder if he'd ever seen her do it before. "*¿Qué pasó?*"

"What do you mean?" She paused before mounting Red.

He told her in Spanish he couldn't miss her drooping shoulders and sad expression, then demanded again to know what had happened between her and David.

"We'll talk later." Before the cook could ask more questions, she headed toward the horses.

Some days it was a downright disadvantage Eduardo knew

her so well. But if he could tell something was wrong, she'd best get hold of herself. She didn't dare give Toby any more ideas about how she felt about David. If he figured out for sure how much she loved the partner he so feared and loathed, she hated to think what he'd do.

David kept his distance when they stopped at noon. She caught him watching her a time or two while she and Eduardo were cooking. But he didn't direct a single comment her direction while they ate.

Her miserable afternoon dragged by as she herded the *remuda* up the trail. Sweat soaked her shirt. She wiped her gritty neck and face with her bandana. No use worrying about smelling like a horse with no chance of David caring about it.

"You silly goose." More like a silly fool for not listening to her head about David.

Jumper twitched his ears. Good thing he couldn't tell anyone she'd resorted to talking to herself. She'd been bracing for telling David goodbye in Abilene. Steeling her heart against him telling her goodbye. Not speaking to him already was better. The less time she spent with him, the fewer memories she'd have to forget or wish she couldn't remember.

She wanted to scream. Or spur Jumper and ride back to Texas without stopping. But she couldn't do either one. She was stuck. Stuck in her misery. Stuck in her loneliness. And it was all her fault for not being sensible about David Shepherd from the start.

DAVID TRIED his best not to think about a certain wrangler as he scouted for a spot to spend the night. The feel of her soft cheek beneath his fingers wouldn't let go of him. Brushing her tears away must have offended her. She wouldn't look at him after they'd crossed the river.

The hot breeze blew the grass in waves as he scanned the

horizon for Indians. He wanted no more surprises like the one they'd had yesterday evening. She'd galloped straight for him then. After last night, she'd probably run full speed from him.

If that weren't enough, the hurt he'd caused her while dredging up his painful memories would be enough to make her want to stay away from him. She hadn't cried after shooting a mountain lion or almost drowning in the Red River. So he must have caused her tremendous pain last night. Which made a lot of sense. She'd lost her mother and brother during the war, plus her father this spring.

If only such a tenderhearted woman weren't so bullheaded about working a ranch with a brother who didn't care if she lived or died. Shivers coursed through his body. *He* cared if she lived or died. Too much. Whether Charlie cared for him or not, he'd still keep her safe.

He rode toward the trees in the distance. This time he'd check for more than just a good creek to water the herd. Seminoles were peaceful, but he didn't want any Indians, peaceful or otherwise, around the red-headed wrangler.

The creek had plenty of water, one good thing about all the rain this area had gotten lately. He rode up and down the bank a few minutes. No signs of any other human beings around. The buffalo wallow looked fresh. But as long as the big brutes kept their distance and didn't scare the *remudas*, he didn't care how many of them there might be.

He circled back and waited until Eduardo was in sight, then waved his hat in the air to show him where to stop. The wranglers would be heading in soon. Just thinking about Charlie not speaking to him made his mouth go dry.

Yet not speaking to her would be the best thing for his heart. He couldn't endure the agony of losing another woman the way he'd lost his wife and every other woman in his life. Since caring for her would hurt him sooner or later, he might as well make it sooner.

Once Charlie brought the *remuda* into camp, she acted more

than happy to oblige him about ignoring him. She and Schmidt settled the horses then rode off to look for wood.

While getting his pots and cooking utensils from the wagon, Eduardo kept looking his direction. Nothing got past the shrewd cook, so he had to have noticed the lack of conversation between David and Charlie. Maybe she'd told him what had happened last night.

The last thing he needed was to talk to the kind, matchmaking Mexican who had no idea how hopeless things were between him and Charlie.

While reaching into his saddlebag for his Bible, his hand brushed the bag of candy. So much had happened lately, he'd forgotten about buying enough to last till Kansas. Maybe he should try sharing it with Charlie again. Giving her candy would allow him to touch her hand for a moment or two without being too forward—if she'd let him anywhere near her.

No, he had no business getting the least bit close to her again, much less touching her.

———

CHARLOTTE CAUGHT David staring at her as she and Eduardo cleaned the last pot. He'd barely acknowledged her existence the last two days. No smiles just for her. Not one request for a Spanish lesson. With less than a half-hour of daylight left, soon she wouldn't be able to see him so well, and he couldn't see her.

The cook clucked his tongue at her as if he could hear her silent thoughts. "*Hable con el hombre esta noche.*"

"*No puedo. Es imposible.*" She couldn't talk to a man who wouldn't talk to her and told her friend so. He couldn't deny that David had worked harder to avoid her lately than he worked scouting the trail.

"*Ay yi yi.*" He shook his head as he likened her and David to stubborn mules who wouldn't budge even for their own good.

Whatever their differences were, they wouldn't solve anything until they talked to each other.

She grabbed the clean pot and stomped off to put it in the chuck box. Eduardo headed toward the fire, where the other men lounged as usual. No need for her to follow the cook even for a little while. The man she'd enjoyed covertly gazing at no longer wanted anything to do with her.

Watching the stars come out held no appeal. She sighed and closed her eyes. What a mess she'd made of things.

"Charlie?"

She jumped at the sound of David's voice, chiding herself for being so deep in thought she didn't hear him approach. She should have kept her eyes shut. Maybe he would have thought she was praying and walked away.

But he didn't stop until he was close enough to look straight at her. No matter how much she told herself she should, she couldn't look away from him. Oh, he looked wonderful in a full moon. If only she dared reach up and push his hat back.

"Eduardo said you told him you'd like to teach me more Spanish."

"He did?"

"You didn't tell him any such thing, did you?" He didn't take his eyes off her.

Hoping he wasn't about to walk away after learning the truth, she shook her head.

"Do you want me to stay?"

"Please." *Forever and always.* His tender tone set her heart racing while her mind screamed for her to be sensible and remember how foolish such longings were.

"I was hoping you'd say that. I mean, I've been hoping you weren't upset with me. And I missed ... I missed our Spanish lessons."

His nervous-little boy-sounding explanation made her wonder just exactly who or what he'd really missed. "Why would I be mad at you?"

"For touching you and being so forward the other night."

"I'm not mad, not at you." She shouldn't have said it like that. If he ever guessed how much she'd enjoyed his touch, this wonderful man would be gone before they reached Abilene.

He fished a piece of candy from his vest pocket. "This is sorry pay for what our lessons have been worth."

"Um, thank you."

Her fingers brushed his as she took his offering of peace. If only she knew just how much he thought her Spanish lessons were worth. Such strange words from a man who considered her only a friend he'd soon bid goodbye.

"So, what do you want to teach me tonight?"

Not the words of love welling up in her heart. "Well, more weather words ... and you should know the seasons."

"All right."

As Charlotte went over all four seasons, David alternated shifting his weight from one foot to the other or running his hands up and down his trouser legs. For a man who had just given her a candy peace offering, he acted as if he still didn't want to be here.

"So Fall is the only one that doesn't have an *r* in it?"

"That's right."

"Good thing you're the only one around to hear me make a fool of myself trying to pronounce *r*-words."

"You're no fool, David. You could never be."

"You have no idea ..." He let out his breath as he stared down at her. "I have been, and I could easily be again."

"Um, no ... I guess I don't." And she didn't, since she couldn't begin to understand what he meant. "We should get some rest since we never know what tomorrow might throw at us."

"Yes, we should."

He turned and walked away—just as he'd done so many other nights, leaving Charlotte to ponder over what he had and hadn't said. Instead of leaving the instant he realized she hadn't wanted to talk to him, he'd stayed. For a little while.

Such odd behavior from a man who acted as if he wanted to be at peace with her again. She sighed. Since her heart refused to let go of David despite the pain waiting at the end of the trail, she doubted she'd find peace for a long time.

21

The evening sun glinted in her eyes as Charlotte checked the horizon for Indians, just in case. Settling the Dutch oven in the coals, she stood and wiped the sweat from her gritty face with her bandana. Ever since they'd crossed into Indian Territory, she hadn't managed a real bath. It wasn't safe for just her and Eduardo to wander too far from camp. This evening would be no different.

Another thing she hadn't anticipated when she'd decided to come on this drive. But if the Lord had shown her ahead of time everything she'd face, she'd have stayed home and tried to find another way to save the Tumbling G.

Especially if she'd known she'd have to sacrifice her love for David. Making peace with him the other night hadn't brought her a moment's rest. She should have left well enough alone instead of talking to him again.

But God knew best and already knew everything she'd encounter, including David. So somehow she'd keep trusting Him, even in the face of the heartbreak that waited in Abilene.

"Hey, Schmidt, we're heading down to the creek before supper." Tyler interrupted her thoughts as he walked over to the other wrangler stacking the firewood he'd finished chopping.

"Sounds good." Schmidt propped the ax against the wagon wheel as he grinned Charlotte's direction. "Charlie, looks like y'all have supper going fine. Let's go cool off."

Staring into the fire, she sent up a quick prayer for what to say. "That's not what I signed on for. I can't leave Eduardo to finish by himself."

"Boy, you don't look or smell any better than the rest of us." Tyler grinned as he winked at Schmidt.

He grabbed one arm and Schmidt grabbed the other as if they'd drag her off to the creek. A couple of other hands laughed from nearby.

"No!" Eduardo's dark eyes snapped as he seized the pothook and pointed it like a weapon at the men.

They released her and backed away, staring with open mouths at the usually soft-spoken cook.

"No one hurt Charlie. *Nadie. Nunca.*" His low, menacing tone left no doubt he'd use the pothook he still gripped.

Taking another step back, Tyler eyed the cook as he held his hands out palms up. "Whatever you say."

"What's going on here?" David trotted toward the small group by the fire.

Charlotte was the first person he looked at the instant he halted.

"Nothing until this crazy Mexican threatened us." Schmidt kept his eyes on Eduardo.

"Yeah, we was gonna see Charlie gets the bath he needs." Tyler quickly glanced at David.

"That's your side. Eduardo, what happened?"

"They try drag Charlie to creek after Charlie say no. I stop them."

David nodded. "Fellas, it doesn't matter how much Charlie smells like a horse. You'd best keep the cook happy. Every cowboy knows that."

Neither of them looked pleased with the foreman's pronouncement, but they left with the other men who had paused to see what might happen. After insulting her so thoroughly, David had sense enough to follow his hands. She resisted the urge to pelt him from behind with a handful of the sharpest rocks she could find.

Her temper boiled as hot as the pot of stew simmering over the fire. David had protected her and her secret, rescued her. Again. For which she should be grateful.

She would be, if he hadn't said she smelled like a horse. Mentioning keeping Eduardo happy would have been enough to keep her safe. If her cheeks got any hotter, they might catch fire. She could bite the head off a two-headed rattlesnake. *Men!* Some days she wondered how David Shepherd had captured her heart.

As soon as the words left his mouth, David wished he'd chosen them more carefully. Charlie had shot him a withering look that shouted he was in dire trouble. Since he'd have a hard time thinking of a more insulting thing to say about a lady, he didn't blame her.

Especially since he'd spoken in front of so many other people. He'd probably need a lot more than peppermint and horehound tonight to get back in her good graces.

Yet he had to keep peace with the men and keep her secret safe. He hoped and prayed she understood that. Fearing he might further alienate his hands if he went back to explain things to Charlie and Eduardo, he stayed with the men at the creek.

"Charlie's the hardest working boy I ever seen, but the strangest one I ever seen too." Schmidt sat on a log to remove his boots.

David seated himself next to the wrangler. "The kid's been doing a man's work long before he should have. You'd see things differently too, if you'd been through what he has."

"Maybe so, but that don't mean he shouldn't have some fun once in a while."

"Yeah, but leave that to Eduardo if you like to eat. The cook worked for Charlie's father for years and thinks of that boy as his own." David hoped his brief explanation would help them be more sympathetic to the pretend wrangler.

Once the men stepped into the refreshing creek, talk changed to which of the native Texans had seen the hottest summer. Hot might be an understatement for what he'd probably face tonight when he tried to talk to a pretty redhead. He'd better enjoy the cool water while he could.

The rest of the men, including Grimes, soon joined the others at the shaded creek. No one mentioned the incident with Charlie. Maybe they assumed it best not to say anything to the volatile older brother they assumed would either defend the kid or mercilessly ridicule him. Whatever the reason, he didn't mind not discussing Charlie with his partner.

"All the rain doesn't make river crossings any fun, but I'm glad the creeks are running so good." Grimes stepped into the water.

If not for appearing unsociable, David would have left as soon as his partner arrived. But he couldn't try to make peace with the man if he avoided him. So he deliberately took his time drying off as the others gradually made their way back to camp.

Grimes hung back until just he and David were left. "For a man who says he owes me for saving his life, you don't listen very good."

"What do you mean?" David finished pulling on his boots before rising to face his partner.

Grimes fixed him with an icy stare as he finished buttoning his vest. "Just because I haven't seen you talking to Charlie for a couple of days, don't think you're fooling me."

Staring into the man's cold brown eyes, he prayed about what to say. "I've been thinking about all that ever since you mentioned giving up on God."

"God hasn't got one thing to do with what I'm talking about."

"Sure He does. Maybe if you'd listen to the Lord again, you wouldn't be so jealous of a scrawny kid." He kept an eye on his partner's balled fists, wondering if he should get ready to duck, dodge, or fight back.

"I'm not jealous of Charlie."

David shrugged. "Sure looks that way, especially as much as you hate for any of the hands to praise him."

"Stay out of our family business. And stay away from Charlie." Grimes's words hissed through gritted teeth.

"As I've said before, I'll be happy to do that whenever you start treating the boy the way you should."

Grimes pointed his finger at David's chest. "You want more than Spanish lessons from the kid if you can figure out how to trick him into it."

Why the man was so sure David was trying to trick Charlie made no sense. Unless he suspected David knew the wrangler's secret and would take advantage of her? "I have no intentions of tricking Charlie into anything. And if you'd listen to the Lord, you'd know that."

His partner's eyes narrowed to slits. He stared down at David a moment or so more, then whirled and stalked off.

"God's the only one who can help you," David called to the retreating man.

Grimes needed to turn back to God. If he didn't, David feared what might happen to Charlie after he wasn't around to protect her.

Such dire thoughts slammed into him like a giant fist landing a punch to his gut. Since Charlie insisted on keeping the promise she'd made to her father, he'd only be able to watch over her for a couple more weeks or so. Letting go of the woman he couldn't not love was already harder and more painful than he'd imagined.

If you love her, why let her go?

Whether the words came from God or were just his own wishful thinking, he couldn't tell.

He had a multitude of good reasons to let her go. The most unladylike woman he'd ever met loved her ranch enough to sacrifice what had to be unimaginable hardships to save it. Which meant she might cause him unimaginable heartache if she had to choose between him and eight hundred acres.

Which brought him back to the promise he'd made to protect himself from such pain by never loving anyone again, especially not the woman he loved. Add in the problems with Tobias, and he had a promise for nothing but trouble if he didn't quit loving Charlie.

He yanked his vest off the bush he'd draped it over. His treasured watch from Mr. Bentley fell out of the vest pocket, landing just at the edge of the water. He dropped to his knees to grab the chain.

As he wrapped his fingers around the timepiece, thorny brambles growing at the bottom of the bush cut into his hand. A little blood trickling down his hand was better than losing the most precious thing he owned. He clutched it with all his might as he rose.

Son, all of us have caused the good Lord more trouble and hurt than we're worth, but that's never stopped Him from loving us. You got to learn to do the same with people again.

Mr. Bentley's often repeated words to him echoed so loudly through his mind that he wondered the whole camp couldn't hear them.

His hand trembled as he maintained his grip on the timepiece, staring at the blood now almost down to the end of his fingers. No matter how much pain she might cause him, Charlie was much more precious than any watch. He couldn't let her go. Not without a fight against Tobias or anything or anyone else in his way.

But what if the fight he needed to wage was not against her brother? He'd been the one she'd defended when he and Tobias had come to blows. She continued talking to him no matter how much her brother disapproved, so she had to want to be with him more than she'd say. If he could fight for and win Charlie's heart, she might walk away from Grimes and their ranch and run to him instead.

The first thing he had to do was figure out how to convince her he loved her. He well knew how to woo a hoop-skirted southern belle. Courting a woman in trousers and boots without giving away her secret would be about as easy as leading her in a dance while blindfolded.

But if he didn't try to win Charlie, he'd lose her for sure.

22

A fter the way David had insulted her, Charlotte didn't care to speak with the foreman tonight or any other time. She'd stayed by the fire until the men headed for their bedrolls. She shook her quilt out, then laid her head on her saddle and hoped she could sleep. The last month or so, a certain blue-eyed man had cost her so many hours of rest she'd lost count.

She pulled her quilt up to her chin. Oh, she reeked. A body would be hard pressed to know if they were standing next to a human being or a horse if they got close to her. But David still had no business insinuating such a thing to every hand around this afternoon.

While she ground the coffee the next morning, Eduardo bombarded her with his opinion about her ignoring David the night before. Too bad this chore couldn't be done on the run.

He patted her shoulder as she tried to explain her reasons for not speaking to the foreman, maybe ever again. *"Pobre chiquita mía."*

His whispered sympathetic comment about his poor little girl made her feel some better. She stuck close to Eduardo while they cooked. David let her be during breakfast.

She doubted anyone thought anything of how fast she ate

since she needed to have the morning mounts corralled and ready to rope. Wolfing down her food was another unladylike thing to do.

As soon as possible, she guided the *remuda* toward the trail. Talking to Jumper was better than saying one word to most of the men around her, especially after yesterday.

By the time she rode up to help Eduardo with the noon meal, sweat had already soaked her shirt. Today might be hotter than the day before. Maybe that was why the wagon had stopped sooner than usual.

Eduardo patted the spot next to him on the wagon seat. "We fill water barrel first."

"Now?"

He nodded.

After dismounting and ground tethering Jumper, she scrambled up beside him. He headed the mules toward the trees where she assumed a creek flowed. He explained in Spanish he'd talk to *el jefe* while she brought in the morning horses.

So David had been kind enough to find a secluded spot on the Cimarron River they'd cross after lunch. He'd said it should be suitable for her to clean up. The foreman had already scouted the area for signs of Indians and had also volunteered to keep Schmidt occupied and away from the water.

The more Eduardo explained, the warmer her cheeks became. Relying on help from a man who was like a father to her was one thing. But David was a completely different bundle of problems. He should not be thinking of such personal things for her even if Eduardo had been the one to ask.

No matter how much she appreciated David's kindness and consideration, she couldn't imagine mentioning such gratitude to him.

Half an hour later, she finished buttoning her vest over her clean shirt. It would be damp with sweat as soon as she helped cross the *remuda*, but oh, how wonderful to be clean again. Her hat hid the dirty hair she dared not wash even if she had the time. That luxury would have to wait until Kansas where there was no possibility of Indians slipping up on her.

"Please tell David thank you for me." She climbed up on the wagon seat next to Eduardo.

"*Sí*, I tell him."

And no telling what else. Eduardo was still so intent on his matchmaking, she shouldn't have asked him to give any kind of message to the foreman. But David deserved her thanks in some form or another. Knowing Eduardo, it would definitely be a matchmaking form of another.

The rest of the afternoon went by smoothly, somewhat making up for the unseasonably warm temperature. The Cimarron cooperated much better than the Canadian had for crossing. Charlotte shaded her eyes from the glare as she looked toward the wagon stopped about two miles ahead.

David stood next to Eduardo by the chuck box. No doubt the cook was delivering her message. She should talk to the foreman tonight. He deserved a civil conversation.

A short time later, she rode into camp. David grinned her direction, causing her cheeks to warm. Thank God for her wide-brimmed hat. As soon as she dismounted, she busied herself helping Eduardo. She watched with relief when David grabbed his Bible from his saddlebag and went toward the edge of camp.

The cook spent their time together urging her to talk to David. His grin spread ear to ear when she assured him she would.

"*Bueno. Es muy bueno.*" He bent to stir the beans while she went back to the chuck box to get the plates.

Spurs jingled behind her. Water coursed over her shoulders. She yelped and whirled to see Tyler and Schmidt holding their canteens. Several laughing men stood a few feet behind them.

"That should help you, boy, since you didn't get a decent bath crossing the river this afternoon." Tyler laughed.

"You'll feel even better with a wet head." Schmidt reached for her hat.

Eduardo jumped between her and the men, grabbed the other wrangler's wrist in one hand, and knocked his canteen to the ground with the other. His stony glare rivaled one of her brother's scowls.

"You not want me help you remember what I say yesterday about Charlie."

"You gonna poison my food, crazy man?" Schmidt jerked his arm free.

In rapid Spanish, Eduardo told the man he'd do no such thing because Schmidt's poisoned flesh would harm the buzzards coming after him.

"Now what's going on?"

Charlotte jumped at the sound of Toby's gruff voice behind her. He looked from her to Eduardo to the other men.

"They bother Charlie. I take care of it." Belying his calm voice, Eduardo's stoic features shouted he wouldn't be cowed by her brother or anyone else.

Toby looked to be still studying the situation. "I'll handle my crazy cook and my foolhardy brother, men."

Schmidt picked up his canteen and hurried off with the others.

"What did you do to cause trouble now?" Toby glared at her.

She returned his scowl with what she hoped was a look as hard as his. "Nothing. You're the foolish one, not me." She turned back to the work table and her biscuits.

Toby grabbed her upper arm and yanked her around to face him.

"Let go of Charlie. Now." David charged onto the scene.

Toby released her.

Each man stood with clenched fists, exchanging stony glares.

"*Señores*, the men no eat if Charlie and I no cook." Eduardo looked from one man to the other.

"You're right, *amigo*." David unclenched his hands.

Toby relaxed his stance and turned to walk away.

"Grimes." David's terse use of his partner's name sounded like a barked order despite his quiet tone.

Her brother whirled to face them.

"Never. Jerk Charlie around. Again." David's near-whisper didn't disguise the intensity of his words.

"You and I will settle this and more in Abilene." Toby stalked off toward the other men.

"Thank you, Eduardo. And thank you, David." Charlotte waited until her brother was out of earshot before speaking.

"*Sí, gracias.*" Eduardo added his thanks.

David's entire countenance softened as he looked at her. He patted her arm. "He'll never hurt you. I promise."

"But what about you? He threatened you."

"I handled men like him during the war." He flashed a broad, lone-dimpled grin. "You and Eduardo finish supper so we don't starve."

As had become her habit, she stared at his retreating back several moments after he'd walked away. Those fascinating eyes weren't the only thing about him that mesmerized her.

"Biscuits no jump into oven themselves." Eduardo chuckled.

Heat rushed from her neck to the roots of her hair.

"*El jefe te ama muchísimo,*" he whispered before heading toward the fire.

David didn't love her. He'd never contradicted her when she called him her friend. But his gaze had been so tender when he'd promised Toby wouldn't hurt her.

DAVID DIDN'T BLAME Charlie for not leaving the fire until after Grimes headed off for his watch. Her brother was getting recklessly bold to threaten her in front of Eduardo.

He rose to find her. He still needed to apologize for insulting her. Defending her from her brother seemed to have diluted the anger he'd seen flashing at him yesterday. Eduardo said she'd appreciated his part in helping her clean up at noon. Not exactly the way he'd have thought to court a woman.

When he came around the back of the wagon, he found her staring up at the stars with her back to him. "Charlie?"

She turned toward him. He halted in front of her. How he wanted to take her in his arms and declare his love.

"You want to learn more Spanish?" She stared up at him.

"After I apologize."

She looked down.

"I should have chosen my words more carefully yesterday. Staying in good graces with the hands is important, but I'd rather stay in your good graces."

"You would?" She tilted her chin up to look at him.

Oh, she looked beautiful with the moonlight playing across her face. If he could take her hat off and ... He stuffed his hands in his pockets to keep from crooking his finger under her chin and bending to kiss her.

"Um, you want me to teach you more Spanish?"

He forced his thoughts from her tempting lips that he could almost taste. "Uh, yes."

She nodded.

He could rope the moon as long as she wanted him near. "Mind if I ask you something personal?"

"That's only fair after the questions I've asked you."

"How long have you been working your ranch? You rope and ride like you were almost born in a saddle."

Hopefully, she'd only started working with her father out of necessity during the war. If not, he doubted he could ever convince her to give up her share of the ranch for him.

"Pa had to have help after Pete, my younger brother, died in '63. My sister, Belinda, wouldn't think of trying to learn. So the chores fell to me."

"You've lost so much, but you're not angry. You don't blame God or anyone else." He liked her answer for more than one reason.

She shrugged. "You're not bitter. You lost your grandmother, your wife, and son during the war. Did you lose your mother and father then too?"

Hot anger raged through him. He'd done his best for years not to think about the man who'd given him his last name and no more. Or to wish too often he could have known his mother. He sucked in a ragged breath. "The war didn't ..."

A horse nickered not far away. Both of them looked toward the herd. If Grimes were near, he'd positioned his mustang where the wagon blocked him from their view.

"*Hace calor*. That means the weather's hot." She raised her voice enough to be heard by the men still sitting around the fire, or anyone else close by.

He repeated her words as best he could while listening for his partner to go back where he should be.

They worked on Spanish until they heard Grimes's bass voice singing to the cattle.

"Guess he's tired of listening to us." Charlie tilted her face toward him again.

Once more, his thoughts turned to her full lips, shadowed by the night. But unless the Lord worked a miracle in her heart, he'd never be able to do more than imagine kissing her.

"David?"

He focused on the eyes shaded by the shadows of her hat. "What?"

"If it's hard to talk about your father or mother. You don't have to tell me."

"How do you tell what I'm thinking?"

"Your whole body got stiff."

"You remind me of Grandmother, the way you pay such close attention to me."

Her shoulders sagged. "She was a good woman, wasn't she?"

"A wonderful woman. Could I tell you about my parents another night?"

"I'm sorry if I pained you again with my questions."

"You could never pain me." Well, she could, worse than anyone had ever done if he lost her. But he couldn't tell her that.

"Goodnight, David."

"Goodnight."

She made her way to the stack of bedrolls.

Comparing her to a woman as wonderful as Grandmother was a high compliment, but not the kind of romantic words a man said to win a woman's heart. He should kick himself. Even in the dark, he couldn't miss the listless tone of her voice or the way her whole body had slumped after his misplaced words of praise.

Saying all the wrong things when he had such precious little time left to be alone with her wouldn't help his cause.

Courting an imaginary cowboy was more difficult than he'd imagined. Flirting with her in front of the men was out of the question. He couldn't tell her in private how he longed to take her in his arms until she'd come to love him.

If she came to love him.

23

Charlotte soaked in the peace of early morning as she mounted Jumper, ready to start the *remuda* on the trail. A slight breeze rippled across the grassy plain, stretching to the cloudless horizon.

A half dozen or more startled prairie chickens flew up in front of her. Jumper spooked and galloped toward the herd as if the grass had caught fire. The rest of the horses took off in every other direction.

Of all the days for Toby to be riding flank and be close enough to see what happened. She barely managed to pull Jumper up short before he stampeded the longhorns. Even from a good fifty feet away, her brother's rigid body signaled his anger.

She turned her back to him. She had a good three dozen or so mustangs to gather up as well as her thoughts about her conversation with David the night before. His gentlemanly consideration of her needs to clean up meant a lot. Maybe he *did* care for her.

Except she reminded him of his grandmother. Not something a man said to a woman he loved. Yet he protected her at every river crossing, defended her from Toby, and so much more. He'd even saved her life.

If only he did love her. But if he didn't, she was setting herself up for terrible heartbreak. So she'd continue to hide her feelings as carefully as she maintained her ruse of being a boy. Revealing either secret held risks she didn't have the courage to face now. Dealing with everything in Kansas would be bad enough.

She spent much of her day praying for answers or direction. She'd never dreamed following God could be so precarious. That afternoon, she walked toward the wagon to help Eduardo and spied David standing next to the cook.

The dazzling smile he flashed her direction took her breath away. "I'm looking forward to another Spanish lesson."

She couldn't help grinning back. "I'd like that too."

Eduardo beamed at them both as he reached for a pot in the chuck box.

Cooking on the open plain lost all its drudgery with David so close. Too bad he walked away as soon as the first of the men came into camp. But they both knew Toby would be in soon.

After unsaddling his afternoon horse, her brother charged her direction. "Where's that jug head of yours that almost caused a stampede this morning?"

"Your best horse would spook if a bunch of noisy prairie chickens flew up in his face."

"None of my string is that stupid." He jerked his gun from its holster as he marched toward the *remuda*, grazing at the edge of camp.

"What are you doing?" Charlotte tossed the pot hook to the ground before running after him.

"I'm fixin' to put a bullet through that churn head so he won't cause more problems."

"No!" She grabbed his free arm.

He shoved her to the ground. She jumped up and ran ahead of him, planting herself between him and Jumper when he halted.

"Move." He glared down at her.

"No." Looking him in the eyes, she squared her shoulders.

The muscles in his jaw twitched. He didn't lower his weapon.

"You don't want Jumper around 'cause he threw you and embarrassed you. You don't want me around. Which one of us would you rather shoot?" Her heart pounded as she stared him down.

He clamped his open mouth shut.

Maybe she should have kept quiet, but it was past time for her brother to face the truth his shocked expression signaled he was denying. Past time for her too. She'd never be able to work the Tumbling G with Toby unless the Lord performed a miracle in his heart soon.

"Drop the gun, Grimes." David cocked his revolver as he crept up behind Toby. "You'll be the first man I've ever shot in the back if you so much as nick Charlie."

"I'm aiming for a horse that almost caused a stampede after you'd taken your leave this morning, not Charlie."

"Shoot Charlie's favorite mount, and I'll only graze your shooting hand enough to keep you from using that gun again."

As she glanced past her brother to David, his easy-sounding southern drawl belied the hard look in his usually gentle eyes. He would kill for her if necessary. Cold shivers prickled up and down her spine.

"Charlie, move over here with me, so I don't have to worry about him shooting more than a horse." David's icy tone should be enough to even scare some sense into a man as stubborn as her brother.

Toby's Adam's apple bobbed as he swallowed. But when he kept his pistol aimed just over her shoulder, she inched her way over to the foreman. The instant she was in reach, David shoved her behind him with his free hand.

Turning to face them, her brother's shoulders sagged as he holstered his gun. "I would never shoot *you*, Charlie."

"I'm not sure about that anymore." She held his gaze. He wouldn't win this battle he'd started.

Toby stalked back toward camp.

When David started to follow behind Toby, Charlotte brushed his sleeve with her fingers. He paused and looked into her eyes.

"Thanks." She kept her voice low since they were so close to camp.

"You're more than welcome. I'd do it again. For you."

Why? She barely shut her mouth in time to keep from asking her question out loud. He'd put himself in harm's way going against Toby and his already drawn gun.

If that didn't prove his love for her, she was hard-pressed to know what else it could mean. This was not the time or place to try to get the answers she craved. Yet all she could do was stand and stare at him, wishing she could say exactly what she was thinking.

"As much as I like talking with you, we'd better not get too far behind your brother and draw more attention to ourselves than we've already done."

"Yeah." She forced her boots to move again. He matched her pace.

Doubts about David's real motive for watching over her plagued her with every step she took. He'd either acted out of duty to watch out for a good friend or protected the woman he loved and wanted to spend his life with.

Until she could figure out his true motive, she'd keep hiding her love for him.

Every still, silent cowboy looked as if they'd turned to statues in their various places as they walked into camp. Since Toby and David hadn't shouted at each other, she doubted they'd heard what was said. But they'd seen plenty.

"We had a misunderstanding over a horse." Toby tossed the men a stiff-looking smile.

No one offered the slightest grin in return.

Charlotte went back to helping Eduardo.

By the time everyone sat around the fire to eat, the men were talking cows and weather as if nothing unusual had happened. Whatever opinions they held about the Grimes brothers, they kept to themselves.

Toby was the only quiet one. His downturned mouth and sad eyes made her wonder what he was thinking. He hadn't frowned at her once after threatening Jumper.

After she and Eduardo finished cleaning up, thoughts of enjoying the sound of David's Georgia drawl replaced her concerns about her brother. Eduardo teased her in Spanish about her plans as they put the plates and pots in the chuck box.

"Could we talk?"

She jumped as Toby lightly touched her shoulder from behind. She turned to face him. "We haven't got anything to talk about."

"I do. Please."

Please? He dared to be so civil to her now? "I said everything I needed to say while you held a gun on me."

"That's what we need to talk about." His voice cracked as he shifted from one foot to the other.

She stared up at him, trying to decipher his sudden kind behavior.

"Please, Charlo—Charlie."

Eduardo patted her arm. "I watch and pray. Talk to him."

"All right."

She followed her brother to the eastern edge of camp. When she glanced back, two men stood at the back of the wagon.

Toby halted and faced her. "I couldn't shoot you. Wouldn't even think about it. Never."

"Really? You didn't lower your gun until David aimed his at you."

"David!" He spat the name out. "Can't you go five minutes without talking about him?"

"Why do you hate him?"

"Why do you love him?"

"What?" She stepped back. He might as well have slapped her.

"I'm not blind."

"Yes, you are. David is only a friend."

Since she had little hope for more than his friendship, she wasn't misleading her brother.

"You're the blind one. That smooth-talking man will hornswoggle you out of your half of the ranch and make us both miserable." His sad tone reminded her of someone trying to reason with a wayward child who refused to listen.

"No. You're the one who'd be happy to get my half if I'd be kind enough to drown in a river or let some other accident happen to me."

"That's not true. I love you just like I always have. I'll explain everything in Abilene." He held his hands out, palms up. "Please believe me. Everything will make sense at the end of this trail."

She hadn't heard him speak so gently in years. If only he'd let go of his unwarranted hatred for David ... "I don't know what to believe about you anymore." Spinning on her heel, she went back to camp.

Toby didn't try to stop her.

24

Not long after sunrise, Charlotte saddled Jumper and headed off to bring in the morning horses. A slight breeze rippled across the grassy plain. It had cooled down a little overnight. Maybe today wouldn't be so unseasonably hot.

The last few days had been blissfully uneventful. If they made as many miles today as they had been, they'd probably spend tonight in Kansas. She wouldn't mind being safe and not having to watch for Indians every time she checked the horizon. Except every day she counted down meant she was closer to heartache and the day she had to tell David goodbye.

A wild turkey gobbled in the brush nearby. The startled bird took off just as she halted Jumper. Her horse didn't spook this time. She urged him through the brush again then reined him in.

"Look at that, fella. A nest." She dismounted then stooped to better examine her find. Sixteen eggs. What a treat for breakfast. Except she didn't dare remove her hat to take them to the cook.

She jumped back in the saddle and galloped toward camp. She spied David talking to Eduardo. "I'd be happy to guide one of you back to a nest full of turkey eggs."

"I'll be even happier to follow you." David grinned. He soon rode bareback beside her.

"I'd have brought them back myself, but I couldn't take my hat off to carry them." She kept her voice low.

He nodded. "We'll tell everyone I found them so no one wonders why you didn't bring them back."

"Thank you." She showed him the location of the nest before going after the *remuda*.

When she rode toward camp again, David urged his horse alongside hers as if he'd been waiting for her. He cradled his hat in front of him. "This is quite a find."

She nodded.

Toby glared at the two of them as they came in together. How he always managed to know if she and David were anywhere near each other gave her chills. Regardless of how many times he tried to convince her of the good reasons he had. He must watch her every move.

"Mr. Shepherd found turkey eggs." Charlotte made sure her words could be heard throughout the camp.

Before Toby had a chance to say anything to her or David, the men clamored around them.

"There's enough here for an egg apiece and one left for us to fight over." The foreman handed the eggs to Eduardo before dismounting.

"You found 'em. You get the extra." Jessup grinned as he finished tucking in his shirt.

Half an hour later, the men lined up for Eduardo to fill their plates. David got the last plate then waited for Charlotte to fill hers.

"Come here, kid." He cut his second fried egg in half. "You're still growing." He brushed her fingers as he slid the treat onto her plate.

It took every bit of willpower she could muster not to stare into his smiling eyes any longer than she should. "Thanks, Mr. Shepherd."

"You're welcome."

She sat next to Eduardo to puzzle over David's barely-disguised flirtatious looks. The cook's eyes twinkled. One glance at Toby's scowl said he'd interpreted his partner's generosity the same way Eduardo had.

Toby reminded her of a circling vulture while he stayed in sight of her the whole time she and Eduardo cleaned up from breakfast. He waited until she'd roped horses for all their hands before walking up to claim his mount.

As she coiled her lasso, Toby leaned in close. "Open your eyes and see what Shepherd's trying to do. Listen to me or—"

"Or what? My eyes *are* open. I don't like what I see about *you*."

David rode over to them, scowling straight at Toby. "I saw plenty of signs of buffalo yesterday afternoon. We'll need to keep an eye out for stray ones cutting through the herd." His frown reversed as he turned his attention to Charlotte. "I've already told Schmidt to watch so the *remudas* don't get spooked again."

"Thanks, Mr. Shepherd." Ignoring the dark glares the two men exchanged, she lassoed her brother's horse as if everything were right as rain in the spring.

Charlotte spent the morning on edge as she watched for stray buffalo that might spook the horses. Her sharp words with Toby didn't help her feel any better. She hated being at odds with her brother. But she no longer trusted him or believed him when he said he loved her.

For someone who wouldn't consider shooting her or harming her, he had a strange way of not convincing her of that. He'd never liked the idea of her dressing and working like a man, but he'd been so much harder to deal with after finding out Pa had left her half the ranch. Only God knew how she'd manage Toby after they got home.

Thoughts of home caused her heart to ache. Only a week or so left to be with David. He'd soon have the money to fulfill his dream, and she'd have the money to keep her promise. But at such a tremendous cost.

Back on the trail, she continued watching for buffalo. A rider headed toward her and the other *remuda*. He sat his horse like David. But the sun showed it to be around two, much too early for the foreman to be coming back.

"There's a huge herd of buffalo up ahead. We'll have to hold the cattle and *remudas* and let them graze till after all those shaggy beasts pass." He reined in his horse beside hers.

"How long?"

He shrugged. "All I could see was one buffalo after the other. Ride over and tell Schmidt. I'll pass the word to the rest of the hands."

"Sure."

"One more thing." He tossed her a beguiling, one-dimpled smile. "Spanish lessons tonight?"

Her heart raced faster than an untamed mustang. "Yes."

What had to be a good two hours later, they were still waiting for the huge herd to pass. Charlotte wished she could ride closer to the front of the grazing beeves and get a better look at the fascinating buffalo, but she couldn't do that and her job at the same time.

David rode up to her a while later. "I told Eduardo to make camp since there's a creek not far from here. We'll have to wait till tomorrow to ride into Kansas."

"All right."

He looked disappointed. She wasn't. Buffalo had given her one more night with him.

"I'll help Schmidt with the horses so you can help Eduardo."

"Thanks."

"Thank me tonight, uh—with Spanish lessons." He grinned.

Staring into his intense blue eyes made her wonder if his stumbling words might cover up what he'd really like as a thank you. The kind she'd gladly give him if he'd try to steal even one kiss from her. Her cheeks heated. She urged Red into a canter and headed toward the wagon.

DAVID FORCED himself to stay by the fire until after Grimes left to start his watch. "I'd better see about a Spanish lesson while I can." He rose.

As if he had the rest of the night to get there, he ambled toward the wagon. "Something wrong the way you left so quickly?" He made sure his voice was too quiet to be overheard.

"I'm all right."

Her strained tones said otherwise, but he'd come to court her, not argue.

"*Todo es bueno ahora.*" Eduardo grinned as he turned down the lantern. "*Buenas noches, mis niños.*" He picked up his quilts.

Charlie glanced toward the retreating cook.

"What did he say besides goodnight? Something's good. What?"

"He thinks everything is good now that you're here."

"Maybe not everything, but something, rather *someone* is very good." He grinned into the beautiful brown eyes obscured by gathering nighttime shadows and the hat he longed to remove.

She gasped and stepped back.

He'd said too much too soon. "Horehound is good. Right?" He fished out the candy in his pocket.

"Um, yes."

He pressed the treat into her palm. She didn't withdraw her hand from his. Good thing the half-moon wasn't up very far so her brother couldn't see exactly what they were doing.

"I want to talk about something besides Spanish."

She nodded as she stared up at him. "I'd like that."

"And I suppose you'd like to enjoy your candy." He released her hand.

"Thank you." She popped the horehound into her mouth.

No candy could be as delicious as her lips had to taste. But he'd come here to completely answer her earlier questions, not make a fool of himself.

"You deserve to know all the reasons I left Georgia."

"Only if you want to tell me."

"I want to." He looked toward the rising evening star. "My grandparents raised me because my mother died the day after I was born."

"Oh, David." She placed her hand on his arm.

Her soft words soothed him while her touch ignited a flame that traveled up to singe his shoulder.

"My father left just days after. Grandmother tried her best to explain her son's deep pain over losing my mother. But the truth ..." He took in a ragged breath.

"I'm so sorry." Her fingers rubbed his wrist, fanning the sparks beneath his shirt sleeve.

He gulped in more air. "My father couldn't stand the sight of a baby who looked so much like the wife he'd lost. The war took away everything and everyone I loved." He closed his eyes, praying for the strength to finish his story.

"You don't have to tell me more." Her quivering voice signaled she might be close to tears, close to crying for him.

"I went to fight, leaving behind my bride of six months. My father-in-law's letter said she died during childbirth. Our son lived two days. Grandmother died soon after. I sold my family's plantation to the first carpetbagger who came along, then left for Texas.

"Why did you tell me this?"

"Because you've been so honest with me." Because he wanted the woman he loved to truly know him. "Plus, you're easy to talk to."

"Thank you, but I don't deserve such praise." She slid her hand from his sleeve, letting her arm hang limply at her side.

"You deserve a lot more than that."

"I do?"

"Yes." He resisted the urge to kiss her. "Maybe I can explain better once we're in Kansas, and we can walk out away from everyone safely."

"Kansas?" Her voice cracked. "Uh, we should both get some sleep."

"Yeah. I guess we should. Goodnight." *My love.* He bit his lip to keep from saying the last two words aloud.

"Goodnight." She snatched up her bedroll and scampered away.

He hoped he hadn't scared her off. She hadn't acted the least bit afraid when she allowed him to take her hand or when she'd reached out to touch him. The next few nights inside Kansas where they could go off to themselves should be interesting.

25

Watching the wranglers head the *remudas* into camp at noon, David reminded himself not to pace. Eduardo flashed him a broad smile. Courting a woman without letting the other men figure out what he was doing while praying *she* figured things out was getting the best of him. He'd done more praying than sleeping last night. Again.

Eduardo shaded his eyes as he stared in the same direction. "She look for you."

"It's hard to tell from a mile away."

The cook waved to Charlie. She waved back. "She watch. For you." His grin spread ear to ear.

"I wouldn't mind if you're right."

"Is right. Very right."

"Keep praying about that, *amigo*."

"Last night good. This morning she blush when I ask." He bent to check the beans simmering over the fire.

Such encouraging words made David wish he could gallop out to meet the pretty redhead. But her brother rode at point today. He wasn't the only one who could see for miles with nothing but waving grass stretching to the horizon.

His partner wasn't just a thorny problem. He might be a real threat to the woman David loved and to David himself. If only the scoundrel would prove him wrong and turn out to be all bluster, like his cantankerous sergeant during the war.

Charlie smiled straight into his eyes as soon as she walked toward him and the cook. "You think this nice weather will hold?"

"You never know this time of year." Keeping his voice sounding normal took tremendous effort. How he wanted to take her in his arms and give her a greeting she'd never forget.

Instead, he remained in the vicinity and watched her help prepare the meal. Thank God, Schmidt kept to his habit of staying away from the wagon or fire lest Eduardo put him to work.

"Spanish lessons tonight?" Coffee pot in hand, she halted in front of him.

Breathe, man. He drank in her sparkling brown eyes, her tempting lips. The heat he felt didn't come from the nearby fire. He leaned closer. "Keep looking at me like that, and your brother won't have to wonder if I've discovered who you are." He kept his voice low enough for only her ears.

Her face flushed.

His heart pounded in his ears. "You and your secret are safe with me."

"I'm not so sure, judging from the way you're looking at me." Her saucy smile left no doubt about the meaning of her whispered words.

"We'll talk tonight." Not doing more would take every ounce of willpower he could muster. Kansas needed trees. An entire forest.

She nodded before returning her attention to cooking.

When he saw the herd approaching, David took a few steps back. He wanted to throw his hat in the air and shout for joy. Charlie had openly flirted with him. But his partner wouldn't be his only audience soon.

After Grimes dismounted, he wasted no time inviting

himself to stand as close to his sister as he could. David smiled. Tobias offered his usual stony glare. He might not recognize the man if he didn't look like a fierce storm brewing all the time.

Eduardo said something to Charlie in Spanish. She laughed before replying. David caught a few words. *Bueno* meant good.

He chuckled as if he understood every word. Grimes turned his scowl toward David.

"*Sí, es bueno. Muy bueno.*" He grinned. "Your brother's lessons are coming in handy. You should let him teach you."

This little incident wasn't planned, but maybe he could convince Grimes that Charlie was teaching him more Spanish than anything else and keep the man at bay for a while longer.

His partner mumbled something to himself and then left.

"Nothing like being afraid of the truth." Charlie stared at her brother's retreating back.

Part of the truth. But he still wondered how close Grimes might be to knowing that he and Charlie discussed a lot more than Spanish lately.

CHARLOTTE CHECKED the sun in the afternoon sky. Thank God for clear skies and no rain. Four o'clock or thereabouts. Time to move the horses toward wherever Eduardo had stopped the wagon to start supper. Another earthen mound with a Texas flag stuck on top of it lay just ahead. She'd lost count of how many such signs she'd seen since they crossed into Kansas.

Markers for the trail to Abilene. Markers counting down the few days she had left with David.

She'd spent her day reliving her recent moments with him. The wonderful feel of his hand covering hers when he gave her candy. His compliments. Whatever he'd left unsaid last night, he'd offered to explain now that they'd left Indian Territory. Her cheeks heated up even with only horses for an audience.

But thoughts of how things would change in Abilene chilled

her as if a cold blue norther had blown in. She had no idea how to accomplish what needed doing in a cattle town. Shadowing Toby. Finding a buyer. Negotiating prices and being taken seriously as a woman by her brother and everyone else concerned.

David. She sighed. They needed to talk tonight, but not about the things he'd hinted at while she helped Eduardo at noon.

Whatever Abilene held, she had to be prepared. David was the only one she could turn to for help. How she wished she could turn to him for more. But since God wanted her to keep her promise to Pa, that came first. Working things out with David might not be a close second if he couldn't come to terms with her intentions to continue ranching.

Hard, cold reality slammed into her, robbing her of breath. How anything else might work out was also up to the Lord. Thinking she might have such a short time left with David made it hard to take in air.

She forced herself to return her attention to the gently rolling plain stretching to the horizon and urged the horses toward the wagon stopped a couple of miles ahead. If only she could see her way as clearly as she could see the miles of prairie stretching in front of her.

By the time she turned out the *remuda* to graze close to camp, Charlotte had managed to control her emotions. She dismounted and headed toward Eduardo, hoping she looked as if she didn't have a care in the world when she grabbed the coffee grinder.

"*Buenas tardes.*"

She jumped at the sound of David's voice behind her. She turned to face him. He flashed his mesmerizing grin. If only she dared trace that dimple with her finger. She'd have no problem reaching him as near as he was ...

"Uh, we need to talk tonight." She whispered, lest Schmidt or anyone else hear her.

He nodded. "I'll be waiting, but not patiently." He ambled off to watch for the herd coming in.

Even with David keeping his distance, Charlotte had a hard time focusing on her chores. Eduardo chuckled when he caught her staring at David's back.

She concentrated on the biscuit dough she was supposed to be stirring. The cook had no idea she'd be stirring up problems tonight instead of romance. Judging from the looks and hints David had been giving her lately, asking him about cattle prices and sales was not the kind of discussion he had in mind. She wouldn't blame him if he ran the other direction.

After supper, Eduardo rushed through cleaning up while she tried to take her time. Tonight, she could wait forever to talk to David. Dousing his hopes might chase him off and ruin what little time she had left with him.

Around sunset, Toby headed off to start his watch. David sat cross-legged on the ground, watching her from his spot by the fire. She waited until the evening star appeared to walk behind the wagon.

David soon joined her. "What would you like to teach me tonight?"

Hoping he couldn't see how red her hot cheeks must be, she fiddled with the lantern on the folded-out worktable of the chuck box. His husky tone left no doubt he wasn't thinking about Spanish.

"*Buenas noches, mis niños.*" Eduardo grinned at them as he picked up his bedroll.

"No lessons tonight." She looked up into his eager face. How she hated to disappoint him in only a few moments. If she hadn't let her emotions run wild and flirted with him, she wouldn't be in this fix.

"Why not?"

"We need to talk about what happens when we go into Abilene."

"All right."

Thanks to the lantern, the shadows from his hat couldn't completely disguise his tender expression as he gazed into her eyes. How she hoped her imagination and heart weren't playing tricks on her.

"I don't want to be seen or overheard. Go for a walk with me?" She turned down the light.

"I'll take a walk with you under the stars anytime." His husky tone was not her imagination.

Heart racing, she made her way to the *remuda*, not stopping until they were in the midst of the grazing horses. "Toby shouldn't be able to see us or hear us this way as long as we talk softly."

He turned to face her as he halted. "Why the change tonight?"

"I don't want my brother to know my plans ahead of time."

"Your plans?"

Off in the distance, coyotes howled as she wrestled with thoughts of the best way to say what needed said. She swallowed hard. Best get this over with and face whatever consequences the truth might cause.

"I won't be pretending to be Charlie once we're in Abilene."

"Is that so?"

She nodded. "My best dress and hat are in a carpet bag in the wagon. I'll look a sight in such wrinkled clothes, but no buyer will take a fourteen year-old boy seriously. I'm going to be as much a part of selling our cows as Toby."

He sucked in a breath. "You can't go anywhere in that town alone safely."

"Why not? Surviving this drive proves I can take care of myself." She braced herself as she waited for him to object to her unladylike idea of selling longhorns.

"You don't understand." He covered her hands with his.

Regardless of how much she dreaded what he might say next, the warmth of his touch radiated through her entire being.

"Abilene is bound to have even more scoundrels who don't

respect a lady than it had last year. I insist on escorting you wherever you go."

"Escort me. Like a lady?"

He nodded as he caressed her fingers with his.

"You really think I'm a lady?" With her elation growing with every beat of her heart, she worked to continue to keep her voice low. No one needed to overhear this conversation.

"Why wouldn't I?" He crooked his finger under her chin and tilted her face up toward his.

Breathe. She had to breathe. "What real lady wears trousers, boots, and spurs? Look at me."

"Oh, I am."

Even with only starlight to see by, the way he looked her up and down in no uncertain terms could not be misinterpreted. He brushed her neck with his fingers, sending chills and sparks through her at the same time. Then he took her in his arms and kissed her, devouring her lips with a hunger she'd never expected.

He stepped back, tracing her lips with his fingers. "Did I answer your question?"

"Yes." She had to catch her breath before she'd be able to say more.

"Good." He caressed her cheek.

She closed her eyes as she placed her hand over his and pressed it to her face, savoring his kisses. If only this moment could last. "But I have other questions."

"Later. Not now." He placed his lips on hers and pulled her to him again.

As if they had a will of their own, her arms wrapped around his neck while she returned his sweet kisses with a fervor she couldn't rein in. Tonight she'd pretend there would be no *later* with all its uncertainties and questions.

Later would come much sooner than either of them wanted.

26

C harlotte shaded her eyes from the glare of the hot afternoon sun glinting off the bank-full Arkansas River. At least Schmidt no longer teased her about leaving her shirt on. He'd gotten so used to her methods of crossing rivers that he paid little attention to her at all now.

She looked downstream toward the shirtless cowboys starting the herd into the water. David rode toward her. Memories of last night and his wonderfully sweet kisses crowded out any thoughts of what she was supposed to be doing. Closing her eyes, she relived every glorious moment in his arms.

"Ready, Charlie?"

David's voice jerked her back to the present. She jumped and gripped her saddle horn to keep from losing her seat.

"Um, yeah."

"You looked lost in your thoughts. Were they good?" He grinned.

She nodded. Her cheeks warmed as if she were standing next to a roaring fire.

"Glad to hear that." He winked.

She plunged Red and the other Tumbling G mounts into the river. Cold water splashing her trouser legs brought her back to reality. But last night had been real too. The sandy-haired man riding a few feet from her was delightfully real. Delightfully determined to keep her safe the way any gentleman treated a real lady.

If only her unvoiced, unanswered questions would quit running through her head every time her mind cleared. She had no idea how she'd run their ranch with Toby. She loved David. Lately, he'd been acting very much like a man in love, especially considering the way he'd kissed her last night.

But he'd soon have his own land. And she'd secure hers. After that ... only God knew.

Half an hour or so later, every mustang grazed on the other side of the Arkansas. All the beeves would be across in an hour or less. Charlotte dismounted and grabbed dry socks from her rolled-up jacket.

David rode between her and Schmidt before she lifted her wet trouser legs and exposed her bare ankles. While pulling on her boots, she couldn't miss his undisguised admiring glances her direction.

Schmidt grinned as he rode closer to them. "Too bad every river hasn't been this easy."

"Yeah." She looked toward the wagon halted about a mile ahead. "We should have time to gather up extra wood while we can find it."

"Good idea, boy." Schmidt roped a nearby dead branch and headed toward the wagon, leaving her alone with David.

Instead of enjoying the sight of the handsome foreman so near, Charlotte swung up in her saddle and turned Red toward a sparse stand of cottonwoods upstream. David wouldn't consider her a lady if he knew her current thoughts. Focusing on her job was much safer. She'd drag in as much of the scarce wood as they could find. The fewer buffalo chips she had to use, the better.

David rode her direction as she lassoed a nice-sized fallen limb. "I'll be happy to help."

"I'd appreciate that."

"Not as much as I'd appreciate time with you tonight." His low, throaty voice left no doubt he planned on more than Spanish lessons.

"I think I can arrange that." His single-dimpled grin sent wonderful shivers all through her.

He looked away from her just long enough to throw his rope around a nearby branch.

"I figured I'd find you with Charlie after I saw you leave the herd, partner."

Charlotte jumped at the sound of Toby's voice from behind them. Good thing she and David were in the habit of speaking softly to each other. She'd been so engrossed in David's presence she hadn't heard her brother ride up.

"There's quite a bit of wood here if you'd like to help." David started dragging the limb toward the wagon.

As Charlotte headed her bay in the same direction, Toby turned his black into her path and blocked her. "Ride with me. Not him." He reached over and grabbed the reins from her.

"Grimes, let Charlie go. Now."

Charlotte looked over Toby's shoulder to David, halted just behind them. The foreman's narrowed eyes had a treacherous-looking glare she didn't know he was capable of. If her brother could see behind his back, he wouldn't look so sure of himself.

"This is none of your affair. Leave me and Charlie alone." Toby tightened his grip on her reins.

"It is as long as you're threatening the boy. Your quarrel's with me, not Charlie."

"What makes you say that?" Toby tossed the reins toward her and twisted to look at David.

"Not what, who."

"I never liked a man who talked in riddles. Spit it out, Shepherd."

David looked straight at Charlotte. "Take that wood back to camp and let us talk."

"You sure?"

He nodded. "I'll handle this."

"All right." She guided Red around her brother's horse. Toby did nothing to stop her.

She prayed David knew what he was doing. If Toby would grab her reins and block her way with Eduardo and Schmidt so close by, she feared what he might do to David.

DAVID STARED at his scowling partner. The man's hatred oozed from every stony feature of his sweaty, bearded face.

"You didn't talk much last night since Charlie turned the lantern down so soon. Not like the night before when you talked so long."

Like the sun warming his shoulders on a cold day, relief washed through David. Charlie's ruse of dousing the light had worked. The man had no idea David now knew how well his sister could kiss. He fought to keep his face from showing how broadly he was grinning on the inside.

"I assure you that you have nothing to worry about when I'm with your brother."

Grimes's seldom used laugh sounded brittle. "You aren't fooling me."

"I don't have to when you deceive yourself." He looked his partner in the eyes. "I don't want a single blade of grass on your ranch."

The man's jaw went slack. "How'd you ... Charlie's been telling tales."

"No. Charlie doesn't lie, and what you almost said confirms that."

Hearing out loud how right Charlie was about her brother sent prickly chills through him, making his heart pound in his chest.

"We've got a lot to settle in Abilene." Grimes continued glaring into David's eyes.

"Yes, we do."

The man's upper lip curled into a snarl, reminding David of a circling, bad-tempered dog.

Ready to pounce. For reasons only the cur understood, he gave a quick nod then turned his horse toward camp.

"One more thing, Grimes."

His partner halted and twisted in his saddle to look at him. "You got more of my family business to tell me that you shouldn't know?"

"No. My business. You once told me to watch my back in Abilene. I'll be there in plain sight. Watching you and guarding Charlie. If you hurt that kid, I promise you won't have to watch *your* back."

"Charlie's not setting foot in Abilene."

The cur was also a fox. He probably suspected what his sister might do. David fought to keep his face blank and unreadable. Confirming Charlie's plans before she was ready to reveal them wouldn't do. "I'll protect Charlie wherever, whenever. In or out of Abilene."

Without another word, Grimes kneed his mount and headed toward the wagon.

The rest of the evening, David did his best not to pay too close attention to Charlie. He'd probably riled Grimes more by promising to keep Charlie safe. But keeping quiet would have let the man think he could do as he pleased concerning his sister. She needed to know about his conversation with her brother, but biding his time was best for both of them.

After supper, he followed her from the fire as soon as she left. She halted behind the wagon and waited for him to catch up to her.

"Don't turn the lantern down yet." He placed his hand over hers as she reached for the light on the work table.

Eduardo grinned as he bid them goodnight.

"Why do you want the light?"

"Your brother." He repeated Tobias's words about watching

the lantern. "Let him see us talking a while. After you put out the light, we'll separate and meet up in the middle of the *remuda* again if you'd like."

"I'd like that. Very much."

So would he. He could taste her sweet lips already. But first, he needed to warn her about her brother. "I told Tobias I don't want your ranch."

"Why?"

"Sometimes letting your enemy know what you know makes him realize he doesn't stand a chance of getting by with anything, and you're the one who's outfoxed him."

"But he didn't believe you."

"He looked even angrier because he knows you told me what he'd said to you. He also let it slip that you won't be in Abilene, so he figures you'll try to go with him."

Shadows from her hat hid her eyes, but he had no problem imagining how wide those eyes must be. She took a couple of deep breaths. "He'd know ... in a few days, anyway."

Did he imagine the crack in her voice as she mentioned a few days? He hoped not. More than he'd yearned for anything in a long time, he wanted her to not want to live without him.

"I promise I'll be there with you." He reached for her hand.

She pulled back. "The lantern."

"Don't turn it down yet. We need him to think we talked a little longer than this."

"I can teach you a few more Spanish words."

He could think of some he'd like to know, such as how to tell her he loved her. But he'd better not rush there yet.

The ranch she was so desperate to save that she'd risk her life for might be a wall between them she wouldn't breach. A wall of separation and pain that could make him regret tossing aside his fear of loving her. He had to be sure what she'd do before he declared himself.

Although kissing her last night until neither of them could breathe had said so much more than he should have.

"You're not thinking about Spanish one bit, Mr. Shepherd."

Her saucy tone told him what *she* wasn't thinking about too. He'd gotten himself in one more fix last night. Still, if he wanted to woo her, he had to let her know how he felt. Courting any woman was hazardous. This one was well worth the risk.

He hoped he survived.

"Mr. Bentley keeps several coon hounds. What's the word for dog?" He turned the topic to something safe. Things would be dangerous soon enough when they walked out to the *remuda*.

"*Perro.*"

"Another *r*-word." He did his best to repeat it.

The way sounds carried across the prairie, her brother wouldn't have any trouble hearing her laughter. She taught him the word for cat and a few other animals as well.

"Enough of this." She doused the lantern. "You promised me a walk in the moonlight even if we will be surrounded by mustangs."

"That I did, Miss Grimes." He whispered as he touched his fingers to the brim of his hat, stopping just short of tipping it to her.

He walked one direction. She went another.

NOT FAR FROM JUMPER, Charlotte halted to wait for David. She should be sensible and ask him the questions bothering her about selling cattle in Abilene. His heated discussion with Toby this afternoon meant her problems weren't going away. But sensible was miles away from her mind right now.

David wove his way around the horses, only a few feet away.

Her heart raced as he halted in front of her. Shadows from his hat obscured his face as he gazed down at her. Tucking a wisp of hair behind her ear, he tilted her hat back then let his fingers linger on her tingling cheek.

"You might be more dangerous than Toby."

"Perhaps." He took her into his arms, kissing away all her questions and doubts.

Oh, she shouldn't be kissing him back and wrapping her arms around his neck. But her heart refused to listen to her mind.

Jumper snorted. They jerked apart.

"I don't see anything. Do you?" David whispered.

"No. If Toby had seen us, he'd be charging in faster than an angry longhorn."

"Yeah." He lifted her fingers to his lips. "We should say goodnight. I'd escort you back to camp if I could." He squeezed her hand before walking away.

She took a different path toward the wagon to get her bedroll. If only he could escort her to a preacher as soon as they could find one in Abilene.

Abilene. That town held too many unanswered questions. Letting David kiss her senseless two nights in a row was not the way to figure out anything.

Knowing he considered her a real lady in spite of her unladylike ways still didn't solve her problem of what to do with the ranch. Dealing with Toby and cattle buyers could be the easiest thing she had to handle. Working the ranch with Toby afterward looked to be next to impossible.

She groaned as she shook out her quilts. Figuring out what God wanted for her and David and hoping her heart didn't get broken in the process was the hardest part of all.

27

Sitting inside the wagon a little before noon didn't give Charlotte the best of light as she surveyed herself in Eduardo's small shaving mirror. But just feeling her clean hair made her grin at her reflection. After breakfast, David and Eduardo had seen that she got a chance to wash her hair in the Smoky River not far from Abilene. She finished braiding her hair into a single long plait before letting it hang down her back as she listened to the men loitering around camp.

They'd separated the herds yesterday. Other herds could be seen in every direction. The men were chomping at the bit to spend the hard-earned money they'd soon receive and sample everything the cow town had to offer. With their crude descriptions of last year's escapades, Jessup and Schmidt fueled the fire of anticipation. No wonder David insisted on escorting her in such a place.

She sucked in air. Toby planned to ride into town this afternoon. No more pretending to be a boy too young to speak his mind. She'd anger her brother and shock the other men. But Toby would have a much harder time being disrespectful to a woman and ruining his reputation in front of everyone in camp.

One deep breath. Another deep breath. One last look in the

mirror. She scrambled out of the wagon to help Eduardo with the noon meal.

"*Bueno, chicquita mía, muy bueno.*" The cook grinned as she put her hat on. As he set the coffee grinder on the worktable in front of her, he reassured her everything would work for good.

"Not just *bueno. Hermosa. Muy hermosa.*"

She jumped at the sound of David's low, husky whisper from behind her. Eduardo must have taught him the word for beautiful. As he bent close, her cheeks heated. His warm breath on her neck sent delicious chills up and down her back.

"I've spent many an hour imagining how it would feel to tangle my fingers up in that beautiful red hair." His hand brushed her braid near the nape of her neck for just a moment.

"Shush. Somebody might hear you." She couldn't begin to make her whispered rebuke sound the least bit threatening. Having him so near made it hard to breathe.

"Does it matter today?"

"Just don't kiss me."

His low laugh tickled her ear. "I'll save that for later, no matter how tempting you are." He straightened. "You can tell me your real name now."

She smiled as she turned to look into his eyes. "Charlotte."

"Charlotte Ann." Her brother's gruff voice sounded more like a growl as he marched around from the other side of the wagon.

They whirled to face him.

"How long have you known about my sister?" Toby's fingers rested on the handle of his gun.

"Long enough." David stepped in front of Charlotte.

Voices of the other men drifted their direction. Toby's gaze shifted toward the campfire everyone would gather around soon. "We'll talk later."

"Yes, we will." Charlotte moved to David's side. "For now I'll help the way I usually do."

"Not with that hair hanging down your back."

She looked him in the eyes. "It's past time for the truth about a lot of things."

David didn't leave her side until after Toby stalked off toward the men gathering to wait for their food.

A short time later, Charlotte's hands shook as she carried the coffee pot to the fire in plain sight of the men.

"Charlie?" Schmidt stared open-mouthed as she bent to set the pot on the grate.

"Charlotte, really."

"I'll be hogtied *and* whipped!"

Similar expressions came from the others as she straightened then pulled her braid over her shoulder, allowing the gaping men to see her hair trailing down past her vest pocket.

"We needed a wrangler." She squared her shoulders as Toby glared at her from behind the other men. "Since Pa left me half the ranch, I thought it was only fair I do my share."

David sauntered over to her side. "I'm sure you'll all agree she's done an excellent job."

"She sure has, but I never thought I'd see such a sight in all my born days." Wilson continued to stare at her.

"You have now." Charlotte rubbed her damp palms along the side of her trousers. "I'd better help Eduardo."

The cook grinned at her before stooping to stir the beans. He spent the rest of their time together reassuring her and telling her how proud he was of her.

While they cleaned up after the meal, his praise continued. He was sure the awed, befuddled admiration the men had expressed as they ate was only the beginning of better things.

She kept her doubts to herself as she stacked the clean tin cups on the work table.

"Charlotte, come with me. Now." David rushed toward them. Grabbing her arm, he tugged her in the direction of the grazing *remuda*.

"What's wrong?"

"Hurry, but be quiet." He whispered as he pointed to the horses just outside of camp.

With his back to them, Toby tossed his saddle on his already bridled black.

"Where you going, partner?" David's voice was loud enough for everyone to hear as he and Charlotte approached.

"I have a herd to sell." Toby cinched his saddle then placed his hand on his gun handle before slowly turning to face them. He stared slack-jawed at Charlotte as she and David halted in front of him.

"You aren't going to Abilene without me." Preferring the rest of their business not be heard by everyone, she kept her voice low.

"That town's no place for a decent woman. This would-be swindler next to you knows it." Toby's quiet tone didn't hide the menace lurking in his snapping brown eyes.

Hands on her hips, she glared up at her brother. "You're the one trying to sneak off and sell my half of the herd behind my back. So who's the real swindler?"

"Not me. I'm trying to take care of you, look out for you, for our ranch the way I've always done."

"Like you did when you sold the horses this spring? The way you'd cheat me again if we didn't have so many people watching us?"

As he looked past them toward camp, his hand moved away from his gun. His shoulders slumped.

"I'll be ready as soon as I get my things from the wagon and saddle my horse. David, will you see that my brother doesn't leave without me?"

"Happy to be of service, Miss Grimes." Grinning, David tipped his hat to her before she turned to walk away.

A short time later, Eduardo and every other man in camp watched as she jumped from the wagon seat then reached for the carpetbag holding her dress and hat.

"Charlie ... uh, Miss Charlotte, you need help with that?" Jessup reached toward her.

"No, but thanks. I don't have much in here."

"Be real careful. Abilene's no place for a lady," Miller said.

"David's promised he'll escort me wherever I need to go."

"David, huh?" Jessup grinned.

Heat rushed up her neck and cheeks. She gripped the handle of her bag. "I'll see y'all later."

Before falling into step with her, Eduardo took her bag. He placed his hand on her arm as they reached the edge of camp. "*Vaya con Díos, chiquita mía.*"

"*Gracias.*"

"Will be good. I pray."

"I pray you're right." She kissed his cheek as she took her carpetbag from him.

Tension rose like heat waves in August as she approached the two rigid, silent men. Standing where she'd left them.

"Sorry I couldn't rope and saddle your horse for you." David reached for her bag as she halted beside him.

"That's all right. Toby's still here." Pretending not to notice her brother's stony glare, she grinned at David. Toby was probably wishing he could turn her into a rock right now or anything else to keep her from interfering with his plans.

David handed his rope to her. The entire time it took to lasso then saddle Jumper, she felt Toby's scowl on her back. She positioned her horse between the two men before mounting. Her brother sat his saddle as stiff as a statue when they rode off. Their cowboy audience was the only thing preventing Toby from tearing her apart, verbally and maybe physically. She'd avoid being alone with him while they were in Abilene.

Then how are you going to run a ranch with him? The unbidden, haunting thought taunted her as they turned their mustangs toward town. She used the tense silence surrounding them to pray. God held everything and everyone in His hands.

"Our partnership is over." After they lost sight of camp,

Toby's lip curled into a snarl as he looked over at David. "I won't have you interfering with selling the herd."

"Yours and Charlotte's, so you mean *our* herd."

"Yeah, not yours. Which means we part ways now."

David held the man's gaze. "Not until after the two of you make a fair sale, and I see your sister get her rightful share of the proceeds."

"I aim to see you don't cheat my sister, and I'll do whatever I have to do to protect her and her share of our ranch." Toby snorted.

"Then we should do better in Abilene than either of us anticipates since we both have Charlotte's welfare in mind."

"Her welfare is not what you have in mind."

Suppressing a groan, she tried to think of something to say to end their war of words. "Can't we just enjoy this beautiful, clear day without a single river to cross?"

"Charlotte, open your eyes. Why won't you see what this man is trying to do?" Toby reined in his horse.

David halted his bay beside her brother. Wishing she could again maneuver between the feuding men, Charlotte jerked on Jumper's reins,

"I'm tired of your high-falutin' words and how you think you're better than me." Toby looked his foe in the eyes.

"Treat your sister as you should, and I'll leave you alone."

"Let's settle this here and now, Shepherd." Toby's fingers grazed the handle of his gun.

"No!" Charlotte jerked her brother's arm back.

He turned his attention to her. "Make your choice, little sister. Ride with him or ride with me."

A GIANT FIST of uncertainty tried to squeeze David's heart in two as he waited for Charlotte's answer. He swallowed hard.

Anguish filled her eyes and twisted her pale, full lips. He'd suspected something like this would happen—had to happen.

But not here. Not now.

He'd envisioned finding a private place at the Drover's Cottage to talk with her. Hold her. Kiss her breathless again and convince her of his love. Convince her they should be together the rest of their lives.

Staring at her brother, she gripped her saddle horn as if she might lose her seat. She took in a couple of shaky breaths as she twisted to look at David. "I ... I promised Pa. I have to take care of the ranch first. I can't tell you anything until after that." Her voice cracked.

"*You* take care of the ranch?" Grimes's derisive snarl again reminded David of a circling cur ready to pounce. A cur with no regard for his sister's obvious pain.

Sucking in air, Charlotte returned her attention to her brother. "Just before he died, Pa asked me to do my best to save the Tumbling G, so we'd never have to worry about a Yankee offering to buy us out again."

"He never said anything like that to me." The angry look in Tobias's eyes softened.

"He couldn't. If you sold those horses for what you claimed, then you got took. If you got more than you said, what did you squander the rest of the money on? Pa knew you lied. So do I."

The scoundrel's face blanched. As hard as he was, his sister's words must have hit their mark. "I won't discuss family business in front of this would-be swindler you think you love."

Grimes spurred his horse, leaving David and Charlotte no choice but to do likewise if they wanted to keep up. David's thoughts galloped faster than his bay. Charlotte loved him? Tobias didn't sound as if he had the slightest doubt how his sister felt about David. He hoped and prayed her brother was right.

Except if the lady chose her ranch over his love, he was heading full speed toward the worst kind of heartache he could imagine. Maybe worse than he could dream in his most terrible nightmare. If he had any sense, he'd rein in his mustang and let the other two go into town without him. But Charlotte wouldn't be safe.

He slowed his horse only after Grimes did his.

The short, silent ride was worse than the longest, most grueling march he'd endured during the war. Halting his horse just outside of Abilene, he stared toward the bustling town teeming with cowboys, cattle buyers, and riffraff. To his relief, Tobias did the same. Charlotte pulled Jumper up on the other side of him, away from her brother.

"The white, three-story building with the green shutters is the Drovers Cottage. We'll stay there tonight." He pointed toward town.

Grimes snorted. "Any place that fancy has to be expensive even for someone as full of himself as you."

"It's the only place in town suitable for a lady. I'll pay for her room." David looked the man in the eyes.

"No. She rides with me. I'll take care of her."

David swallowed his words of argument. Only God knew which man she'd pick. But for now, he had to pacify a snake to stay close enough to guard his intended victim. "If that's the way you want it."

"Both of you quit talking about me as if I'm not here or can't decide things for myself." Charlotte's rigid shoulders signaled her irritation.

"Forgive me?" The instant he looked into her eyes, her stiff body relaxed. "I only want what's best for you. Nothing more. Nothing less."

"I know. Thank you."

"You two can jaw all day. I have business to tend to." Tobias jerked on his reins and urged his horse ahead.

"Thank me later." He whispered.

Her slight smile didn't reach her sad eyes. Snapping her reins, she rode to catch up to her brother. David followed.

Just as he feared, men ogled and pointed at Charlotte and her long, red braid as soon as they got into town. Tobias guided his horse beside his sister. David rode on the other side of her. Gunshots rang out from somewhere close by. She glanced over at him, wide-eyed.

"Stay close to me."

She nodded.

Maybe she'd choose to ride with him. She'd turned to him instead of her brother, but the giant fist of doubt still squeezing so hard on his heart made breathing almost impossible. He'd keep praying.

A few minutes later, he opened the door for Charlotte to precede him into the Drover's Cottage. He couldn't thank Grimes enough for insisting he'd take care of his sister and grabbing her carpetbag before he could. Empty hands gave him an advantage the scoundrel hadn't intended. As every cowman who caught sight of Charlotte eyed more than the red hair hanging down her back, he extended his arm to her.

"This is no cottage." She whispered as she placed her hand near the crook of his elbow.

He grinned as he led her and her gawking brother toward the desk. The fine furnishings reminded him of his grandparents' plantation. But Charlotte would be the only one he'd share any thoughts of his old life with.

David tipped his hat to the lady at the registration desk. "Mrs. Gore, if I remember correctly?"

"That it is, young man." The matronly woman behind the desk beamed.

Glad to see the lady was still here managing the place with her husband, David returned her kind smile. "Please forgive us for coming into your fine establishment before cleaning up, but as you can see we need to see to a lady first. My partners and I would like a room apiece, please. As close together as possible."

She quirked an eyebrow Charlotte's direction. "We have two

rooms left next to each other and another just across the hall on the second floor."

"I'll take the one next to my sister." Toby placed his hand on Charlotte's shoulder.

"And I'll be happy with the other room." Happier than he'd mention. Such an arrangement would make it easier for him to keep an eye on Charlotte as well as her brother.

After they signed the guest book, David motioned toward the carpetbag at Tobias's feet. "Could you help Miss Grimes get her dress ironed? It's had quite a journey."

"Of course. I can have someone tend to that while you settle into your room, Miss Grimes."

"Thank you." Charlotte's happy grin lit up her beautiful face.

How he'd like to take her off somewhere private and taste those gorgeous, smiling lips. But that had to wait.

Mrs. Gore had insisted she'd see to Charlotte's safety, have her clothes ironed and procure anything else she needed. One important thing accomplished. Next he had to stick with the man he longed to be rid of and be sure the scoundrel didn't find a way to sell his herd without including Charlotte.

David headed west toward the heart of the crowded town. Staring at the sights as they walked, Tobias followed.

"We'll clean up and buy new clothes before we return to your sister."

"You can't order me around like some wet-behind-the-ears boy." Halting in front of the Bull's Head Saloon, Tobias stared at the red bull painted on the large sign. He licked his lips. A wanton-looking woman smiled at them from the doorway. He looked her over thoroughly.

"You can indulge yourself in any sort of debauchery you choose after Charlotte gets her share of the money." David grabbed his arm and pulled him away.

Grimes stiffened. "You've got Charlotte fooled, but not me. I'll take care of my sister."

"I'll see that you do, along with Eduardo, who'll look after her on the return trip."

Thoughts of Charlotte going back with her brother wrenched his gut. But he had to try to get Grimes to think he wouldn't have everything his way going back to Texas. Especially if Charlotte chose her ranch over David and went back without him.

"That grimy little Mexican's all smooth talk like you."

Cringing on the inside at Grimes's derogatory description of such a fine man, David stared straight into Tobias's eyes. "Eduardo will kill you if you hurt Charlotte. As will I."

Grimes's tanned face lost all color.

"No smooth-talking words, just fact." David dodged a drunken cowboy before resuming his march down the street. Tobias silently fell into step next to him. "The sooner we make ourselves look like presentable businessmen, the sooner we can be rid of each other."

"What about my sister? You sound like you're ready to throw her away like yesterday's coffee grounds."

Now the man was worrying about David deserting his sister? He clamped his mouth shut. Saying nothing might be the best and safest thing for now. He'd talk to Charlotte later, but Tobias didn't need to know that. Or that David planned on more than talking with her tonight.

"Since you don't have any fancy reply, I must be right."

"Charlotte is an intelligent woman. She'll make up her own mind about me and about you."

Grimes replied with his usual silent glare.

Getting rid of his former partner couldn't come soon enough. But the looming decision Charlotte had to make had the unrelenting giant fist now trying to squeeze the life out of him. He sent up another desperate prayer as he walked into a crowded barbershop advertising baths as well.

"We'll be here longer than either of us wants." Tobias

frowned and stepped back toward the door. "Maybe some other place isn't this busy."

"They're all the same with this many herds coming in." David blocked his partner's retreat. "Might as well get in line here."

They emerged from the shop an hour or so later.

"Our next stop is the Great Western Store for new clothes, then the emporium for boots." David turned toward Texas Street.

"I'm here to find a buyer as soon as I can, not dude myself up for a woman the way you're doing."

"You'll get a better price if you look like the owner of your ranch instead of just another cleaned-up cowboy roaming the town." He resisted the urge to punch the man and ram his words down his throat.

David took his time selecting his purchases at both stores. Unlike his partner, he was in no hurry. If he dawdled long enough, they wouldn't have time to sell their herds until tomorrow.

Which he prayed would give him one more chance to talk to Charlotte tonight. One more time to hold her. The opportunity to openly tell her of his love, to persuade her to come with him.

Stepping out of the emporium, he checked his watch. Both of them now sported new boots to go with their new clothes. "It's so close to supper, we should head back to the Drover's Cottage and treat Charlotte to a good meal. She deserves that and more after what she's endured the last couple of months."

Tobias's rusty-sounding laugh chafed David's soul. "I'm going into the first buyer's office we pass on the way."

"Not without your sister."

"No one will take her seriously." Tobias quickened his pace.

David matched his former partner's stride. "They will when I march in with you and tell them you're trying to sell a lady's herd behind her back. I have papers proving my partnership with Mr. Bentley. What do you have other than your brand?"

The scoundrel closed his open mouth and halted in the street.

"So I assume we enjoy supper with your sister?" David forced what he hoped looked like a jaunty grin and started walking again. Tobias fell into step with him.

If only he felt as sure and carefree as he pretended. But a beautiful redhead who had yet to make up her mind held his entire future in her hands. Maybe he should quit delaying things and get it all over with.

Only God knew if he'd soon be enjoying wedded bliss or enduring the kind of agony he'd promised himself he'd never go through again.

28

Charlotte sighed as she leaned against the ornate headboard and closed her eyes. Skimming Bible verses for most of the afternoon hadn't helped her answer the jarring question Toby had tossed at her before they rode into Abilene. She'd ridden in with him and David. As much as she hated to think about it, riding out with both men looked to be impossible.

Who would she choose?

With all her heart, she wanted to tell David of her love and ride with him the rest of her life. But would Pa understand if she abandoned the Tumbling G to Toby? If only there were some way to save the ranch as well as her heart. She groaned.

No answer dropped down from above.

A light knock sounded on her door. She jumped, sending the Bible in her lap to the carpeted floor.

"Charlotte?" David's unmistakable Georgia drawl drifted through the door. "We'd like to take you to supper."

We must mean her brother was at least agreeing to eat with David. "Uh, yes. Let me check my hat and things."

Buttoning her shoes took longer than tugging on a pair of boots, but if she greeted David in her stocking feet, he might change his mind about what kind of lady she was. Her heart pounded in her ears as she took one last look at herself in the washstand mirror before going to open the door.

Toby glared at her.

"Ohhh." David's smile spread across his face, accenting that fascinating lone dimple. Leaving no doubt how pleased he was with her transformation, he looked her up and down. "Could I escort you to the dining room, Miss Grimes?"

Unable to quit staring into his shining eyes, she nodded as she placed her hand on his extended arm. He led her toward the staircase, leaving Toby to follow them.

"Don't be taken in by a bunch of fancy manners, Charlotte Ann."

Toby's low hiss sent chills up her spine. He'd said he'd explain himself and his so-called good reasons for his hateful ideas once they got to Abilene. But the menacing tone of his voice made her doubt she wanted to hear whatever he had to say now that they'd arrived.

"That green dress is perfect for your hair and eyes." David patted her hand with his free one as if trying to reassure her.

"Thank you." In spite of her simple calico dress, his words and admiring glances made her feel pretty.

As soon as they descended the stairs, Toby stalked over to her other side. She chose to ignore him and concentrate on David, enjoying his company while she could. Her heart lurched into her throat at such thoughts. She sent up another desperate prayer for guidance, for a way not to lose David and keep her promise to Pa.

When they walked to their table, David pulled out her chair and seated her as if she were royalty. Oh, she could get used to this. Toby took the chair across from her.

"We're celebrating the end of the trail, so both of you order whatever you'd like. I'm paying." David's grin included Toby.

Charlotte opened her mouth to protest. David laid his hand on hers. "I insist. Please."

"I'm not stupid enough to turn down a free meal in a place like this." Toby's eyes narrowed.

Resisting a strong urge to kick her brother from under the table, she turned her attention to David. "Thank you." She hoped he understood how much those few words conveyed.

"You're more than welcome." He squeezed her hand before releasing it.

Toby's intense scowl knitted his eyebrows together, but he stayed quiet.

Until their food arrived, David talked about weather and other unimportant things. The delicious-looking roast beef served on fancy china left her hunting for words. So many nice things to savor and remember. How she prayed her memories of tonight would be as wonderful as their meal looked.

"I want to help you be as prepared as possible for selling your herd tomorrow." David gave Toby a brief glance before resting his gaze on Charlotte.

"All right." She sipped her coffee as she looked into his intense eyes. If she kept staring at him too long, she'd forget about cattle and anything else. But looking away was impossible.

"I suggest we go to the office of Kimball and Jones tomorrow. They dealt fairly with Mr. Bentley and me last year. From the talk I heard today, we should expect about twenty-eight dollars a head."

Charlotte sucked in her breath. She couldn't even think how much money that would be for almost seven hundred longhorns. Their ranch would be safe. But would she? The bite of bread she'd just taken nearly choked her.

"I'll talk to whoever I think best." Toby stabbed a piece of meat so hard his fork clanged on the china.

Staring tight-lipped at Toby, David laid his knife on his plate, aiming the point toward his former partner. "Go wherever you'd like. But I will be sure Charlotte's name is on every bank draft, and half the cash advance us in her saddle bags. Minus what you owe me for supplies."

Toby's eyes flashed as he swallowed hard. Without another word, he finished the rest of his meal. Maybe David's menacing tone and looks got the best of him, or he didn't want to cause a scene in public. Either way, she was happy to enjoy David's attention without her brother's usual interference.

After eating every spoonful of his strawberry ice cream, Toby pushed his chair back. "With you insisting on paying for all this, I've got money to enjoy some other entertainment." He stood and glared down at Charlotte. "Since you're bound and determined not to listen to me, I'll leave you to whatever ruination you and this man have planned for the night."

David jumped to his feet. "Never insinuate such things about your sister. Ever. Go—now—before I do something to get us both thrown out of here."

Toby clenched and unclenched his hands, then stomped out of the room.

"I'm sorry." A boyish grin crept across David's face as he seated himself again. "Not completely." He leaned close as he whispered his confession. "I've been praying all day for time alone with you."

"Is that so?" She twirled her spoon through her melting ice cream.

He nodded. "We can enjoy the rest of our dessert in peace."

The loving looks he'd been giving her had her thinking about something other than ice cream for dessert. She studied the sweet treat in front of her as heat warmed her cheeks.

After paying the bill, David led her into one of the private lounges available for business discussions. "We'll leave the door open for propriety's sake, but ..." He pulled her to stand with him almost behind the door, obscuring the view of anyone passing by.

Cupping her chin in his hand, he gazed into her eyes. "If anyone were to see me kiss you the way I've done on the trail, I wouldn't just damage your reputation—I'd destroy it."

"Um, well..." Just the way she'd dreamed of doing so many

nights, she traced his lone dimple with her finger. If she weren't careful, she'd be the one ruining her reputation by wrapping her arms around his neck and placing her lips on his in a way no lady should do in public.

"Charlotte. Such a beautiful name for an even more beautiful woman." He pulled her close and kissed her until they both stepped back to get some air in their lungs. Looking straight into her eyes, he placed his hands on her shoulders. "I love you."

"I love you."

He caressed her cheek. "Marry me, please."

Her heart skipped several beats as she stared up into his eager, shining eyes. How she wished God would shout from a cloud and tell her what to do. How to save the ranch and keep this man too.

"When?" The one squeaky word she could manage almost choked her.

"Tomorrow. Unless we can find a preacher tonight?"

"Oh, David ..." A searing pain ripped her heart. She took a step back. "What about my promise to Pa?"

"What happens after you keep that promise?" His shoulders slumped as his hands hung limp at his sides.

Unable to look into his pain-filled eyes, she stared at the floor. "I don't know ..."

"Look at me, please." He sucked in a shuddering breath.

Her eyes gazed up at him as if they had a will of their own.

"You have to choose. Tobias or me. Working together is impossible for either of us. Impossible for you and me as well."

"I'm still praying for answers." She blinked back tears.

He gave her one last forlorn look then turned toward the doorway.

"David." She grabbed his arm.

He turned back to face her.

The stinging tears in her eyes blurred her view of his dejected face as she looked up at him. "Please, don't leave without ..." Her breaking heart wouldn't cooperate with her to finish the sentence.

"Without you or without telling you goodbye?" Woeful blue eyes held her gaze.

"I don't know yet. But please ..." She swallowed a sob.

"Make up your mind." His voice cracked. He whirled and marched from the room.

Why wouldn't God show her what to do? She prayed she wasn't watching him leave for the last time.

STUMBLING from his bed in the dim predawn light, David's eyes burned as if someone had ground gravel into them. He leaned over the basin and splashed water on his face, hoping to wash away the signs of his sleepless night. The nearby lamp on the wall barely gave him enough light to see to shave.

He had to leave here as soon as possible. Before Charlotte awoke. Seeing her again would be like stabbing himself in the heart and twisting the knife with both hands. Last night couldn't have ended any worse. If she loved him, choosing him over a piece of land and a brother neither of them trusted shouldn't have been so hard.

By not choosing, she'd made her choice. She'd save the ranch she loved regardless of her own safety or happiness. Regardless of his happiness. He couldn't say or do anything to stop her. Keeping her promise to her father promised him no future with a woman whose brother begrudged David's every breath.

The razor nicked his jaw. He winced. He'd leave her to do the best she could with Tobias. Last night he'd done as much as possible to prepare her to sell her herd. Staying long enough to be sure Tobias didn't cheat Charlotte was out of the question now. He couldn't handle another painful rejection.

After he finished shaving, he stuffed his things into his saddlebags. He snatched the note he'd written for Charlotte. Her last chance to come to him. He didn't have the strength to talk to her face to face again. He slipped the folded paper under her door.

Coward.

During battle, he'd marched unflinching toward possible injury or death but now couldn't manage to raise his hand high enough to knock on Charlotte's door. No doctor could amputate his aching heart to heal the wounds she'd inflicted.

He strode down the hall, praying for God to touch her, bring her to her senses. Rather than risk her seeing what he'd just done, he took the stairs two at a time.

29

A s the garish sunlight roused her, Charlotte groaned. She must have finally cried herself to sleep, but what time was it now with the room completely light? Jumping out of bed, she threw her clothes on. She'd heard Toby come to his room at some ungodly hour last night, so she prayed he too had overslept instead of slipping off to find a buyer without her.

A few minutes later, a muffled animal-like moan answered her insistent knock on his door.

"Toby?"

"That you, Charlotte?"

"Yes."

Words he shouldn't say singed her ears. "Give me a little time. I want some breakfast before we tend to business."

"All right. I'll wait for you in my room."

Just as she walked inside, she spied a folded piece of paper lying on the carpet. She'd been in such a hurry to check on Toby's whereabouts, she must have stepped over it. In case her brother tried to sneak away from her, she left her door cracked open enough to see into the hallway. Her first name was written on the outside of the page. David was the only other person here who knew her well enough to call her that. Her hands shook as she opened the note.

My dearest Charlotte,

Don't wait for me or look for me. I'm meeting with my preferred buyers first thing this morning. If you follow my instructions from last night, you should do fine selling your herd. I pray all goes well for you today and in the future.

My leaving is best for all of us. As I told you, your brother and I could never work out a way to share you or your ranch. I'd rather walk away now than chance coming to blows with Tobias again, or possibly worse, with so much bad blood between us.

I'll drive my cattle to the stockyard as soon as the sale is final, pay off the men I no longer need, and allow Jessup and Schmidt a short time in town.

We'll be back at camp no later than three o'clock. If I don't hear from you by then, I'll start my horses toward Texas.

Love,
David

Closing her eyes, she leaned against the wall by the bed, lest she collapse on the floor. A flood of tears blurred the room as she clasped the paper to her pounding heart. She'd prayed and cried most of the night, begging for answers. God had never been so silent or so far away.

"Dear Lord, show me what to do. Please." A choked-back sob ended her whispered prayer.

She reread the short note before retrieving her reticule from the nightstand and placing the precious letter inside. Noises from next door told her Toby was out of bed.

After glancing at her pale reflection and puffy eyes in the washstand mirror, she did her best to rinse away any signs of tears. If Toby had any idea how badly she was hurting, he'd try to take advantage of her distress.

Deciding to deal with a brother she'd likened to a copperhead while losing a loving, godly man like David Shepherd had to mean she'd gone crazy. She groaned. Honoring her father was exacting a horrible price. *God, why?*

A light knock interrupted her morose thoughts. "Let's get some breakfast."

Taking in a shuddering breath, she walked over to open the door for her brother.

"I'm starving, and we're getting a late start." He looked her over but said no more.

She nodded as she stepped out of her room, turning her back on Toby only long enough to lock her door. "Let's go."

Before heading down the hall, she couldn't keep from glancing at the door of the empty room across from her.

"I expected you and *David* to be gone already." As they descended the stairs, his sarcastic words hissed in her ear.

"He's gone." She fought to keep her composure.

"Is that so?" His brown eyes lit up as a boyish grin spread across his face. She hadn't seen him look so happy in years.

As they walked into the dining room, she fisted both hands to keep from slapping him in front of everyone. He had the good sense to gloat in silence while they ordered their meal and waited for the server to set their breakfast on the table. She picked up her fork and pushed the eggs around on her plate. Her churning stomach rebelled at the thought of trying to choke down a few bites.

She glanced at the clock on the wall near their table. Almost ten o'clock. "David should have his herd sold by now. He'll be leaving by three."

Toby's beaming smile made her want to throw her coffee in

his face. Instead she gripped the cup with both hands, praying for self-control as she sipped the tasteless beverage.

"And what about you, partner?"

Now I'm his partner? She set her cup down so quickly the coffee almost sloshed onto the tablecloth. "We need to talk."

He nodded. "First I'm going to finish our first decent breakfast we've had since we left Texas."

The small bite of eggs she'd forced into her mouth stuck in her throat. *Our* breakfast. He was so cocksure of everything. She wasn't sure of anything.

Such a short time away from finally keeping her promise to Pa, but not one ounce of elation coursed through her shattered spirit. Paying for a ranch with her blood and sweat was one thing. Paying with a broken heart was something she'd never anticipated.

"We can talk in my room whenever you're ready." She let her fork clatter onto her plate then picked up her napkin to dab her mouth.

As if relishing every bite, he took his time eating. "If you're not hungry, no use letting good food go to waste."

She shoved her plate toward him. He finished off every bite she hadn't touched.

After paying for their meal, Toby walked with her upstairs. Neither of them spoke as she shoved the brass key into the lock to her room. He followed her inside. She closed the door and turned to face him. For the first time in years, his brown eyes showed no trace of anger. Not the slightest sign of a frown on his face.

"If we're really partners, it's your turn to be honest with me. Nothing but the truth about how much you got for the mustangs you sold this spring. And I want to hear every one of your so-called good reasons for hating David."

"I'm happy to oblige now that your *friend* won't be in the way." He smiled.

"David was never in *my* way." In spite of her efforts at self-control, her voice cracked.

His brittle laugh enraged her. Lord help her, she could picture her hands around his throat squeezing out every ounce of air he tried to take in.

"He'd have been in my way and yours if you'd married him."

"You're still not making any sense." She fought to keep her voice steady.

"Let me start with those horses you won't forget about."

"All right." Trying her best not to lose her battle to remain calm, she sucked in a deep, shaky breath.

"I got a good price, and—"

"You cheated your own pa?"

He held his hand up. "I can't explain if you won't quit yapping long enough to let me talk."

"Finish this story you've had three months to dream up." She made no effort to soften her sarcastic tone.

A flash of his customary anger lit his eyes for a moment. "Every cent I didn't spend to get ready for this drive is in the bank in San Antonio in my name."

"Your name? Why?" She forced the words from her dry throat.

"Pa's idea of being fair and leaving half the ranch to you wasn't fair to me."

"Yes, it was. I've worked as hard as you have." She squared her shoulders and stood as straight and tall as she could.

"No. Belinda proved you and Pa wrong."

Her brother had gone crazy. Yet he stood looking down at her with a calm, gentle expression she hadn't seen since before the war. Shivers radiated up and down her spine. She didn't know whether to stay put and listen to the rest of his senseless explanation or run for her own safety.

"You really *are* daft. Our sister hasn't got a thing to do with this."

"Sure she does. Everything. She gladly traipsed off to

Galveston with her husband. If you'd gone with Shepherd, you'd have done the same thing since he'll soon have his own ranch. While still owning half of *my* ranch. It would have been *my* sweat and work to keep the place going while you two enjoy his land and tell me how to run what should be all *mine*."

As his words penetrated her pain-dulled mind, she slumped against the door behind her. Now she understood why he resented her so much. Why he so intensely disliked the man she still loved with all her heart.

He folded his arms across his chest. "If you're still thinking about finding him after we sell the herd, I promise I'll never sell my land to anyone with the last name of Shepherd."

Another thing David had been right about. She and David could never work out any kind of arrangement with Toby. Yet she'd promised Pa ...

Toby pulled his watch from his waistcoat pocket. "We should find a buyer. Anybody but the ones David mentioned since he could have told them who knows what about me or you by now."

"Who we talk to doesn't matter since we know what price we should get."

She didn't have the strength to argue with him or remind him that David was the one who had given them such good advice last night.

"Yeah. Do whatever you'd like to make yourself presentable. I'll come for you in half an hour."

"All I have to do is check my hair." She wasn't about to let him out of her sight for half a minute, much less half an hour.

"Then do it." His huge smile lit up his face, making him look years younger.

She stepped over to the wash stand mirror.

Two hours or such later, Toby hoisted his saddlebags full of coins over his shoulder as they headed toward the Drover's Cottage. The bank drafts made out to her and Toby were in her reticule. He'd insisted she keep both of them.

"I'll put your share of the cash in your saddlebags as soon as we get back to your room."

My share? Of what? Continuing down the crowded, dusty street full of cowboys giving her looks that made her cringe was like walking through a nightmare.

She'd kept her promise to Pa.

But her insides felt hollow. Empty. Without one bit of satisfaction. Still, the ranch was safe as Pa had wanted. Just not the way he or she had thought it would be.

In his own misguided fashion, her brother had made the drive and fought as hard as she had for their land. Every bit as hard as Pa and Ma had. Toby would continue that fight with or without her. As the revelation penetrated her tormented heart and soul, she halted by the hitching post.

Stopping next to her, Toby gave her a quizzical look.

She glanced up at the sun a little over halfway across the clear blue sky. "What time is it?"

"No need to rush driving the herd to the stockyard." He shrugged. "We'll pay off everyone, let Miller and Tyler enjoy Abilene a while since they're coming back with us. We can start the horses toward home whenever we'd like tomorrow. Maybe the day after if we want."

"The time?" Instead of giving in to the temptation to grind her heel hard enough into the toe of his shiny new boots to make him yelp, she stomped her foot.

He pulled his watch from his vest pocket. "Almost two o'clock. Why are you staring at me as if I just grew two sets of horns?"

"Because I finally figured things out and got the answer I've been praying for."

"What answer?"

"The best answer. I have to ride now."

Toby's jaw dropped. "Now?"

"Now."

"But you're not dressed for anything but riding in a buggy."

"I don't have time to rent a buggy. That would be too slow anyway."

Gathering up her skirt, she ran toward the hotel stable, leaving Toby to trot behind her. She burst through the door. "I need my horse right now."

The man working there closed his open mouth as he stared her direction. "Don't think I heard you right, Miss." He made no move toward the stall holding her mustang.

Charlotte marched past him. With the reticule dangling on her wrist, she threw her saddle blanket on Jumper's back.

"What are you doing?" Toby grabbed her arm.

"What I should have done last night." She jerked her arm free.

"You're the one not making sense now." Her brother looked from her to her horse.

"Everything makes perfect sense if I don't run out of time first." Ignoring the dirt and dust flying onto her dress, she heaved her saddle up on Jumper's back and cinched it as quickly as possible, then grabbed her bridle hanging on a nail in the stall.

She turned to face her dumbfounded brother. "Boost me up?"

"Why? You owe *me* answers now."

"If I hurry, maybe I can catch David before he leaves. Help me up, or I'll climb up on the stall and cause a scene that will embarrass even you."

Helping her up in her saddle, his eyes narrowed to slits. "And you keep calling me crazy."

"Guess it runs in the family." She grinned down at him, his dour expression not bothering her one bit.

"I still won't share my land with any Shepherd."

"I know. Don't worry about putting money in my saddlebags. I don't care if they're empty when I come back for them."

She left him standing in the livery stable, shaking his head at her. As soon as she rode outside, she urged Jumper into a gallop and headed out of town. Let everyone around gawk at the ridiculous woman with her hairpins coming loose and her petticoats showing. David had been so broken-hearted when he left last night. How she prayed he'd stayed and waited for her.

When she spotted the Tumbling G herd and two *remudas* still right where they should be, her heart raced faster than her horse.

"David!" She called to him as she reached the edge of the camp.

He jerked his head her direction but didn't move an inch.

Every man turned to stare at her. The closer she got, the wider Eduardo's grin spread across his face. David's forlorn, stern expression didn't change. He didn't move a muscle toward her.

She hauled Jumper to a halt next to the man she loved.

"What are you doing here, Charlotte?"

"I'll tell you if you'll help me down."

The instant he set her on the ground, he dropped his hands to his side. His letter had left her with a glimmer of hope. His stiff posture signaled nothing of the sort.

Looking up into his pain-wracked face, she took a deep breath and prayed. "I made my choice, but I wanted to tell you in person."

"All right." His voice cracked. He didn't budge.

"I choose *you*. I love *you*." Wrapping her arms around his neck, she kissed him full on his mouth in front of everyone.

Whoops and shouts erupted throughout the camp as David pulled her to him and deepened their kiss into the heart-stopping kind she'd longed for.

Stepping back to catch his breath, he placed his hands on her shoulders as he looked into her eyes. "I assume this means you accept my proposal of marriage?"

"Yes! And I'll be happy to explain everything."

He caressed her cheek. "That has to be a very interesting story."

"It is."

Keeping her promise to save the Tumbling G only to lose it to her brother hadn't been in her plans. But gaining David's love meant more than any piece of land. She laid her head on his chest and soaked in the wonderful feel of his arms encircling her.

David twirled his fingers in a loose lock of her hair. "Before we find a preacher, let's go for a walk. I'd like to hear that story you promised to tell me."

Lifting her head, she smiled into his sparkling eyes. "I'd—"

"What are you doing, Charlotte Ann?"

She spun to see Toby galloping his horse into camp.

WHEN TOBIAS DISMOUNTED and charged their direction, David pushed his fiancée behind him. He did not want to fight the man. But the fight looked to be coming to him, so he'd do whatever necessary to protect the woman he loved. He made an obvious show of dangling his fingers just above his revolver, praying for safety and calm. A few feet away, Eduardo rested his hand on the handle of his gun.

"What are you doing here, Grimes?"

"I came to talk some sense into my sister. You have no say about anything between us."

Tobias glanced down in the direction of David's gun hand but didn't make a move toward his own weapon. Maybe all the people watching would cause the man to think twice about starting anything.

"Whatever you'd care to say to my fiancée, you can say to me too."

"The bank drafts in my sister's purse have my name and hers on them, not yours." Shifting his gaze toward the reticule dangling from Charlotte's wrist, he folded his arms across his chest and swore.

Stepping to his side, Charlotte gripped David's hand with her free one. "Let's go for a walk where we can talk, just the three of us."

Grimes's lip curled. "No, just you and me. He's not my family. Never will be."

Her grip tightened on David's hand as Grimes shot her a glare. "Talk with the two of us, or ride out of here alone. I've made my choice. You make yours." Unflinching, she stared him down.

As Tobias looked toward the silent men taking in the whole scene, he shifted from one foot to the other. "I haven't got all day. Let's get this over with so we can drive the herd we sold to the stockyard."

Leading the way out of camp toward the nearby creek, she kept her hold on David's hand. She stopped at a spot where the *remudas* partly blocked them from Eduardo and the other men's view.

Since they were out of pistol range now, David prayed the cook had his rifle handy. He'd witnessed more than one instance when Charlotte had shown more spunk than sense. He prayed this wouldn't be another one of those times.

"In case you didn't notice, Eduardo is watching out for me as usual. His hand hasn't moved from his gun since you rode up." She looked straight into her brother's angry eyes.

"Speak your piece. The day's wasting." Grimes spat out his words.

David squeezed her trembling hand. The only sign of how she feared her brother. Her raw courage continued to amaze him. It probably always would.

"You want to keep the Tumbling G as much as I do, so the ranch should be safe with you just like I promised Pa."

The scoundrel's brows knit together. "What do you mean?"

"I mean I'm willing to turn the ranch over to you."

"For a fair price." David hoped speaking his thoughts out loud wouldn't cause Charlotte more problems, but he had to stick up for her. Be sure she got her fair share of what she was willing to turn over.

"You stay out of this." Tobias kicked a rock and sent it flying.

"No, David's right. I worked for that land. As hard as you."

The grass should have wilted at Grimes's next choice words.

David draped his arm around Charlotte's shoulders. "This conversation is finished if you insist on speaking to my fiancée in such a crude manner."

"Fiancée!" The man swore again. "All you want is our ranch. You don't care about my sister."

"Who was the first one to see about me when I shot the mountain lion? Who risked his life for me at river crossings or with the Comanches?" She stepped up and poked her finger in his chest. "Not you, Toby."

Every man left in camp had to have heard each word she'd just shouted at her brother. But family business or no, it was past time for Grimes to face the sorry man he'd become. She stepped back from him.

"You've got it all wrong. I do care. About you. About our ranch. He's the one who doesn't care." Toby pointed his finger at David.

Without flinching, David stared straight into Grime's hardened eyes. "You're right about one thing. I don't care about your ranch."

Grimes opened his mouth as if to speak. David held his hand up.

"I don't want a single blade of grass or speck of dirt on your ranch. I want, I love, your sister. Charlotte is the one who matters. The one I care about and would give my life to protect if necessary."

The instant Toby's hand brushed the handle of his gun, a rifle cocked a few feet behind him. David had been so intensely concentrating on the threatening man in front of him he hadn't noticed Eduardo moving toward them.

"I promised *tu padre* to watch out for Charlotte. Don't make me do that *ahora*." Eduardo's steely calm voice left no doubt he was more than willing to keep the vow he'd made.

Grimes let his hand go limp at his side. He closed his eyes. His shoulders slumped. "All right. Let's talk about a fair price."

"*Bueno*. I leave to let you talk family business. *Familia* is three people now. But I keep watch." The cook nodded at Charlotte before turning to go.

The muscles on either side of Grime's tightly drawn lips twitched. "Family is still only you and me." He focused his gaze on Charlotte as if David weren't there. "But since you're determined to leave everything you've worked so hard for and go with this man instead of being my partner, I won't stop you."

"And I won't stop praying for or loving you no matter how hard you're making it for me to do either one." Charlotte's soft voice sounded as if she'd had to choke out her words.

David squeezed her hand.

"We're talking about me buying you out. Nothing more. I'll get the ranch I've wanted to work the way I want. I hope you don't end up with more trouble than you're bargaining for."

A slow smile spread across her face as she looked into David's eyes. "What I'm getting, money can't buy."

A short time later, Charlotte's string of horses had been cut from the other Tumbling G mustangs. Her share of the gold advance they'd gotten rested in David's saddlebags. He hoisted them into the back of the wagon he and his soon-to-be bride would drive back to Texas.

Grimes exhaled a shaky breath as his sister placed one of the banknotes with her and Tobias's signatures back in her reticule. David had never seen the man look so dejected. So defeated.

But perhaps being forced to face what he'd become would show him how badly he needed to return to God. He prayed the Lord would send someone like Mr. Bentley to the man and help him change before his bitterness and rage ate even deeper holes in his heart.

"I've got beeves to drive to the stockyard." Grimes put his signed note in his waistcoat pocket.

"And we need to find a preacher." David lifted Charlotte's hand to his lips.

He grinned at her despite the seriousness of the situation. Now that everything concerning the Tumbling G looked to be settled, he couldn't wait to return to Abilene. He was as glad for Charlotte to be rid of the land that had stood between them as Tobias was to gain it all.

Much happier, judging from the other man's solemn expression. David was getting something, rather *someone*, so much more valuable than the eight hundred acres Grimes would sell his soul to own.

CHARLOTTE ALLOWED David to help her up onto the wagon seat as Toby and his men rounded up his beeves. She might be seeing her brother for the last time. Deep inside, she'd known this day might come no matter how hard she'd worked not to think about it.

Yet even with the sadness, she had peace. The Tumbling G was safe just as she'd promised Pa. Her heart was now safe too. Wrapped in David's forever love for her and her forever love for him. Toby was in God's hands, whether he wanted to admit it or not. Which was the best place for anyone to be. Where she needed to leave her wayward brother.

David interrupted her thoughts as he jumped up beside her. "This isn't the buggy a lady should have, but it has to be better than the way you left town a while ago."

"Much better." She grinned as she focused on her soon-to-be husband. "My ride out of Abilene probably still has people talking."

Eduardo beamed at both of them as he mounted Jumper to ride along and witness their upcoming marriage.

Toby reined his horse in next to the wagon then looked from Charlotte to Eduardo. Again ignoring David. "Eduardo, I've always taken you as a smart man. I'm sorry you decided to stick with Charlotte instead of trying to talk her out of making such a bad mistake."

"Is no mistake for Charlotte or for me. I make *my* choice. Is sad, but you make yours."

Eduardo quoted in Spanish the Bible verse about a man reaping what he sows.

"You know I don't understand your jabber."

Looking over at her brother, Charlotte sighed. "You wouldn't understand the meaning in English, either. But I pray someday you do."

"Don't waste your breath praying for me."

"We all intend to do that, but you're the one who decides if it's a waste or not." David bent to unwrap the reins from the wagon brake. "Jessup and Schmidt will be watching our horses. They said they'd keep an eye on yours while you're gone."

"Guess I'll let them do that since they're both more honest than you," Toby growled, then turned his mount toward his cattle.

Her brother's sad eyes and sagging shoulders betrayed his true anguish. His harsh words were only a mask to hide the pain he wouldn't admit to or deal with. Instead of riding off alone, he should be coming with her as a happy witness to her wedding.

"Toby!"

He twisted in his saddle to look back at her.

"Would you meet us at the Drover's Cottage when you're through? Please." She looked at David, assuming his nod signaled his agreement. "We can wait for you if you'd like to see us get married."

"I'd rather watch a hanging." He turned his back to her and urged his horse into a canter.

Eduardo looked over at her. "All be right someday with him, *chiquita mía*. God tell me He will send someone to help him. And He tell me you belong with this man." A slow grin spread across his face.

"Better listen to our wise *amigo*." David caressed her hand.

Blinking away threatening tears, she looked into David's tender eyes, full of love for her. A woman should cry only happy tears on her wedding day. Toby's anger might or might not bring his ruin, but his problems wouldn't spoil her special day.

"We both made our choices. I still choose you, David Shepherd."

"I promise to do my best to see you never regret that." He pulled her into his arms and kissed her.

Delightful kisses the likes of which she'd never received before almost robbed her of her breath. She moved away just enough to see his face and trace his lone-dimpled smile with her finger.

"I'll hold you to that promise for the rest of our lives."

ABOUT THE AUTHOR

Betty writes encouraging stories for a discouraging world. Never give up on what God has planned for you. Stepping out in faith can be an amazing journey. Take one step at a time. If or when you stumble along the way, remember the Lord upholds his children with his hand. Psalm 37:23, 24.

She's a member of American Christian Fiction Writers (ACFW) and active in her local chapter. Her debut novel, *Love's Twisting Trail*, won first place in the 2013 ACFW First Impressions Contest. She's also won or finaled is several other contests over the years.

An incurable history buff, Betty can roam for hours through historical sites and museums. She often loses track of time while researching on the internet. The story of a woman who actually went on a cattle drive disguised as a man inspired Love's *Twisting*

Trail. Plus, Betty can tell you more interesting tidbits about the past than you might want to know. While answering her grandchildren's questions on a family vacation, she was mistaken for the tour guide at historical Old Town in Cody, Wyoming.

She's enjoyed writing since childhood. If friends or relatives would sit still long enough, she'd hand them something she'd written. She still has the notebooks of handwritten stories. Her love for writing has taken several detours along the way—marriage, children, grandchildren, even great grands. Wonderful detours she wouldn't trade for anything.

When not living in her make-believe nineteenth century world, Betty enjoys time with family. Especially family RV trips with her three adult children, grandchildren or great grands. She and her husband share their Texas home with a spoiled Chihuahua who is sure they're making the payments on *her* house.

Find more about Betty at www.bettywoodsbooks.com.

MORE HISTORICAL ROMANCE FROM SCRIVENINGS PRESS

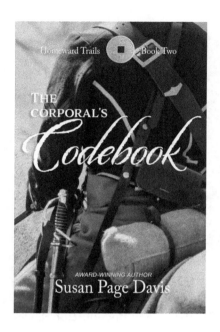

The Corporal's Codebook
by Susan Page Davis
Homeward Trails Series
Book Two

Jack Miller stumbles through the Civil War, winding up a telegrapher and cryptographer for the army. In the field with General Sherman in Georgia, he is captured along with his precious cipher key.

His captor, Hamilton Buckley, thinks he should have been president of the Confederacy, not Jefferson Davis. Jack doubts Buckley's sanity and longs to escape. Buckley's kindhearted niece, Marilla, might help him— but only if Jack helps her achieve her own goal.

Meanwhile, a private investigator, stymied by the difficulty of travel and communication in wartime, is trying his best to locate Jack for the grandmother he longs to see again but can barely remember.

Dogwood Winter

by Candace West

Valley Creek Redemption Series

Book Three

He is walking away while she is fighting to walk.

After a springtime swim, Ella Steen is stricken with a dire illness, leaving her without the use of her legs. Meanwhile, Dr. George Curtis, the man she secretly loves, faces ruin. For over a year, the crusty New York City bachelor and vivacious spinster have exchanged dozens of letters and formed a wary friendship.

Neither are willing to open their hearts completely. Until they face each other. The past looms between them, however. Does George still love another or is his heart completely free?

A trip to Valley Creek holds the answers. Instead, when George and Ella arrive, they encounter obstacles that force other truths to the surface. Is George brave enough to confront what he fled in New York?

Can Ella confess why she hates dogwood winters? Will their hearts survive?

If only their pasts would keep out of the present.

Beyond These War-torn Lands

by Cynthia Roemer

Wounded Hearts Book One

While en route to aid Confederate soldiers injured in battle near her home, Southerner Caroline Dunbar stumbles across a wounded Union sergeant. Unable to ignore his plea for help, she tends his injuries and hides him away, only to find her attachment to him deepen with each passing day. But when her secret is discovered, Caroline incurs her father's wrath and, in turn, unlocks a dark secret from the past which she is determined to unravel.

After being forced to flee his place of refuge, Sergeant Andrew Gallagher fears he's seen the last of Caroline. Resolved not to let that happen, when the war ends, he seeks her out, only to discover she's been sent away. When word reaches him that President Lincoln has been shot, Drew is assigned the task of tracking down the assassin. A chance encounter with Caroline revives his hopes, until he learns she may be involved in a plot to aid the assassin.

Scrivenings
PRESS
Quench your thirst for story.
www.ScriveningsPress.com

Stay up-to-date on your favorite books and authors with our free e-newsletters.

ScriveningsPress.com